Some books are for pleasure,
others are to live by—
FIVE FOR SORROW, TEN FOR JOY is both.

"Another compelling story told by a marvelous writer . . . Ms. Godden's use of visual imagery is, as always, unique. She has the eye of a poet, focused precisely to catch nuances of beauty."
                    —*National Catholic News Service*

"Exciting . . . rewarding . . . celebrates the life of the spirit."
                    —*The Albuquerque Tribune*

"A beautifully executed and moving story of a woman who finds peace with herself."
                    —*Colorado Springs Gazette-Telegraph*

"Eloquently written . . . a very special novel."
                    —*Santa Cruz Sentinel*

FIVE FOR SORROW, TEN FOR JOY

a novel

by

Rumer Godden

FAWCETT CREST • NEW YORK

FIVE FOR SORROW, TEN FOR JOY

THIS BOOK CONTAINS THE COMPLETE TEXT OF THE
ORIGINAL HARDCOVER EDITION

Published by Fawcett Crest Books, a unit of CBS Publications,
the Consumer Publishing division of CBS Inc. by arrange-
ment with The Viking Press

ISBN: 0-449-24372-9

Acknowledgment is made to Oxford University Press for
permission to quote from "Caged Skylark" by Gerard Manley
Hopkins.

Printed in the United States of America

First Fawcett Crest Printing: February 1981

10   9   8   7   6   5   4   3   2   1

This book is for Dorothy Watson with love and thanks for all it owes to her adventurous encouragement, endurance—and endless patience with its author.

Author's Note

The characters in this book are fictitious except for Père Lataste, Mère Henri Dominique and Soeur Noël who are part of the history of Bèthanie; also five other characters of today who have consented to be portrayed—with fictional names—simply because I could not imagine them as any other than they are. Their stories, though, are typical of what I heard, saw and learnt through the generosity of the Sisters. In fact the book is, I hope, a truthful reflection of the life and work of the Dominicaines de Bèthanie, that unique Dominican Third Order of the Congregation of Saint Mary Magdalen conceived by Père Marie Jean Joseph Lataste in the eighteen-sixties.

Père Lataste held the belief, as did the first sisters of Bèthanie and many others, including the writer, that in the New Testament the Mary of the Mary and Martha story at Bethany was the same Mary Magdalen, the sinful woman from whom seven devils were driven out, who anointed Christ's feet at the supper given by Simon the Pharisee; she anointed them again with spikenard at another dinner just before his death when Judas Iscariot objected to the ointment's cost. Many contest this belief, but clues to its possibility can be found, not only in the gospels but in contemporary Jewish history.

In actuality, France has now only one Maison Centrale for women, that of Rennes, but for the purposes of the plot in this novel there are two such prisons, Vesoul and Le Fouest.

To explain the title: a rosary has fifteen "decades"— ten beads in each—of which five decades are the "sorrowful" ones, five "joyous" and five "glorious." The Sisters of Bèthanie wear the full rosary, which has three strands, one for each "mood." What most lay people use is really a "chaplet" or "chapelet," a single strand of five decades told bead by bead, three times over.

My grateful thanks are due first of all to Maître Luba Schirmann, Avocat au Barreau de Paris, whose influence and kindness opened many doors for me; to Monsieur l'Avocat Général Robert Schmeck for permission to attend the Cour d'Assises in Paris; to Monsieur Chapiteau of the Ministère de la Justice (Directeur de l'Administration Pénitentiaire) who allowed me to visit the Maison Centrale for Women; to the personnel of the prisons for their friendship, invaluable help and the trust with which they allowed me to see and question as I wished; to my agent, Georges Hoffman of the Agence Hoffman, for his indefatigable care and interest; above all to the Sisters of Bèthanie and their Reverend Mother-General who have given me riches that go far beyond this book.

November 1978   R.G.

They that be whole need not a physician, but they that are sick. . . . Go ye and learn what that meaneth.

Jesus, in Matthew 9, verses 12–13

The Pretty Beads

PERHAPS IT WAS RIGHT THAT Lise should first see the beads as they lay in the dirt and debris of a table outside the cheapest kind of café among the rubbish of the Paris night.

Brought up in England—her Aunt Millicent was Protestant to her firm bones—Lise had never touched a rosary before. Patrice would have shrugged and smiled: "Quelle dévotion sentimentale!" but, "Many of our girls had a 'chapelet,' " Lise was to tell Soeur Marie Alcide. "Some of them were devoted to it."

"Filles de joie—to give them their happiest name— prostitutes, often are," said the Sister.

"Yes. Often ours would climb up to the Sacré Coeur in Montmartre, all those steep steps, to light a candle," said Lise. "I used to think it ironic that it was usually to Saint Thérèse of Lisieux, the pure Little Flower. They were far more reverent than many people in the world."

"In the world": that is the phrase nuns use of people

outside the convent, but we, too, lived in a different world from other women, thought Lise.

It was the silver glint of the cross that had caught her eye, or was it the hard little hand that held it? A ragamuffin hand, almost a child's. "I don't know. I never shall know," said Lise. "But I couldn't bear to see either of them in that pool of vomit and stale beer. I unclenched the fingers, picked up the beads and wiped them and put them in my handkerchief. Then I took Vivi home."

Chapter
One

THE SOUND OF THE BELL carried far over the orchards and fields of the convent of Belle Source.

It was the first bell for Vespers, not a bell in a bell-tower but a hand-bell, rung outside by the Soeur Réglementaire, the bell-ringer, and, in ones and twos, the nuns came in, those from the farm and garden shedding their heavy boots and dark blue overalls, all taking off their aprons. Each sister washed her hands in the basin at the end of the corridor, straightened her veil or took off her blue work head-handkerchief and put on her veil, then went to her place in the line where all the community stood. This was the time when each told, before them all, of any fault she had made.

"What—every day?" asked Father Marc, the new Aumônier. "That seems a little over-scrupulous. What faults could they possibly have?"

"Only faults against charity and I'm sure not many." The Prioress smiled. "But at our Béthanies we need charity as perhaps nowhere else."

"And, perhaps, as nowhere else," Marc was to say when he knew them better, "these Sisters understand the creeping power of sin; if you allow the least crack. . . ."

"I lingered in the garden after recreation and so kept two of my sisters waiting."

"I answered Soeur Marie Christine back and was rude." Soeur Marie Christine made a swift movement of reconciliation.

"I spoke sharply. . . ." They were those "least cracks"; but, like an echo from far far back, far from the steadfastness of Belle Source:

"She wouldn't stop crying so I stuffed my handkerchief into her mouth, down and down until . . ."

"He came in drunk, the third time that week. He sat down and vomited all over my clean table and his food. . . . I took a kitchen knife—it wasn't big . . ."

"Very well then, if you want to know. I went to bed with five boys in one night. Why shouldn't I? Everyone at the College did it."

"The first time I tried was when a man used to come outside the school. A lot of us did it but I . . . at first it was only a sniff but soon . . . soon I was getting zunked—high—more than I knew, then it got so that I had to have it, but it was six hundred francs for thirty grammes and I hadn't any money. That's why I . . ."

They were only echoes and, of course, only for some, and no one knew for whom. All alike, the Sisters stood in their white tunics and black veils, no difference between them.

In chapel for Vespers the sacristan had lit the candles on the three-branched candlestick that stood by the altar; on the altar itself was a bowl of roses, otherwise it was bare though a lamp set on the floor burned before the tabernacle all else was quiet and simple, the arched, whitewashed ceiling, the polished floor, plain wooden stalls.

The Prioress inclined her head and the nuns came in, their white tunics seeming to fill the chapel with light while the black of the veils picked out faces, some old, some young, pale or rosy or sunburned like Soeur Fiacre who looked after the gardens. Some wore spectacles; some strode, some limped; all, as they took their places, kept their hands under their scapulars which made them more anonymous.

Towards the end of Vespers came, as it always did, the Magnificat, the Virgin Mary's words of exaltation:

> *Mon âme exalte le Seigneur;*
> *exulte mon esprit en Dieu, mon Sauveur . . .*

> My soul magnifies the Lord,
> and my spirit has rejoiced in God, my Saviour.
> He has regarded the lowliness of His handmaid
> and He, who is mighty, hath done great things in
> me.

and in me . . . and me . . . me . . . me. . . . Another echo, glorified, that ran through the ranks of the nuns.

Great things. "Impossible things," most would have said.

"Father, I should like to introduce you to our Sisters." After Vespers the Prioress walked with Father Marc into the corridor. It was the Year of the Rabbit. "Fitting, because I have become a rabbit," said Marc.

He had celebrated the Chinese New Year in Hong Kong or, rather, Kowloon, in his parish "of huts and sampans," as he called it. The Dominicans had only just come there, "and were so sorely needed." Now, only in April, he was in France again, "sent back ignominiously."

"Not ignominiously," said Father Louis, Marc's best friend, once his novice master.

The long row of nuns seemed formidable. "Soeur Marie Hilaire de la Croix . . . Soeur Magdaleine Joséphine . . . Soeur Marguerite . . . Soeur Marie Alcide," a very old nun but with small black eyes that penetrated among her wrinkles. "Soeur Magdaleine de la Trinité

15

. . . Soeur Marie Agnès . . . Soeur Thecla . . . Soeur Fiacre . . . Soeur Marie Magdaleine de l'Enfant Jésus . . . Soeur Marie Lise." So many Maries and Magdaleines, thought Marc. "Well, if you were they, wouldn't you like to have those names if you could?" asked Father Louis. "Soeur Elizabeth, Soeur Lucie. . . ." The big brown eyes glanced timidly at Marc and were immediately veiled.

"I sometimes have to believe," Marc said that evening to Louis, "that being celibate does bring its dangers; one can stay a child. That little Soeur Lucie. . . ."

"What makes you think she is celibate?" asked Louis.

Marc had not wanted to come to Belle Source. When the Father Provincial had told him of this appointment Marc, in his dismay, had gone straight to his friend, now Prior of the great house of Saint Dominic, near Paris.

"Louis, help me out of this."

"I can't, Marc."

"You have influence, Louis. Please."

"No." The brusque answer made Marc blink. Then, "There they were beginning to know me," he said,— "there" meaning Kowloon. "I was learning the dialect, beginning to be able to understand them. They were so pitiful, Louis, the poverty and despair. I couldn't do much, but at least I was there for them, day and night."

"And what will you be at Belle Source?"

"For forty-five or so nuns! In Kowloon, that God-forsaken hellspot, there were hundreds, thousands, of poor souls. . . ."

"The Sisters work for souls too," Louis reminded him. "You haven't a monopoly."

Marc flushed and Louis put an arm round his shoulders. "Cheer up. It isn't the end of the world, mon ami—my friend. Think of the salads you will have," he said. "You can help with the hay and the apple-picking. It's part of their healing."

"I don't want any more healing, thank you."

"I wasn't thinking of you." Louis said it in the old

16

mild way that at once brought Marc to quietness.

"I'm sorry—but, mon Père, why? Why? Why?" demanded Marc. He had given Louis the old novice master title and, indeed, there was something of the novice still in Father Marc for all his forty-one years—the eagerness, passion and rebellion. "Why?" he demanded. "Why?"

"You know why. Typhoid is no joke, Marc, and then that formidable heart attack—three months in hospital." Louis rose from his desk and put his hand on Marc's shoulder. "Come and sit down. Let's have a drink. My scallywag friend, Jules Carpentier, who runs the betting-shop here keeps me in armagnac, bless him."

They drank out of the Prior's liqueur brandy glasses, unexpectedly fine old glass, "left to me by my Aunt Tilde."

Marc smiled. "Something you didn't sell to give the money away."

"No. I was fond of Aunt Tilde. Odd," said Louis. "I have scarcely ever bought anything in my life. It has always been given. Of course," said Louis, his eyes twinkling, "I know how to take."

"Is that a hint?"

"Maybe." Louis looked into the gold of the armagnac, savouring the aroma as the glass warmed in his hand. "To begin with, couldn't you enjoy your drink?" But Marc burst out again.

"To drop out of life when I had scarcely begun."

"Out of life?" Now it was Louis who smiled. "I can guess Béthanie will give you a few surprises."

At seven o'clock, the morning after his introduction, Marc said his first Mass at Belle Source. Father Louis was server.

"I should serve you, as I always did."

"Not now. You are the chaplain, confessor and, if you really care, general factotum, Father Marc."

He says Mass beautifully, thought Soeur Marie Lise

17

with relief. Instinctively she liked this new priest— But how ill he looks, she thought, thin and sallow and the strangely tonsured hair. "It isn't a tonsure," Marc was to tell her. "It's just that after typhoid my hair wouldn't grow again."

It was Soeur Marie Lise who cleared the altar after the Mass, carrying out book and vessels. Then she brought in the monstrance, shaped, on its tall stem, like a star. Vested in a stole, Marc put in the Host and knelt for a few moments before it, while behind him the soft voices sang. Though the monstrance was of gold, the chapel, he noticed, was plain almost to poorness; there was not even an organ. As he left, a sister moved a prie-dieu to the middle of the choir; from now until Benediction, there would be Perpetual Adoration of the Blessed Sacrament, the nuns keeping vigil, perhaps several at a time, perhaps only one, but the Presence was never left alone, and in the chapel silence, absolute and peaceful, reigned. Double glass doors shut off all sound from the ante-chapel.

Soeur Marie Lise brought a small rack of candles that would burn all day on the altar, then another bowl of roses. There was an inner and outer sacristy; to the inner one the sisters never came, except to clean and to lay out the vestments of the day; here Marc and Father Louis made their own silent prayer. Then they walked down to the aumônier's small house for breakfast.

In the domaine, a dew mist was drying off lawns and paths, flower-beds and well-kept vegetable plots. Not a nun was to be seen—"I expect they are at their breakfast—I'm sure more frugal than ours"—but the cows had been driven out to the paddocks—"Jerseys," said Louis, "and what beauties. I can guess they are part of the income of Belle Source." The hens were out too and in the pheasantry the cocks strutted in the brilliance of their feathers. Ducks quacked from the moat that ran along the walls. Last night, taking an evening stroll, Marc and Louis had passed a pen with a notice: *"Attention! Je couve,"* and had trod delicately by so as not to disturb the brooding pheasant hen. "She's another way by which Belle Source earns its living," and, "Marc, I envy you this," said Father Louis. At a turn of the path they met the sacristan, her arms full of daffodils for the chapel. "I wanted to pick them before the sun took off the dew," she said.

Marc had noticed this sister the evening before because of her height and the grace with which she moved. Later, he had gone into the wrong sacristy and found her there polishing the silver and had asked her name. "Soeur Marie Lise du Rosaire."

It was another of these, as he was to learn, anonymous names—no surnames or family names were given at Béthanie—but he had asked, pleasantly, as he would have asked any nun, "You have a particular devotion to the rosary then?"

"No." It was brusque, almost rude and, to his dismay, two red patches appeared on her cheeks. "I'm afraid I haven't learnt that devotion." She put the chalices away and shut the cupboard. "Good-night, Father," she said, and was gone, but this morning she was smiling and "buoyant with happiness," as Louis said afterwards.

"It was a lovely thing for me, mon Père," she said to Marc with complete friendliness, "that you should have said your first Mass here this morning. For me it's an anniversary. Eighteen years ago today, I entered Béthanie."

"Congratulations, Sister." Both men said it warmly and Louis added, "I envy you being sacristan."

"I'm not sacristan. I'm only filling in for Soeur Magdaleine Baptiste who is ill. I'm the convent dogsbody."

"Also, I'm told, one of the missionaries, the prison visitors." Louis had an extraordinary way of finding things out. Without questions, thought Marc. "A very special work," said Father Louis.

"Just work." As she moved away towards the chapel a puff of wind caught her veil, blowing it back, and they saw she had a scar on her left cheek, running from her brow to the ear. Marc had already noticed the poise of the tall figure; and found himself wondering how old she was; the line of hair that showed was as black as the veil that hid it; she had had eighteen years at Béthanie, but one could enter at any age, twenty, thirty, forty or more, so that told nothing; all the same Marc sensed there was some deep gulf between this Soeur Marie Lise and the girl she must once have been. Her blue eyes were direct, steady, but there was the scar and, There are dark feelings here, thought Marc, feelings that not even control can hide. He was not surprised when, over coffee, Louis said, "That sacristan of yours . . ."

"She's not sacristan and she's not mine."

"Soeur Marie Lise then," and Louis said, "I have seen that face before. . . ." He brooded. Then, "Yes," he said, "it was quite long ago. It must have been soon after World War Two." Father Louis had been in the First. "You could only have been twelve years old or so, Marc, too young to know, but . . . Yes, I remember her."

Chapter Two

BEHIND LISE THE DOOR SHUT. It was the small exit door set in huge bolted gates of iron from which the walls of Vesoul, closed prison for women, stretched away, forbiddingly high and angled with arc-lights at every corner and curve. The small door was locked too and the guard had a grille so that he could look through.

He had let Lise out just after six o'clock in the morning, motioning her through without a word of congratulation, not even a "Bonne chance"—Perhaps he had seen too many women come and go and wanted to get back to his newspaper—but, Never mind, thought Lise. She was outside.

It had been cleverly managed, announced for the afternoon; but if she had come out of Vesoul then, there would have been a barricade of cameras and journalists waiting. A crowd probably hostile. "La Balafrée released." "La Balafrée."

"Yes, that was my nickname," said Lise. "La Balafrée.

The branded one, gashed for life." "La Balafrée, Madame Lise" . . . "Madame Lise gets off after only ten years." Lise could imagine the headlines, the talk revived; commuters reading their daily papers in trains, comments from politicians, gossip in cafés and factories, shops: women at home pronouncing over their coffee, "Something wrong with our penal service . . . It's not justice. Far too soft . . . only ten years!" Let them try just one, thought Lise. Would any of them have said "Poor woman"?

But she was not poor; she, Lise, now, at thirty-seven, had no surname she wanted to own, no family or old friends to greet her, no possessions except what she had in her suitcase, no money except the few hundred francs she had earned in the workshop; in fact, nothing except hope, but she stepped out into the April morning buoyant with the happiness Father Louis was to see all those years after. She stood on the pavement and took a deep breath.

"Will you be frightened?" Marianne Rueff, the Assistante Sociale or Welfare Officer, had asked her. "It would be only natural after so many years." But Lise was not frightened, only a little giddy, and feeling a stranger, as she had felt when, after the few discreet goodbyes, she had crossed the prison outer courtyard with its trees and lines of parked cars to the gates.

It was the first time she had set foot on that courtyard ground since the day when the great gate had opened to let in the police van, the "panier à salade," with its load of miserable occupants. She had not noticed the trees then; it had been too difficult getting down from the van because she had been chained to the woman next to her, as they had been chained on the long train journey, two by two like miscreant sheep; Lise's wrists had been marked for days. It had also been raining, a cold dark afternoon, And I was dark, black dark, with no feeling as if I had been made of wood, wood not iron thankfully, she thought now, because there is a tale, or is it a sentence that someone

22

once said when speaking of a lute, that anything made of wood has an affinity with the Cross.

"But why did I take three years to find that out?" Lise had said to Soeur Marie Alcide. "It was only after I had done three years that suddenly your white tunics . . . Why so long?"

"Well, perhaps you were not ready," said Soeur Marie Alcide.

"I suppose if it were the same for everybody it would be very dull," Lise had said.

"I think you will find God is never dull," said Soeur Marie Alcide.

"You are put down as Elizabeth Fanshawe," the Directrice had said that first night at Vesoul. To Lise it had sounded almost like another accusation. The Directrice and Sous-Directrice were in ordinary but well-cut suits; they looked not like senior prison officers, but everyday women, except that both had unmistakable authority; the clerk, writing down particulars as the forms were filled in, was in white, and Lise had caught a glimpse of Madame Chef, the chief wardress, her white uniform gold-starred on the lapel, and over it a dark blue cloak. The new arrivals had gone in to the office one by one. "Elizabeth Fanshawe, but you are know as Madame Lise Ambard." Mercifully the Directrice did not add "La Balafrée," though that had screamed from the headlines in every newspaper. "Quinze ans pour La Balafrée" "La Balafrée condamnée à quinze ans . . ." "fifteen years" "La Balafrée."

"I am Elizabeth Fanshawe," said Lise.

"Then you are English!"

"I was English once."

"But of course you are English," Patrice used often to say. "Anyone not a fool should see that."

"Most people think I'm an American."

"Americans don't often have that long-legged grace." Lise knew she carried herself well. That was from years of Aunt Millicent's "Sit *up*, Elizabeth. Don't slouch," and I was taller than most French girls, "Nor do they often have fine bones like a racehorse," said Patrice. "Didn't the English have a king," he teased her, "Somebody Longshanks?"

"Edward Longshanks. That's hardly a compliment."

"You don't need compliments, thank God, chérie. Then there's your voice. Do you remember how embarrassed I was when I first took you into a restaurant? It carried into every corner, that 'county' voice."

"Don't be silly. It's not county. My father was a solicitor."

"But of what family! You have 'family' stamped all over you."

"Well, I don't know them and they certainly don't know me. . . ."

"Next of kin?" the Sous-Directrice had asked.

"No one." Lise could not, possibly, name Aunt Millicent.

"There must be; someone has to be notified in case of illness or death."

"There is no one."

"Then what is to be done in the event . . . ?"

"Put me in the dustbin . . ." but Lise could not say that; she shrugged.

She had told Jacques Jouvin the facts; facts, to her, were the least important; he had had to deduce the rest which was perhaps why, in court, he was so badly defeated.

Jacques—"Jacquot" to them all at the Rue Duchesne —was Maître Jouvin, a well known and eloquent lawyer who, out of kindness, had chosen to defend Lise. "But I have hardly any money, Jacquot. It all belonged to Patrice or, rather, Emile." Emile, small, pale, greasy-skinned, with his quick currant-black eyes and short-cut hair, lived in the shadow of his splendid brother. "But Emile had more power than we thought," said Lise. "He kept the accounts, which really governed everything."

24

"Rosamonde will have to go," Emile had pronounced one day.

"Go? Go where?"

"Where they all go," said Emile without interest: "to a cheaper house if she's lucky. Maybe the streets . . ."

The streets were a different world from a "house," and one despised the other. "But I started like that," said Patrice, "sending out my girls," but even then he had groomed them carefully. "Monsieur always had class," Eugenia, the maid in charge of the rooms, said in pride. He showed Lise in fun. "Stand against the wall—pretend it's a doorway or a porch. Lean . . . look at ease. Pull your stomach *in*, girl. Light a cigarette. Now show me your leg. Lift it . . . higher . . . now show the other one discreetly—you must always be careful of the flics—the police. Now! I'll be the client. Puff your cigarette so that the glow shows your face. Now follow me. No, don't move. Follow me with your *eyes*."

"Coming with me?"

"How much?" and Patrice laughed again. "How much will you charge me, chérie?" But to Lise it was not fun. To be put out of a house to *that*. . . .

"You have had Rosamonde for fifteen years," she had protested to Emile.

"Precisely. Which is why she's not earning her keep; she's too old."

"Milo! She might end up in the Seine!" Emile shrugged.

"If there was no chance of a sou for Rosamonde," Lise told Maître Jouvin, "what hope will there be for me?"

"It doesn't matter," said Jacques. "I don't care about the fee, but please, Lise, be frank with me," and Lise had tried to tell it all, as simply and directly as possible, first for Jacques, later to Soeur Marie Alcide, as one day she would tell it to Marc, "when he had to know," said Lise.

It seemed an interminable dossier. "How absurd," said Lise. "It took me two minutes to kill Patrice, two and a half years to compile the reason why, and three days of public time and money for the Court to find me guilty when I had already said I was."

The dossier—the truth but somehow oddly distorted —had been read out, French fashion, to the assembled Court before the trial began. "In England you are tried first for the particular crime before your disreputable past is made known," Lise was to explain to Marc.

"Where did you meet Patrice Ambard?" That was almost the first question Monsieur le Président had put to her.

"In a fountain." Lise could not say that but it was true.

It had been the night of August the twenty-fourth, 1944, the Liberation of Paris, when the French tanks came roaring down the Avenue d'Orléans, and all bedlam broke loose as the people massed the Avenue, every avenue, the boulevards and streets in a sea of hysteria and joy. Every Place was crowded, the bars were giving free drinks as bells were rung, the deep note of Notre Dame sounding over all.

It was dangerous; bursts of fighting were still going on as snipers shot from the roofs, but every corner was already full of French and Allied troops. They had to protect their prisoners from the crowd who spat at them, kicked and bit, even tried to lynch them. Men climbed ladders to sit on window sills and walls; they sat in trees, as they shouted and sang.

Lise had driven all day, coming up from the coast. "I was seconded to the Motor-Transport Corps, picked to drive the American General, General Simpson. I can see myself now in my khaki tunic and skirt, green flashes, so proud of my camouflaged Ford with its fluttering flag. I was just twenty."

"France." Aunt Millicent had said doubtfully when Lise told her in confidence that she might be going there. "Will it be safe?"

"By then it will."

"Does it mean Paris?"

"I hope so."

26

"Lady Moberly used to know of a good pension where they took English people. I wonder if it's still there."

"Aunt, I'm in the Army; there'll be quarters."

Lise lived with Aunt Millicent, "because I was an orphan. My aunt had hardly been out of our village, Greenhurst," and, "I don't like it," said Aunt Millicent, but to Lise the thought of Paris was the most exciting of her life, "which wouldn't be difficult," she had told Patrice, "brought up in a little Sussex village by a maiden aunt, going to a small private boarding-school for girls. We couldn't afford very much. If it hadn't been for the war I might have turned into a second Aunt Millicent,"she had teased Patrice.

"You! Impossible."

She had driven into Paris that first night, or tried to drive, but the traffic was jammed; people surged round the cars and trucks; soldiers sat girls on the bonnets; they stood on the mudguards and climbed on the roofs, cheering every army car they saw, waving little French or American flags or Union Jacks.

"Why were you waving an American flag when you're English?" Patrice had asked.

"I took it off the car."

Lise had tried to edge along the pavement, the corporal in the seat beside her doing his best to guide her but she could hardly hear him. The General and his A.D.C. were in the back and at last her "old boy" as Lise called him had leaned forward. "It's no good, Liz. See if you can turn into the next side road and stop. We'll walk, or try and walk." After almost an hour, Lise succeeded in that. "Lock the car securely and come back in the morning," the General ordered. "We'll hope she'll still be here. Make a note of the street. You can fetch her, then report."

Lise had failed to report.

As the "old boy" got out of the car with the Captain he had stopped. "You know where you're supposed to be staying, Liz?"

"Yes Sir." In front of the other two she did not call

27

him Simps as she did when they were alone. She gave him the paper with the address.

"Do you know where this is?"

"I haven't been in Paris before."

"I see. Well, I shall need Captain Harlan. Corporal. . . ."

"Yes Sir."

"What's your name?"

"Collins, Sir."

The General gave him the scrap of paper. "Corporal Collins, you will escort Driver Fanshawe to her hostel. Here is the address," and, to Lise, "You speak French, Liz?"

"A little."

"Enough to ask the way?"

"I think so."

"You will take her straight there?"

"Yes Sir."

"Sir . . ." began Lise.

"Orders are orders," said the old boy.

"But . . ." and it burst out, "I have *never* been in Paris before."

He stopped, looking down at her—he was so tall he could do that—and as he looked a surge of people were round them; one woman caught Lise, hugged and kissed her then dared to kiss the General. "Please," beseeched Lise.

"Very well." The eyes below the bushy eyebrows smiled. "Let her have a little tour around first, Corporal, but not too long or too late, Liz. Promise."

Fortunately the crowd swept them apart before Lise could give that promise.

It was ten o'clock. For three hours or more Lise had walked, danced, drunk wine with whom she did not know, in bars and cafés so crowded nobody could sit down. They were giving free drinks. "Take them while you can get them, mes gars. It will never happen again." At first Corporal Collins had held Lise's arm in

28

a grip so hard it bruised but, as with the General and
A.D.C., they had soon been swept apart—and the Corporal had her scrap of paper. Lise still had the name of
the side street where she had left the staff car and its
keys were in her pocket; if she could find her way back,
she could unlock it and sleep in it; she had been too
happy to bother, but now she was getting tired; her feet
were aching. It had been a long day and, "Excusez-moi,
Madame. Est-ce que vous pouvez me diriger . . . ?" but a
band of young Americans, G.I.s and French girls, exu-
berant with joy and wine, pulled Lise away and into
their ranks. "Come on, Polly." Why Polly, wondered
Lise? Perhaps they called all English girls Polly. "You
don't wanna stand there talking that rubbish."

"But I want to go home."

"No one's going home tonight. C'mon," and soon they
were in a chain, dancing and buffeting. They came to a
Place where they could swing the girls high; Lise's cap
came off, her hair fell down. Here, fountains were
playing; perhaps they had not been turned on since the
Occupation and someone had rigged up lights, red,
white and blue, playing on the water. People sobbed
with joy as they saw them. In a final burst of exhilara-
tion, the young men swung the girls into a fountain.

"That's where I first saw you," said Patrice. "Laughing and splashing, rising from the water like a nymph."

"Funny kind of nymph in a khaki uniform."

"It didn't look like khaki—dark. You might have
been wrapped in water weeds and your dark hair, wet
and streaming. I can still see your wet face and the
blue of your eyes. . . ."

All that Lise knew was that the man who helped her
out of the fountain was no ordinary person. To begin
with he was not in uniform—even Patrice did not dare
to wear one to which he was not entitled—and, by his
clothes, she thought he must be someone important.
He was not as tall as she, but Patrice had "presence"—
she did not know what else to call it—and charm; he
rid Lise of her Americans not only with authority but

friendliness—what he said in French she could not then fathom. He was red-haired, something she had not known a Frenchman could be; that, his blue eyes and fair skin were even more difficult to explain when she saw Emile, a "frog" Frenchman if ever there were one. They must have had different fathers or different mothers, thought a more grown-up Lise, but she never knew which. Patrice and Emile said little about their family though once, "It's the Norman in me," Patrice had said of his hair and eyes.

He was far older than she—how much older she did not see until they were indoors under electric lights; He's at least forty, thought Lise; that to her was a great age then, but it did not seem to bother Patrice. "If ever there were a happy hypocrite," he said often, "I am he. I amuse myself as if I were twenty. Worry? I leave that to Emile and take what I want from life with both hands."

At the moment it was clear he wanted Lise.

"Mademoiselle, you are very wet." He had an extraordinarily sweet smile. "Somehow he always kept that," Lise was to tell Maître Jouvin and, for a moment, was not able to go on.

"You are very wet."

Dripping from the fountain, Lise had laughed and thrown back her hair.

"You don't mind?"

"Not tonight. Who could mind anything tonight?"

"I mind that you are probably catching cold. Are you alone?"

"Yes." Lise said it so firmly that he laughed too. "But I think that must not continue. You must let me take you to your—but it wouldn't be a hotel. Where are you staying?"

"That's just it; I don't know. Corporal Collins knew but I have lost Corporal Collins, and my cap. . . ." She could not stop laughing.

"You seem singularly carefree, Mademoiselle."

"Oh, I am—I am . . ." but Lise was beginning to feel dizzy; she swayed and he caught her.

"I think, besides being wet, you are a little drunk, Mademoiselle."

"Well, I haven't had wine—much—before."

"And nothing to eat."

"Not all day." Now her teeth were chattering.

"Restaurants are impossible; also, you are wet. I'm sorry I sent my mother out of Paris,"—Lise was to hear of that fictitious mother again—"but our apartment is quite near and dinner is waiting. Let me take you there."

"But. . . ." "At least I had the sense to hesitate," Lise said afterwards. "I have orders."

"How can you carry them out?" That was unanswerable. "Don't be afraid. Patagon will chaperon us."

"Who is Patagon?"

"My macaw—blue and yellow and big and fierce. He will tear me to pieces if I touch you. Come."

"You are very kind."

"Not at all. It's not often we entertain Ondine, Patagon and I. Come." "And I was hooked like any silly fish," said Lise.

"Your age?" Vesoul's Directrice had asked.

"Thirty-one."

"Religion?"

"None."

The Directrice made no comment. A print of Lise's index finger was taken. On the form she could read "Distinguishing marks," but there was no need to ask that question: both the officers' eyes, trained to take in every detail, had already flickered over her face.

"I wonder if she was in the Resistance," Father Louis was to say long afterwards to Marc when they had first noticed the scar in the Belle Source garden.

"Would she be as old as that?" asked Marc.

"Somewhere near, I should think," said Father Louis, and "That scar must once have been deep. It has paled

31

now," but any emotion, anger, distress, made it redden and stand out again. It was throbbing as Lise had stood before the desk and, "Yes, Madame, I have a distinguishing mark, I'm La Balafrée," and, with all the insolence she could muster—Lise could be vilely insolent—"Would you like me to tell you what we canaille call a scar?" she had asked, and shot out the obscene word. "Oh, I was horrible—horrible," she told Soeur Marie Alcide.

They had looked at her without a change of expression; the Directrice simply sounded the bell on her desk and said, "Next." If only I had known then, Lise thought afterwards, what it is to have pity.

It had been a long afternoon. The Directrice and Sous-Directrice had already seen more than a dozen prisoners, some defiant, some hostile, some stunned with despair, some rude like Lise, all exhausted; a soul-destroying task but Lise had not a thought for the officers then—they seemed not women but ogres. She only knew she was cold to her bones, bruised with tiredness and frightened by the echoing silence, a silence that was unnerving after Sevenet, the Maison d'Arrêt, where she had been kept waiting in two years of suspense before her trial; Sevenet had been bad enough but talking, some independent life, was allowed. At Vesoul it seemed absolute silence was a rule. Oh well! thought Lise. I never want to talk again.

After the supper was eaten in that silence, there were more orders before they were taken to their allotted cells.

"Empty your handbag. We shall list the contents and give you a receipt. Your watch please."

On this morning of her release Lise had been given the watch back, but after all these years, would it go? There is no service to wind up prisoners' watches but—what does it matter?—Lise had thought that first day of prison. If it stops, why bother? Life has stopped too.

"Your jewellery," and the wardress said automatically, "You may keep your wedding ring."

"I have no wedding ring."

Aunt Millicent had, of course, believed she had. Patrice, to Lise's surprise, had gone over to England with her to pay a duty visit to Aunt Millicent. "But why?" Lise asked him afterwards.

"As a matter of fact there was a possibility of our setting Milo up in London."

Lise remembered how out of place Patrice had looked in Greenhurst and had been amused to see how quickly Aunt Millicent had fallen under his charm and his power. He had already succeeded in getting Lise released from the Motor Transport Corps. "How?" asked Lise.

"I have a good many important people in my little hand," Patrice had said and laughed.

Aunt Millicent had even given them her Rockingham tea-set as a wedding present. "At least we believed it was Rockingham. I believed things then," Lise told Soeur Marie Alcide.

"Where does your charming Patrice live?" Aunt had asked.

"I'm afraid in rather an expensive part of Paris, near the Opéra, the Rue Duchesne." Patrice had been astute enough to buy the house when the war was at its worst. Lise did not tell Aunt Millicent that now she, Lise, lived there too—but at first she had thought it was only an apartment.

It was over a nightclub—at least I thought it was a nightclub. Patrice had a private staircase; the flat was almost aggressively masculine with leather-covered sofas and chairs, colours in reds and brown, but there was an odd smell of scent and always, through the night, the sound of music—and there were the silk dressing-gowns, the exotic blue and yellow of the giant macaw in his cage; only Patrice could ever let Patagon out and seemed to take pleasure in his fierce pecks and beating wings. "You must feed him with raw meat but use a pair of tongs," warned Patrice. "Throw the hood over him when you clean his cage."

"I think I had a hood over my head too," said Lise.

Aunt Millicent had stopped her allowance. "You won't need anything now," Aunt Millicent had said. "Monsieur Ambard is obviously rich," and, "The Fanshawe girl who married that rather outré Frenchman . . ." Lise could hear the talk in Greenhurst.

"An exeedingly charming and well-to-do Frenchman." Aunt Millicent, Lise thought, would have defended her but, "What am I to do?" Lise asked in Paris. "I must earn my living."

"On the contrary, you must live and that is what you are going to do—with me."

"But didn't you guess what kind of man he was?" asked Jacques.

"I was as green as a lettuce leaf." True, Lise had been driving for two years, but usually with other girls. "I had never met anyone who was anyone until I was seconded to drive General Simpson. I was a good driver, but he was fatherly and in those days, even at twenty, one could be young."

"There was one thing that did strike me," she told Maître Jouvin, "though I didn't try and understand it then. Patrice looked so well fed—too well fed in a Paris that had been half-starved in those years of the Occupation; some people had gone through the winter living on turnips and a few potatoes, while he had the sleek satisfied look that comes from at least two good meals a day; when I saw that dinner I couldn't believe my eyes—a whole fillet of beef; I didn't even know what it was. In my ignorance I had supposed conditions in France were different from England, not that they were worse for most people. If I had stopped to work it out, it would have told me many things—how, for instance, Patrice and Emile got the money to move from the little house on the left bank to the Rue Duchesne—but I didn't stop. I couldn't, it was all such a whirlwind."

Until she met Patrice, Lise had not been to a fashionable restaurant or to any but a provincial theatre, never to opera, never to a nightclub. "I didn't know men chose women's clothes, dressed you like a model or a doll. Patrice gave me rings, jewellery, furs. I had Coco, a little French bulldog I adored—Patagon was wildly jealous. It was fun and I had never had any fun."

"And you were lovers?"

"Of course," but to Soeur Marie Alcide she said, "Until Patrice, I had never been kissed on the mouth—or . . ." she broke off but it was Lise, not the Sister, who blushed. "I didn't know you made love over and over again, not just once in the night but day-time, any time. I thought that was for whores. It didn't occur to me I was a whore. . . ."

"Put on that gold lamé dress, chérie," said Patrice. "I think you must go downstairs tonight."

"Downstairs?"

"You don't think I live here as a tenant?"

"You mean that . . . that club. . . ."

"Belongs to me, at least to me and Milo—and it isn't exactly a club, chérie. You said you wanted to earn your living. Well, you are going to be a little more generous than that. You are going to earn mine. . . ."

"And it dawned on me," said Lise.

"You mean . . . be like those girls?" She was white with shock.

"They are not 'those girls'. They are the same as you. Many of them started up here, chérie—just like you."

Patrice knew how to hurt physically too, without leaving a mark; when Lise refused he had twisted her arms, holding them behind her back and slapped her face until her ears rang. "But it wasn't that which made me give in," Lise told Soeur Marie Alcide. "I . . . I had thought he loved me—of course I didn't know then what love was—for instance that pride has nothing to do with love and in that first hurt moment I didn't care what I did—or thought I didn't."

35

"I had never seen the rooms on the first floor," said Lise. "I had not even known they were there, a whole line of rooms, opulent and scented, with old Eugenia hobbling up and down." "Number four, Momone." "Number seven." Eugenia was the mother of Gaston, who kept the entrance and did everything else as well from morning to night. Eugenia spied through keyholes and cackled; she carried tales from spite and always had her hand held out. It was her duty to keep the rooms tidy, smooth each bed with her stick or put on a fresh cover as soon as it was vacant and, "Don't let anyone be too long," Patrice would instruct, "As I was to instruct," said Lise. "They're not here for the night, you know—unless they pay."

They usually paid. The Rue Duchesne was expensive. "Fifty dollars for one go!" a young American expostulated and, "There are cheaper houses round the corner," Lise, when she became Madam Manager—Mère Maquerelle—used to say smoothly. "Besides, you have chosen Zoë, one of our best girls, so what did you expect?"

"It was amazing how quickly I learnt," said Lise, "and soon how well I trained them, considering I was something of a fake myself—a whore who wouldn't be a whore." Then she added, "The Rockingham tea-set was a fake too, as I found out when I tried to sell it. They would only take it in the flea-market, where I belonged too."

"Not quite," said Soeur Marie Alcide.

"Quite," said Lise firmly. "Ma Soeur, you don't know it all."

On that first night she had been handed over to a Colonel of the Foreign Legion—"Worse than an Arab and quite drunk," said Patrice. "You may as well go in at the deep end. Now remember. . . ."

Remember! Lise never forgot. The Colonel had had no mercy and finally, leaving him asleep, Lise had escaped, gasping. She had dodged past Eugenia down the back stairs, found a coat in the passage—it had probably been Gaston's—ran through the kitchen like a mad thing, astonishing the cook Marcelline who, loyal even then, never told a word, and, in the street, ran again. She was sore, dishevelled, blinded by tears and it was raining hard. She had seen a church—it would be empty at this time of night. It had been not only empty but locked and then Lise had seen a light in the presbytery. She crept up and saw, through the window, a priest, white-haired, old, but still up, working, writing at a desk. Timidly she had knocked.

"But, my child, I can't let you stay here all night," Père Silas had said.

"Father, *please*." "If he had, would it all have been different?" she asked Soeur Marie Alcide. "He hesitated, but it must have been my looks," the dress, gold shot with green, brilliant and revealing, the scent Patrice had sprayed her with, her make-up raddled, her hair fallen out of its knot and, "I can't," said Père Silas. "I have young priests here . . . and my housekeeper. I'll find you a taxi while you tidy yourself. Here is an address. I'll telephone the Sisters and they'll take you in for tonight. Then come and see me in the morning."

"I have no money, Father."

"They won't want money. Here's enough for the taxi," and the good old man had given Lise a ten-franc note. "That's too much." "Keep it, keep it." Then he had put on his cloak, taken his umbrella and gone out into the streets; he came back with a taxi and put her into it. "Go to the Sisters for tonight and come back tomorrow morning. Ten o'clock without fail."

"Without fail, Father," but the address Lise had given the driver was not that of the hostel but the Rue Duchesne. It was only when she was there again that Lise realised she had no bed of her own. "I should have slept on the kitchen table." Instead she had climbed Patrice's staircase back to the flat. "And for some unfathomable reason I told Patrice about Père Silas."

"I'm going back to see him in the morning."

"Are you?"

"Yes at ten. This is the end, Patrice."

"At ten?" Patrice had made no other comment but, "At ten o'clock I was locked in his office," Lise told Soeur Marie Alcide and, "You're going to learn from another kind of priest," said Patrice.

When it was over he had knocked her on to the floor—she, proud, poised Lise, cowering and bruised. "You'll not be fit to be seen for a good few days," said Patrice. "But if you like, go and show yourself now to your holy man."

"You could have," said Soeur Marie Alcide.

"I was too—ashamed."

"He would have understood."

"Would he? No, he couldn't."

The Sister studied Lise's bowed head. "Was it because . . . you liked it?" asked Soeur Marie Alcide.

The head came up and Lise looked Soeur Marie Alcide in the face. "It was ecstasy," said Lise.

Patrice had said, "Now come up to the flat."

"No."

"Yes."

Upstairs he had wrapped her in one of his own dressing-gowns, the same she had worn the night of the fountain, then given her brandy, and had taken her face between his hands. "Poor bruised face. Terrible black eye!" and, "Do you think I like doing things like this?" he had asked almost virtuously. "Like sharing you? But we have to eat, buy clothes, live. Don't you understand?" said Patrice and, for once, he had spoken seriously. "Don't you realise I'm good for nothing, only bad for one thing."

"And you have no limits."

"Fortunately none," and he smiled, the smile that always left Lise helpless. She tried to fight him. "I hate you."

"No, you love me—and I love you, Lise"—"Which no

one else had ever really done," Lise told Soeur Marie Alcide.

"Why should he love me? Me, among all those dozens and dozens of girls far more beautiful, amusing, desirable. Why me? Of course, he knew he could trust this poor fool."

"Yes, loyalty rates high in that world," Soeur Marie Alcide agreed. "But I think it was for something more uncommon than that. You always gave, Lise, gave through thick and thin."

"Yes, you are right, chérie," Patrice had said seriously. "You are different from the others, from everyone," and, "After that," said Lise, "though I went downstairs every night I didn't go up to the 'rooms.' It was as if I had a label on me—'Monsieur Patrice'; the men kept their distance—except one . . ."—and she said, "Yes, I had five years of Patrice. Only two without Vivi but . . ." She broke off; she could not tell Soeur Marie Alcide, not even her, what else Patrice had said that day.

"Lise, say after me what I shall say to you." He had been even more serious.

"Say what?"

"Just, 'Chéri' and, 'à jamais'—'forever.' Say it."

"No."

"Yes."

"But it's like a children's pact."

"Children have a way of speaking the truth. Say it."

"I can't."

"Please, chérie." No one ever said "chérie" as Patrice could, but Lise has still tried to hold out. "Patrice, not now."

"Now."

And, through her ravages and tears, Lise had whispered it: "Chéri, à jamais."

"Go behind the screen, Fanshawe, undress . . . put your clothes on the chair . . . now take a shower."

"Madame, I had a bath this morning."

"Take a shower. Use the soap."

Then came what Lise, for all her long sentence, never could get used to—the search, when the prisoner stood naked while her body, her hair, her clothes, her cell were thoroughly gone over. It had to happen, she realised afterwards, and at unexpected times. "If there isn't a search, properly done and often done, there will be trouble," Mademoiselle Signoret, Directrice of Le Fouest, twin prison to Vesoul, was to tell her, but now Lise smarted under the indignity.

"Take your uniform," her "trousseau," underclothes of stiff thick woven cotton and, "in those days," Lise was to tell Marc, "we had a long dingy dark dress, a shoulder cape—unmistakably 'prison,' and a black head-handkerchief that most of us refused to wear, stuff slippers for indoors, sabots for outside—mine were too wide for my feet and made blisters."

On the morning of her release Lise's own clothes had been given back to her packed in the expensive dressing-case that had been one of Patrice's early gifts, morocco leather with ivory fittings—"Ivory suits you better than silver"—but dressing in those once familiar clothes had been to Lise like dressing a ghost.

"On the last day of the trial Lise Ambard, La Balafrée, wore a dark red Chanel suit. . . ." Marcelline had brought the suit to Sevenet. She had wanted Lise to wear the black and white check, "So striking, Madame," but Lise was glad now she had refrained; it would have been far too conspicuous for coming out of prison. As it was, she was sure she looked strangely old-fashioned and she had put on weight under the Vesoul régime, so that she had had to pin the skirt band. Her hands too felt stiff in gloves, it was so long since she had worn any. She had left her hat behind. "Hardly anyone wears them nowadays," Marianne had told her. "Use your scarf—it's a beauty." It had been another present from Patrice, long long after the dressing-case, but "After all, you keep my house for me."

"Both houses," she had flung at him.

40

Now the scarf looked as over-opulent as the suit looked out of date. Never mind, they'll find me some clothes, thought Lise. It doesn't matter what, because I shan't have to wear lay ones much longer, or hope I shan't, please God. "Please God," murmured Lise again and stepped into the road.

Behind her, the big building rose above the street, shut off from it by the walls and the gatehouse. The walls in places were double, as Lise knew, and set with those merciless arc-lights. Who would have believed that she, Lise, could come to view those very walls with something like affection, certainly gratitude. What a paradox! she thought. They are supposed to be unyielding, yet have yielded me so much—though I could not have believed it when I went inside them.

Such a weight of despair hung over the Maison Centrale of Vesoul, despair and fear; the despair could be dispelled, as Lise had found out, but there was reason for the fear. "You'll see, when we come out," the other women had told her, "few people, very few, will have anything to do with us, no matter what help we are given and never mind what we have done and how we have paid for it."

The resentment was understandable. There were, of course, the irrécupérables, the unrescuable, who seemed to have evil in their skin, as if the devil had sown the seed that made them bad through and through—but many, Lise was certain, were in prison not because of what they had done, but because of what other people, especially men, had done to them, and some of us, like me, thought Lise, were in prison for their illusions. Well, I have no illusions now. Those first years at Vesoul had cured that, three long years—before I woke up, thought Lise.

Time had passed—but I did not know it; like all the others, for the first three months, Lise had had to be in the Divison d'Accueil—what a name for it, "Division of Welcome"! Solitary confinement. "Terrible, but necessary," Mademoiselle Signoret was to tell her. "We have

41

to find out what each newcomer is like—because of the others." It was always "because of the others" in prison, in the Rue Duchesne as in the convent, sensible and just, but hard. Hard! At first, determined to stay sane, Lise had made a calendar and crossed off the days—But soon I couldn't remember if I had crossed one off or not, "so I crossed another and perhaps another and soon I thought it was Friday and it was still only Tuesday, or thought it was Tuesday and suddenly it was Friday. If I had gone to Mass as I could have, I should have know the days, but it didn't occur to me to go to Mass. Why, when I went to those early morning Masses in Paris?" she asked Soeur Marie Alcide.

Perhaps the worst of the Division d'Accueil was when each prisoner was let out, morning and evening, to take her solitary exercise in a little gravelled courtyard; Lise, of the long legs, who loved to walk, to stride—going round and round like a leopard in a cage. I felt like a leopard or is it a panther that never can be tamed? They were right then, with their walls and locks and keys—I was dangerous.

Yet, even there, in the Division d'Accueil, for Lise there had been her star. "The real prison is the night," the other women had told her when she was allowed to join them. "It's then, after they turn the key in the lock of your cell at eight o'clock and you are alone in that narrow box until half-past six next morning; a box with an iron bed, a chair and table, a locker that has no lock, a basin and sluice in the corner with the bucket you have filled beside it . . . yes, it is then, in the night. . . ." But Lise had not found that.

The cell windows were not barred; they were made of strong frosted unbreakable glass in metal frames, but one pane, too small to get through, of course, had been left clear by some imaginative person—afterwards Lise fathomed it was a suggestion of Mademoiselle Signoret, though Mademoiselle was then only a junior officer at Vesoul—a pane left clear so that Lise could look out, over to the hills, across the shimmer of lights that was the town, near but utterly distant from the inmates of the Maison Centrale.

The high top of the window opened too, the top panes pulled by a cord, but there was no way of getting up to them, unless one pulled the bed under it and set a chair on top, but the vigilante, passing by every few minutes, would have lifted the "judas," the peephole shutter and seen—yet standing on the chair, Lise was tall enough to look up and out to the sky, and every evening she saw the star. They called it the evening star, Hesperus, Aunt Millicent had told Lise in the garden at home when she was a little girl. In Paris Lise had not seen it until Patrice banished her to the fourth floor, when she would stand, with Coco in her arms, her cheek against his black head, and watch it over the rooftops and chimney-pots of the Rue Duchesne. It seemed to give her life a continuity and in prison, locked in so early, she had seen how, in summer, it appeared as the sun went down; then the evening star would shine in the last green of the sunset, *green like a green pearl*"—she had read that, long ago, in a poem. Every evening it was there, steadfast, and, "Somehow, like the Magi, miraculously," said Lise, "I had the wit to follow it."

"Shall we come and fetch you?" Soeur Marie Alcide had asked.

"I should rather make my own way."

For this moment, at least, of her release, she could choose and, at that thought, it was as if the humdrum town street opened like a dazzling path in front of Lise, seeming as wide as the whole world. Then she laughed at herself; she had already made her choice, or been chosen, for a very different path, a narrow and difficult one. First, though, there was one thing she had promised herself she would do, only an infinitesimal thing, self-indulgent perhaps but how precious only someone who had been in a Vesoul could know. She could also choose whether she would walk to the station—I should have to ask the way. Well, why not? I am free to speak, actually speak to a stranger, or I could find a bus-stop and go by bus, take my own ticket—or ask in that shop if I could telephone for a taxi, but I have forgotten how to use a telephone. Perhaps they would do it for me if I tipped them. I can give a tip, thought Lise, almost with a swagger, and she, Lise, had promised herself one little hour of freedom, just one, before she gave that freedom back again. I shall go to a café and order a cup of coffee, real coffee—not prison coffee—I can buy it—not be given it—and drink it, sitting at a table by myself, alone: a cup of coffee and a croissant—she could almost smell the delicious aroma—real coffee, fresh warm bread. I'll walk, Lise decided, my case isn't heavy; by the time I reach the town it will be seven o'clock, more cafés will be open. She had turned to go down the street when she saw Lucette.

A girl was sitting on the old mounting-block beside the prison gates—Vesoul was at least a century old—a disconsolate figure in an ill-fitting and too thin bright green suit, a cheap fibre suitcase at her feet. The whole small body was hunched as Lise had usually seen it, and she recognised the hair, a tangle that would have been fair if it had not been browned with grease—Lise remembered this girl had always been in trouble for not washing. It was a childish face, round with a quivering red mouth and brown eyes wide apart and wide with hurt yet, at the same time, with a curiously innocent wonder.

Of course, thought Lise, I was not the only one to be released today, but why was this girl out so early? Lise knew that she herself was a special case; for most the usual regulations had to be applied.

She could barely remember the girl's name—Lulu? Luci? No, it was Lucette, but Lise scarcely knew her. In a prison the size of Vesoul, when one was in another division, worked in a different workroom, paths did not often cross, but in her last two years Lise had heard a little of Lucette's troubles: slatternliness, careless work,

44

or work left undone. "She seems so helpless," Marianne had often said.

Lucette had served three years; now in that too-thin jacket and long skirt, she looked a cold, miserable little creature; she must, Lise thought, be at least twenty-one, but some frost seemed to have touched her growing—a cruel frost, thought Lise. Lucette seemed never to have grown and looked too frail and naïve to be abandoned. Abandoned? That was nonsense! The Directrice and the Assistante Sociale, Marianne Rueff, would never have let her go without some prospect of help or shelter and, It's none of my business, thought Lise.

She decided to leave her and then was suddenly impelled to go back to the gate.

"Hullo."

"Hullo." It sounded breathless.

"It feels . . . funny, doesn't it—being out?" Lise tried to be companionable.

"Funny?" The brown eyes were startled.

"And how did you manage it so early in the morning?"

"It wasn't early in the morning; it was yesterday afternoon but I knew, all of us knew, there would be some trick about letting you out. You were in all the newspapers, they said, so I guessed, and yesterday I found a room. I thought if I came early, very early, I might be here when you came out—and I am," said Lucette.

"But hadn't Mademoiselle Rueff arranged for you? Surely somebody came to fetch you."

"They did."

"And?"

"They had a room for me, and a job." It was a moment of boasting, then the curious breathlessness came back. "I sent them away."

"*Away?* But—why?"

"Because. . . ." The brown eyes were raised to Lise. "Madame—where are you going?"

45

It was as if she, Lise, had been suddenly warned. Of what, she wondered afterwards? The implications? How selfish, but all the same she drew back. "I have to catch my train." It was brusque, businesslike. Then why should Lise feel it was brutal? Still, "I must hurry," she said. "Well—good luck."

"Good luck." It was spoken into the road as if the road might take the words away, but Lise had turned her back and was walking towards the town.

It was too early for the kind of café where the cups would have been porcelain, the tables set, but the workmen's cafés and the Café de la Gare of every town opened, Lise knew, early in the morning and workmen gathered at the counters to snatch a cup of coffee, perhaps laced with rum or cognac, or to take a nip of pernod and eat a roll. Lise had often stood with them on her way back from her dawn prowls in Paris; with luck there might be croissants, crisp and fresh, perhaps a table to sit at.

In the first café she came to there was a dog, a poodle, sitting by the counter; every now and again it would beg, its eyes beseeching. It was the first pet dog Lise had seen since. . . . She did not go in but quickly shut the door and found she was trembling.

Leaving Coco had been one of the worst partings—no, perhaps the worst. A small French bulldog worse than human beings? But there were no humans, except Marcelline. Coco's black toad face had been crinkled with anxiety when she had had to leave him so precipitately—seldom had they left one another. There had been no time to take him up in her arms, that firm small black brindled body, well stuffed, but not fat—though that was a battle because the girls were forever giving him tidbits. His coat had been perpetually scented with their caresses. Coco bore the scent with good humour but Patrice did not. "If only they knew how they stink. . . ."

" 'Stink'—with that expensive scent? And the customers like it."

"Don't call them customers—they're clients; besides, they haven't had as much of this as I have. Thank God, you don't use this 'perfume' as they call it."

It was true; she had never wanted her hair or her skin impregnated, no matter how good the scent was, how expensive.

"You're a puritan," the girls had teased.

"I don't compete, that's all."

One of the girls, the Russian Magda, had bought Coco a collar at a fabulous price from the Rue Saint Honoré, scarlet kid studded with rhinestones; but, "For all the affection, I couldn't trust him to a girl—their fortunes are too insecure for a dog," Lise had said, so she had given him to Marcelline. "But Madame, my little room—after this."

"He will be happiest with you, Marcelline, and so shall I be—you're faithful."

How faithful, perhaps, only Lise knew. From the beginning, instinctively she had loved Marcelline just as instinctively she shrank from Eugenia with her lame leg and red lips and the stale powder in her wrinkles.

Marcelline was always upright, deep bosomed and with rosy but formidable forearms; her sleeves were usually rolled up to leave her capable hands free and she had kept her country freshness. Marcelline wore a high-necked striped blouse and, sometimes, what Eugenia would not have consented to be seen in, a little crochet shawl on her shoulders and, over her skirt, a clean checked apron. The only extravagant thing about Marcelline was her hair which she kept coiffed in such puffs and combs as her mother might have worn in Edwardian days.

All through those months when Lise had been waiting for trial at the Maison d'Arrêt at Sevenet, Marcelline had come each week to visit her and, long before then, in the times when Patrice had been in one of his rages, "Raw steak is good for a black eye, Madame," and Marcelline had laid on the bloody mess with a gentle

47

hand. "One of Monsieur Patrice's best fillets!" she had said with satisfaction.

"Yes, Marcelline, take Coco please," and Lise had drawn her rings off her fingers—they didn't confiscate our jewellery at Sevenet. "Take these and sell them; here is a letter to prove I gave them to you. I can't give you money. What I have must go to Maître Jouvin for his fees."

"I don't want money."

"Keeping Coco is expensive."

"He'll have what I have," Marcelline had said it gruffly. "That's what he had with you."

"That's all he'll want."

Marcelline had taken Coco down to the village near Varennes where her family lived. "I won't stay on at the Rue Duchesne without you, Madame. I haven't the heart." She had asked the Curé to write and tell Lise when Coco died—"I never knew till then that Marcelline couldn't read or write." The Curé had written again when Marcelline went herself. "She was my best friend in that old world," said Lise. "Perhaps my only friend," but it was only for Coco that Lise had ever let herself weep.

She went quickly on to the next café.

"The coffee was good! And the croissant. I had forgotten. . . ." With a sigh of content Lise sipped and dipped the fragrant little crescent in the cup.

Not that the food at Vesoul had been bad. Long ago, at Cadillac, in that grim Maison de Force, as prisons were called then, when a group of kind ladies, roused by the young father, Père Lataste, had volunteered to give the prisoners a treat for Christmas and asked what they would like, the unanimous request had been for a slice of fresh white bread. "We were well looked after," Lise was glad to admit that. "I believe the Directrice tasted a sample of the dinner every day, but it was distributed to our trays on battered enamel plates; an enamel mug" . . . so this! thought Lise; the thick white smoothness of the warm cup under her fingers; there was a spoon, a bowl of sugar, as much as she wanted, a napkin, though only of paper. She lifted the cup but, for a moment, instead of drinking, shut her eyes to savour the smell, then opened them—and abruptly put the cup down. Pressed against the window was a face; though the glass was steamy, the waif look was unmistakable; the great brown eyes, the tangled curls—Lucette. "Oh no!" breathed Lise. "Please no."

She sat rigidly at her table, turned to wood again. She must have followed me. Can't I have this one hour? Lise wanted to cry. It was all I asked. I was enjoying—for the first time for ten years—real joy. She was defiant, but no matter how hard she tried to make herself hard, the wood still had, for her, that living chord which was quickened and said or, rather, commanded: "Call her in. Give her a cup of coffee."

"If she wants one she can perfectly well come in," Lise told Lise, "and order it for herself. She must have money. No one leaves prison penniless. This . . . this creature doesn't have to hang about as if she were lost." Lise dipped her croissant into the coffee and bit into it, but somehow its savour had gone. The face was still pressed against the window.

Why doesn't she come in?

She doesn't dare.

Why, she's the same as I am?

She doesn't think so.

"Merde!" Lise swore aloud and got to her feet. "Lucette."

"Madame?" It was evidently more than Lucette had hoped for; the face was illumined.

"Better come in and have some coffee. It's chilly standing here."

Lucette still seemed to need to be ordered. "Sit down. Better take off your jacket, you'll feel the wind when you go out. Coffee? A croissant?"

Lucette did not say "Am I intruding?" She had in-

truded and was as pleased as a puppy or a child.
"Thank you, Madame."

"Why do you say Madame? You know my name?"

"Yes, Lise—like a lily." The eyes were adoring. "I
always think of you as a lily," the shy words came out,
"tall and straight and beautiful."

"Beautiful! With this scar?"

"What scar?" asked Lucette, then, "Oh *that*!" and
dismissed it. Vivi had had no such delicacy when,
twelve years ago, she had seen it at once, but of course
it had been more marked then.

"They call you La Balafrée, don't they?"

"I know."

"Someone did it to you."

"I know."

"Who was it?"

"Somebody," but Vivi's eyes were bright and curious
as a monkey's though a monkey has mournful shallow
eyes and can only do what it is taught, or imitate,
while Vivi's were knowing. They were beautiful eyes,
grey and long-lashed. Grey eyes are supposed to be soft
but Vivi's were hard—I should have been warned,
thought Lise—but the first time I saw them they were
dazed, yound, milky with what I thought was sleep—
until I smelt her. "It was Monsieur Patrice, wasn't it?"
asked Vivi.

"As a matter of fact it wasn't," Lise told Soeur Marie
Alcide. "It happened in a quarrel. I had made a friend,
a real friend, of a client. Henri was a good man, clean
in his way, though he was one of our regulars. He
wanted to get me away from the Rue Duchesne. I think
he would have married me—I might have been living
as a quiet respectable wife in some provincial town.
Patrice knew, he always knew everything, and he was
jealous as only he could be. He said—unspeakable
things," Lise shuddered. "Men despised Patrice, naturally, and Henri was not going to allow those . . . those
words to be said to me, and in public. There was a
bottle of wine on the table; Henri knocked the bottom

off and attacked Patrice. I happened to get in the way."

"To protect Monsieur Patrice?"

"I suppose so. Yes." Lise lifted her chin. "If you love the wrong people it's still love, isn't it, no matter what kind of love, and I'm glad I knew it—it makes it easier to understand. Once you have had that appetite, ma Soeur. . . .

"Of course, when the gash was new it showed horribly and I was no more use in the Club. Poor Henri! He offered again. I think he felt he had to, but I said 'No.' Emile, of course, would have sent me away, but Patrice couldn't do without me; he didn't even mind the scar so I became Madame Lise, La Balafrée—and soon was manager. Ostensibly it was Emile but it was really I. Yes, I was equal with characters like Lulu and Madame la Comtesse, who wasn't a comtesse, of course; we were never pretentious, just a good upper-middle-class brothel. How odd that sounds, but it was true; I think I was the youngest Mère Maquerelle Paris had ever seen, just twenty-three, but I suppose I had an air of authority; that was from Aunt Millicent—she had been a headmistress of a girls' school; head of Girl Guides. That seems far away from the Rue Duchesne and yet it wasn't; in a way I was in the same position. Sometimes I wondered if Aunt Millicent had chosen it or if it simply happened, as it happened to me; the broken end of a bottle and I was marked for life, in more ways than one."

"I think if it hadn't been for that scar I wouldn't have dared to speak to you," said Lucette now. "It showed someone had once hurt you too, so to me it only makes you more beautiful. You see, to me, you are someone different . . . somehow pure."

"Pure! My dear child! Why do you think I was in prison?"

"I don't know—and it makes no difference."

"Thank you, Lucette." Lise was so oddly touched that for a moment tears stung her eyes, then she shook her

51

head. It was, she told herself, just the emotion of this morning. "Drink your coffee," she said abruptly.

"Yes, Madame." Lise had never seen a croissant disappear so quickly, and with such noise; then Lucette licked each of her fingers for the last crumb, blew on the remains of the coffee and set the cup down on the table with a bang.

She has forgotten how to use a cup and saucer. That was one of the things Lise herself had been afraid of—in prison we had only mugs. It might betray her. Now Lucette was saying with a smile, the first smile Lise had seen—it altered her whole face almost into beauty—"I used to watch you, Madame; of course you never knew, but I did. I used to dream that one day you would speak to me—but I never, never thought I should be sitting with you, *invited*. Oh, I'm so glad I sent Mademoiselle Marianne's people away."

"That's what I want to talk to you about," said Lise. "Lucette, what are you going to do?"

"What you do," said Lucette with child-like faith.

"Have another croissant," said Lise quickly.

"Please."

"And coffee?"

"Please."

"Coffee for two," Lise ordered and when it had been brought the croissant disappeared as fast as the other. Then, "I'm sure you wouldn't like to come where I'm going," said Lise.

"I'll do anything you do," said Lucette. "I won't mind anything." Lise was silent and, "I have been on the streets too," offered Lucette.

"This isn't the streets."

"Then is it . . . a house? I don't mind about the fric—the money—or if it's hard."

"It's not that kind of house."

"Then . . . Madame Lise, where are you going?"

"Where I shall find just what we have both left," said Lise. "Walls—or, perhaps, not walls, bounds that I mustn't cross without leave. Rules I mustn't break.

52

Times to keep, silence, work, and where I must be obedient, poor."

"You mean—another prison?"

"Not prison, freedom. That's the paradox. I believe it will be such freedom as I can't imagine now."

"I don't understand."

"Neither did I, at first." Lise looked down at the table as if she could not make up her mind whether to say any more but Lucette was waiting. At last, "Lucette, did you see those Sisters who visited us at Vesoul every three months?" she asked.

"The nuns in white?"

"Yes. Did you go in and talk to them?"

"No, thank you," said Lucette promptly. "J'ai mangé assez de ce plat là—I have had enough of that. I didn't want their talk."

"As a matter of fact it was generally you who talked, they listened."

"So they could tell you toshay your prayers . . . ask Our Lady to help you . . . ask to see the aumônier . . . go to the chapel. I expect they gave you little cards and medals, didn't they?"

"Perhaps they did to some. They gave much more to me."

"What? Holy! Holy! Holy!?" mocked Lucette, but Lise did not flinch.

"It is holy, holy, holy. They have given me a chance, opened a way I hadn't dreamed of, yet I suppose really I had, long ago—that's why it found an echo in me. . . ." Lise was thinking still once again of the wood of that lute. "It would surprise you, wouldn't it, Lucette, if I told you that I hope—I pray—that one day I shall be one of them."

"You! Une frangine!" Lucette was aghast.

"Yes. A nun."

"But—you're too old. They catch you at eighteen."

"There are many older than I. Soeur Marie Alcide told me they once had a great-grandmother of eighty

53

. . . a blameless great-grandmother, so she got there more quickly."

"Blameless! But you have been in prison which means . . ." "I committed a crime."

"Yes, and long before that you were a putain, weren't you?" and "It isn't possible!" said Lucette.

"You said yourself it made no difference to you," said Lise. "Why should you be different from the nuns?"

"Because they are holy." Lucette was inexpressibly shocked. "Holy women," she used the word differently now.

"I thought you didn't believe in holiness."

"I don't, or do I—for other people."

"Why not you?"

"Me?" Then Lucette was angry. "You're trying to be holy too. You only asked me to have coffee with you because you were sorry for me. Didn't you? Didn't you?"

Lise could not deny it and Lucette rose; fishing in her pocket she put four francs on the table.

"That's too much," said Lise.

"It will pay for the pity." She turned.

"Lucette, where are you going?"

"Where *I* want," said Lucette. "Goodbye."

Let her go. God, I have had enough of young girls! Sitting where Lucette had left her, with the empty cups and plates, those pathetic four francs, Lise thought suddenly of Vivi—so different from Lucette. Lise saw Vivi's piquancy, the firm short little nose, teeth so small and pearly they looked like milk teeth, the pretty mouth with lips that were naturally red. Yet Lise knew they could curl, grow thin and twist almost like a little snake that is ready to strike, and Vivi could strike. Perhaps the whole of Vivi was false: her dimples that were not soft but traps: the glow of the skin looked warm like a ripe apricot and yet was cool, and Vivi's beautiful eyes might have been made of glass; like glass, they could light with a gleam, a glint that was shrewd. All this Lise knew, had soon known, and yet Vivi could so easily disarm her. Why? Perhaps, Lise thought now, Vivi wasn't false but simply and naturally herself, as unashamedly shameless as a child. Lise had thought of Lucette as another child, but Lucette could never have been just a child; from the beginning, Lise guessed, she would have been a waif, forlorn and puny. Vivi would never have consented to be a waif; even in the streets, dirty, tattered, hungry, she would have enjoyed herself, kept her cocksure independence, and she must have been beautiful as a little girl, more beautiful still when Lise found her—drunk.

It had been towards five in the Paris morning when it was still not quite light; the debris of the night littered pavements and gutters and dustbins overflowed outside the restaurants, a stale smelly overflow. Cats leapt away as Lise passed, but a rat stayed where it was foraging. A light wind blew through the empty street, Lise felt the coolness on her hot temples and on her cheek where the scar throbbed. She had been on one of the long impatient morning walks in which she escaped from the Rue Duchesne, from the fumes of drink and cigarettes, the close-drawn curtains, over-furnished rooms; from the long pretense of the night, arranging and cajoling upset girls, upset men: from hours of taking insolence or maudlin affection—which was the more disgusting? Every early morning, if she could, Lise escaped when the house at last shook itself free and the girls could go home, or those who lived in, go to bed—alone. Jock, the barman, and Gaston would clean up the last of the ashtrays and glasses, wiping up vomit perhaps, putting bottles in the dustbins. "Everything must be clean, washed and in order." Lise had insisted on this, including the weary girls—it was Eugenia's work to see to that. Patrice, drunk or sober, had gone to bed; if he had a "chosen one" he usually took her to the office, only now and then up to the flat.

"Didn't you mind?" asked Soeur Marie Alcide.

55

"It seldom lasted more than a night," said Lise. "There was a room next to Zoë's where I could take refuge." Those of the girls who slept in had rooms which they shared on the third floor; some went back to their families, taking a taxi or the early métro, others to the apartment of their "old man" whom they kept or helped to keep. By five o'clock usually the house was still. Jock had closed and cleaned the bar; Gaston locked the door before going home with Eugenia; Emile, the last, had put the takings in his safe and gone, himself, to bed—he had to make do with second choice—and Lise was free, to breathe the morning air, fresh as it could be even in the city. She would walk and walk—too far for Coco whom she left snoring in his basket; she walked until it was time, in some church— any church—for the first Mass, when she would slip in at the back and sit in the shadows so that nobody knew she was there.

The trucks had long ago arrived at Les Halles for the market and now there were others; water-trucks to hose the gutters, waste-trucks to clear rubbish and litter, dark blue police vans to pick up human rubbish . . . and it was then that Lise saw Vivi.

It was in a little Place where, outside the shuttered cafés no one had bothered to stack the iron chairs, and the zinc-topped tables had already gathered the dew; at one a girl was sitting on a small iron chair, sitting bent over, head and elbows on the table, fast asleep. It was the elbows Lise saw first, young fresh flesh, soft and vulnerable for all their thinness. She saw the hair, bronze chestnut, tumbled over a neck that was white and, again, so young. "Perhaps it was that little vulnerable neck that first made me love her," said Lise. A girl, little more than a child, asleep over a table.

We were the children of the Maison Dieu, Renée, Pom-Pom, Rico and I—Pom-Pom had to count as a child. A Maison Dieu is where they put the people nobody wants: old people and poor loonies who are out of their minds—and us, not many of us—children only go there for "grave reasons"—I heard the Doctor say that. Renée was hunched from where her step-father broke her back—step-fathers, fathers, they are all the same, Though I was only nine when I came and Renée was fourteen I was taller than she was. Mamaine, who looked after us, said one day someone would take Renée as a servant for nothing, "And do a good deed," said Mamaine. No one would take me, I was too pretty. I am nearly as pretty as Claudine. Claudine is my sister but nobody knows that. I don't want them to know.

Sometimes I shrieked in the night and Mamaine came; poor, sleepy Mamaine, and she held me while I sobbed and sobbed. Next day I saw the Doctor or Madame Lachaume the Superintendent but it was no use.

I should have liked to tell it all t lthe Doctor—I still don't know why I couldn't. I should have liked to live with the Doctor and be his little girl—a proper little girl, not like me, like the little girls outside.

All the same, it was nice at the Maison Dieu. I had a bed all in white and a dress, and pinafores with flowers on them and a hairbrush of my own—I hadn't known my hair could look like silk. I had a toothbrush too—I haven't had one since—Mamaine used to say my teeth looked like pearls! and I was washed and clean. We had breakfast and goûter in the afternoon, milk and brioche before we went to bed and we had dinner at twelve o'clock. Yes, every day we had a real dinner, soup, meat and vegetables, and on Sundays ice-cream. Maison Dieu means the house of God. I used to think God was very kind to have us to live with him. No one else would.

I pretended Pom-Pom was my little dog. Pom-Pom seemed a little boy in blue overall, striped socks on his little legs and felt slippers, a little boy, but not his head. There was a secret: Pom-Pom had to be shaved. I was not supposed to know but I knew; the barber from the men's wing did it and I knew why: Pom-Pom was thirty-four years old.

Rico would have been a little boy but, as Mamaine

said, he was not all there. I think he was not there at all. He would sit at the table and draw but not on the paper—in the air; it was as if he saw far beyond the Maison Dieu to the sea and sky and clouds; I think it must have been sunset, Rico had such a light on his face: it was a shame he would not talk or look at us: it wasn't like living with a boy but with a sunbeam.

Rico did not know who I was but Pom-Pom followed me about and when I talked to him or chirruped like Mamaine's canary or sang one of my songs, slowly, slowly, because things took a long time to get into Pom-Pom, his big ugly face used to break into a smile.

I have two smiles. I wish I had only one but I know I have two. I used to put my arms round Mamaine's fat waist and rub my face against her apron and she stroked my hair. "Pauvre momone, Poor child. She is hungry for love."

Yes, it felt safe and warm in our attic, yet even then I wanted to get out. We couldn't be let out, except for our playtime in the courtyard, partly because we were us and partly because of the Stefans. The Stefans were in the men lunatics' wing with barred windows and iron doors with keys.

I called them Stefans because of Stefan, the Russian. Stefan was young and big and good looking; his hair was gold like Rico's but not in curls; Stefan's was cut short and stubby; his blue eyes followed me each time he saw me. Most of the Stefans were never let out, not even in the courtyard—because of the war there were too few guards—but Stefan was a "trusty" and sometimes he was out in the hall. If he was still there when Mamaine took us out, she hustled past him, but I knew Stefan looked at me.

Every day when it was fine, Mamaine took us down the staircase at one o'clock and through the locked door with its chain, down more stairs into the hall and outside and then we played, at least Pom and I. The old people of the Maison Dieu watched us and talked about us; whenever I think about us, I see those old mouths *talking, some without any teeth. I knew what they said about me. It was supposed to be another secret but I knew. The doctor had a photograph of me; it was in the newspapers though I wasn't supposed to know that, either. "Found sleeping on manure heap"—Madame Lachaume read it out to Mamaine. It wasn't a manure heap, it was turnips and I had a sack on top. I stole up behind Madame Lachaume and Mamaine to look at the photograph and I didn't like it; I wasn't pretty at all. My bruises looked like smudges, my hair not silky; it was caked—I still remember its smell. My dress was an old one of Claudine's like a big sack; it showed my skin through the rents where Papa tore it. He chased me. At first it was only Claudine, then one day it was me too and it hurt. That's why I slept on the turnips—I was afraid to come into the house, but sometimes I wanted to.*

It was because of Papa that I shrieked; I didn't want to make a noise but I shrieked higher and higher and it made me so excited I couldn't stop. I knew my cheeks were red and my eyes so bright they shone, and the whole of me felt light and quick and I had an ache like being hungry, half an ache and half a tingle, and I could have told everybody out flat, "Sometimes I want a Papa to chase me."

There! I was soon small and sweet again. I played with Pom-Pom, sang to Rico, rubbed my head against Mamaine's apron. Madame Lachaume put my hair back. "Poor child. Poor little girl."

The Doctor asked me questions gently, especially after I was given the doll, but I didn't tell him about the baby. It wasn't mine, it was Claudine's. She screamed and screamed out in the shed where Papa had put her; she rolled on the floor and doubled up. We were so surprised when the baby came out. I wanted to keep the baby and love it, but Claudine said we mustn't or the police would take it and her, and Papa. In the end it was Papa and me, but I am still sorry about the baby.

Madame Lachaume told me I couldn't be the Doctor's

*little girl, but it seemed there was someone else—
Monsieur Grebel. Monsieur Grebel was one of the Governors; he was much richer than the Doctor; he had a
beard and a watch-chain, and he was even kinder; he
often came up to the attics to see us and he was all of our
friend. He patted Pom-Pom on the head and dangled
his watch for Rico to catch. He even gave Renée some
knitting wool, bright red, and he brought sweets for us
all. It was he who gave me the baby doll and was
shocked when I had hysterics. I was sorry I couldn't like
it because I loved Monsieur Grebel. He would no more
have chased me than Pom would. I used to think Monsieur Grebel was like God.*

*We were in the courtyard when we heard the people's
voices in Madame Lachaume's office. We were not supposed to hear them but when they argued their voices
grew loud—Mamaine said I had long ears which wasn't
true; they are small and pretty as shells and close to my
head but I stood up on the bench to hear better though
Pom-Pom tugged at my pinafore; the people were Madame
Lachaume, Monsieur l'Abbé who came for the chapel,
the Doctor, one or two ladies and Monsieur Grebel.*

"She cannot be with other children."

"Evidemment, but she shouldn't be here."

"She should be admitted to a Home."

"There would be other children there."

*"We have to take some risks," that was the Doctor and
another voice, sneery, like Renée's said, "May I ask you,
Doctor, if you would allow this child to be with your
own daughters?"*

The Doctor did not answer.

*"In any case, the Homes are packed—all those war
orphans," said a lady, and then, suddenly, Monsieur
Grebel said, "I will take her."*

*They were so surprised there was a silence and I
could feel my heart beating. Then Monsieur l'Abbé
spoke. "It would be a work of great charity."*

*"Not at all. I want her," said Monsieur Grebel—dear
Monsieur Grebel.*

"But—would Madame Grebel . . . ?"

"A woman without children has empty arms. I can vouch for my wife," said Monsieur Grebel.

He came up to the attic that evening with Mamaine. *"Would you like to come and live with me, Vivi?"*

"Would I be a proper girl and go to school?"

"I think you would."

"Would you buy me dresses and a coat with fur on it?"

"Vivi, Vivi. You think too much about these things," said Mamaine.

"But would you? I should need three or four dresses to be a proper girl."

"We'll ask Madame Grebel to help you choose them. I'm bringing her to see you in the morning."

I was taken to the grande salle to meet Madame Grebel. I had been so excited I had had no sleep, but I didn't forget what Mamaine had taught me and I curtseyed to Madame Grebel but she didn't hold out the arms Monsieur had said were empty; she didn't even hold out her hand. She looked at me for a long time, then over my head to Monsieur Grebel and she was angry. Why was she angry?

"Alfred, you didn't tell me."

"Tell you what?"

Her voice was high, as angry people's are, and she had red patches on her cheeks. She got up from her chair. *"Now I understand! You didn't tell me she was beautiful. Too beautiful, Alfred!"* and she turned to go.

I asked in a whisper, *"Madame Grebel has said 'No'?"*

Monsieur Grebel nodded, then he went quickly away, and I, Vivi, was left alone in the grande salle.

"Asleep! Drunk!" The police van had reached the Place and, as Lise came up, a sergeant lifted the girl's head and tilted it back; the eyes opened stupefied, dazed, the mouth lolled. "Drunk. Put her in."

"No." The authority in Lise's voice surprised even her. "I was comparatively new to this then," and,

61

before the gendarmes could touch the girl, "You can't take her," said Lise. "She's one of mine."

"Yours? Never." Morel, the sergeant, knew Lise well, as did most of the flics. "Mère Maquerelle," they whispered among themselves.

"One of yours? Never."

"She is."

"Then what's she doing here?"

"She—ran away. I have been looking for her."

"Ran—why?"

Lise shrugged—an acted shrug. "Frightened."

"She can't be one of yours. She's. . . ." He bent over her and drew back. "Whew! She's filthy."

"I told you—she ran away. She has been out two nights. . . ." but the sergeant was astute.

"Besides, she's too young."

"The little sister of one of our girls," Lise lied glibly. "Pauvre p'tite. Of course, we haven't used her yet."

"She has used herself, Madame Lise." To Lise's face they wouldn't call her La Balafrée. "I don't believe you."

"Why else do you think I'm out this time of the morning?" That was a point: Lise had always taken care to be invisible on her walks. "Why else?" demanded Lise and, "Get me a taxi," she ordered. "Lift her in. I'll take her home."

"I took Vivi home." Why? Lise had asked herself a thousand times. "There's a little church in England," she told Soeur Marie Alcide, "at Southleigh in Oxfordshire, which had an old old mural painting showing a winged Saint Michael holding the scales of justice. The poor soul awaiting judgement is quailing because the right-hand scale is coming heavily down with its load of sins: but on the left Our Lady is quietly putting her rosary beads in the other scale to make them even. I saw it long ago, but in a way I suppose something like that happened to me."

"It happened to me," and Lise started to tremble.

"How did Vivi come to have those beads?" Lise asked that for the thousandth time. "She wouldn't say. She never said. . . ."

Now in the café, Lise seemed to hear Soeur Marie Alcide's firm voice. "Put it behind you. That is one of our first rules. You will probably never see Vivi again," and, "It's time you caught your train," Lise told Lise.

Lise had been taking her ticket when she looked behind her down the line of passengers and, "Oh no!" she could not help saying; there was Lucette struggling with the size of her suitcase, Lucette with her draggled green skirt, thin jacket and tangled hair. "Oh no!" But there was no need to panic. Lucette was too far down the line to hear the name of the town for which Lise asked, And, if I hurry, thought Lise, she won't know which platform is mine.

Platform Number 9. As she reached the train Lise looked back. A small figure was running, dodging, banging into people with the case, stopping to scan each barrier, but getting nearer. In the press of passengers waiting to pass through the barrier, Lise tried tohide herself behind a large man with a duffle bag on his shoulder. She was safe, hidden, and then the man stepped aside and Lucette saw her. Still, perhaps she hasn't the right ticket, hoped Lise; perhaps she won't be allowed through.

Resolute, Lise showed her own ticket, then almost ran herself down the length of the train; at the end she found a corner seat by the far window; she swung her case up on the rack and opened a newspaper she had snatched from a kiosk. There were already three people in the compartment; the other seats were quickly filled and, Lucette would hardly have had time to come as far down the platform as this, thought Lise as the train began to move.

Another anxiety came up: would there be a mention of Vesoul? Of her, La Balafrée. Hastily she scanned the paper. It was a late edition. LES TROIS FRERES CESARO RELACHES PAR LES FELLAGAH—*the Cesaro brothers released . . . held prisoner for forty-seven days . . .* Forty-seven days! Lise almost laughed. TUMULTUOUS WELCOME FOR GENERAL DE GAULLE . . . SENSATIONAL FLIGHT OF THE CARAVELLE . . . *forty-six minutes from Paris to Dijon. . . .*

Nowhere was there a mention—and it would have been a headline: LA BELAFREE RELEASED . . . LA BELAFREE . . . MADAME LISE IS OUT. . . . The secret seemed to have been well kept. If the guard at Vesoul had looked at her more closely, he might have been tempted to give the news—no one knew from whom, in prison, news could leak—as a precaution, Madame Chef herself had come out to see if any pressmen were on the pavement or hidden in a café before she would let Lise cross the courtyard. TROIS ENFANTS . . . PERISSENT ASPHYXIES. *Three little children dead in a farm fire. . . .*

No Balafrée. Lise could sit back, let Patrice's scarf slip down—she had bound it round her head, hiding the scar. When the news did break, perhaps tomorrow, she would be. . . . Where they'll never dream, thought Lise.

Lucette came along the corridor. At every compartment, Lise guessed, she had pressed her face against the glass with the same wistful appeal of the café, but Lise had seen the glimmer of green and shrank back behind her neighbour, holding the newspaper high; the brown eyes, though, were thorough and Lise guessed she had been seen but, She won't dare to come in here, thought Lise.

She had meant at lunchtime to go to the buffet car for a sandwich, one of those crusty French sandwiches with ham, and perhaps a glass of wine. Though it's so long since I have had one it will probably go to my head—but wine! thought Lise. Now, it was too risky to leave the compartment. What would Lucette do? wondered Lise. Stand in the corridor and wait? What ticket had she taken? Where would she have to get off?

Naissances.Fiançailles.Mariages.Deuils—"Hatches, Matches, Dispatches," Lise could hear Aunt Millicent's voice. EISENHOWER TELEPHONES TO J.F. DULLES—but Lucette's face kept coming between Lise and the newspaper.

Unfortunately Lise's station was also the terminus. All the doors opened but there was such a flood of passengers, so many trucks and trolleys, such meetings with hugs and kisses, luggage, mailbags, freight thrown out, that Lise was able to slip through the crowd. She ran down the subway, up the other side, reached the barrier, gave up her ticket and, breathless, stopped on the station forecourt to search the line of cars. There, thankfully, was the blue Citroën she had been told to look for, the familiar white habit, black veil of a Sister of Béthanie. Lise ran across the forecourt.

"Soeur Justine?"

"Yes."

"I am Lise," and the names Elizabeth Fanshawe, Liz, Madame Ambard, above all, La Balafrée, dropped away into an abyss of forgetting. Please God, I shall never hear them again—as, "Welcome," said the young nun with a smile as she leaned across to open the door which Lise had already wrenched open; she threw her case into the back, got in and slammed the door.

There was that perspicacious Dominican look. "Is somebody chasing you?" but Soeur Justine did not say it, only started the car. "You *are* in a hurry," she said instead.

"I couldn't wait to get here." Lise almost said it but she could not enter Béthanie on even the smallest lie and, "It's only that I so badly need to get to Saint Etienne," she said.

Soeur Justine did not waste time; she was already feeling her way through the jumble of taxis and cars and people. Lise, crouching low, looked back; as she thought, or dreaded, Lucette had emerged past the barrier on to the forecourt where she was standing, obviously bewildered, the suitcase at her feet. Lise knew her eyes were scanning, searching, but, I won't, thought Lise. I won't. I have done it before, idiot that I was. . . .

"Bring that guttersnipe in here, cette gamine . . . ? Never." Lise had thought that was what Patrice would say when he saw Vivi, but he had asked in strange excitement, "Have you looked at her? Looked at her face?"

"No, I suppose I haven't looked at her," said Lise.

"That face! Those legs! That whole body!"

"I wasn't thinking of her as meat—to be fed to your lions."

Patrice was too excited to listen. "Chérie, when she's cleaned and fed, dressed and trained. . . . My God!" said Patrice and added, "Do your very best with her."

Lise's "best" was quite different from Patrice's, "or was meant to be," said Lise.

When Vivi was sober, cleaned and disinfected, dressed and fed, Lise tried to coax her into confidence.

"Surely you have another name?" Lise asked Vivi. "Viviane perhaps?"

"No, just Vivi."

"Vivi what?"

"Vivi."

"What was your father called?" A visible recoil. "Your family—when you were a little girl."

"Don't, don't." It was almost a scream. "If you go on, I'll run away," and "Leave her be," said Patrice.

We had run away, Suzanne and me, though there was no need to run because no one was going to come after us. "Don't giggle, Vivi, or somebody will suspect," said Suzanne, but no one bothered to suspect.

Suzanne was almost the same as me, but older; she might have been Claudine, my sister, only she wasn't. No one but me knows there was ever a Claudine—it's one of the things I don't tell. Suzanne had had a Papa

66

who had chased her, too, and she had been taken away and put into a school. I think she had been to even more schools than I had. They had told us Monsieur Ralph was our last hope. They might have saved their breath. Monsieur Ralph was Superintendent of Le Manoir d'Espérance, though it wasn't a manor—it was a foyer. Still, he was kind, poor man. "If these girls can get back to nature," he used to say, "they might be cured." I think he did not know nature, certainly not Suzanne's or mine. Poor Monsieur Ralph. He was the first person who had been kind to me since the days of the Maison Dieu.

I often think of the Maison Dieu and the attics where we were kept—hunchback Renée and Rico, Pom-Pom and I—with Mamaine to look after us, and Madame Lachaume and Monsieur Grebel and Stefan. When I ran away with Stefan they came after us and it was a long time till they trusted me enough to let me come to the Manoir d'Espérance and Monsieur Ralph. He was easy to get round; it was hay-making time on the farm; we were all helping with the hay and he gave permission for Suzanne and me to ride back from the far fields on the hay-floats behind the tractors when they went back to the farm. I loved the sweet smell of the hay and the way Suzanne tumbled about in it.

The men were pleased to have two girls with them but they didn't try any games—they had too much respect for Monsieur Ralph; nor did they know that we had taken their money, poor boys, notes out of their wallets, when they left their coats hanging on the fence posts while they pitched up the bales. We, Suzanne and I, got down from the tractor in the farmyard, but not to go back to Monsieur Ralph. We crept out down the lane to the road and hitched a ride to Paris and we were very polite. "Giggling is bad policy," said Suzanne.

Suzanne knew Paris. She had been born and brought up in the alleys there and she found us a room; it was high up, on the fifth floor of an old house. The landlady, Madame Picou, let us stay even when she found out how young we were, because we did her errands and could be trusted to get her pension for her at the post office when she was too drunk to go herself. We never stole any of that—"It would be bad policy," Suzanne used to say. Everything with her was "bad policy," "good policy," depending how the wind blew.

Suzanne could sing; she had a voice, sweet, like a little canary in its cage. She sang and I collected the money, because I was pretty. "And don't you ever let them off," she told me. "Pester them . . . you can." When we had enough, we went to a stall or boîte to eat, then came back and Suzanne sang some more. We worked different districts but always we used to go first and find out where the police station was, then keep as far away from it as we could. We were never picked up. Perhaps Monsieur Ralph was glad to get rid of us.

Sometimes we could buy a dress or some shoes and Suzanne knew a great many Stefans—not wrong in the head as he was, poor Stefan—but soldiers, sailors, anyone. We had a good time and we were together, Suzanne and I. Then, one afternoon, when we were asleep—we had been out all night—Madame Picou shouted up the stairs at us. We had forgotten to buy her bread. It was Suzanne who went for the baguette; she was still half asleep, and she was run over.

Madame Picou was taken to the morgue to look at Suzanne. They couldn't find me—I had hidden under the cistern in the roof—but I knew Madame Picou had told the police about me and sooner or later they would find me, so I left.

I left just as I was and stayed out in the streets. I don't remember any more.

"Let her be Vivi Ambard," said Patrice and he teased Lise, "All our strays come to be that."

It was true. Vivi Ambard. Lise Ambard. If only she were my daughter, thought Lise, but I'm still too young for that. If she were my little sister—and she pleaded, "Patrice, she's not for us. I'm going to send her to school."

Patrice began to laugh. "Send her to school. Try, that's all. Yes, try. She's been on the streets for two years." Then he was serious. "You'll have to get rid of that roughness, teach her some manners—and pride. It's a miracle she has escaped V.D."

"You have found that out already?"

"Naturally."

"Yes, naturally." Lise was suddenly bitter—she who was never bitter. "I should have known."

"Isn't it my business?" He came and sat close beside her. "Chérie, I think you have brought us a gold mine."

"Patrice, she's only fourteen."

"Jail-bait! A good many have a yen for that."

"What if I inform?" Lise had been cold.

"You won't," said Patrice and Lise knew he was right.

The convent car had left the town and was driving beside a wide river flowing quietly behind its trees; big houses stood in gardens and then gave way to vineyards, little "domaines," the vines carefully espaliered around low thick-walled houses with roofs of rounded tiles. "It's beautiful, our Gironde," said Soeur Justine.

"It *is* beautiful," said Lise, as if she hoped that would distract her.

Soeur Justine glanced at her; the eyes, behind the cheap steel-rimmed spectacles, Lise knew, were taking in the tenseness of the way Lise sat, the way her hands clutched her handbag. "I won't. I will *not*," but soon Lise knew it was no good. "Soeur Justine, would you turn round. I didn't want . . . but there's a girl—not a girl though she seems one—a young woman left at the station. I don't think she has much money, or anywhere to go," said Lise. "Could you take her in, just for tonight?"

Chapter
Three

THE HOLY-WATER STOUP was one of the few relics left. It was shaped like an open shell; the upper half, carved and roughly fluted, protected the lower which was deeper and meant to be filled with water, holy water that brought blessing. Water washes, purifies, as do tears, thought Marc. There must have been enough tears here to make an ocean—when, at last, breaking down the defiance, the bitterness, tears came: there used to be a prayer in our missals for the "gift of tears," thought Marc; I suppose it has been done away with now; he must ask Father Louis for it—but, in any case, the stoup was empty; most of the tourists had not even noticed it.

"Go to the Château of Cadillac and see for yourself," Louis had said when Marc had declared, "I cannot believe it," after his first morning at Belle Source.

"Nor can most people," said Louis. "I can remember a Minister of Justice, a kind experienced man, saying just that. He knew many prisoners do come out, transformed as it were, and make a fresh start: he admitted that an exceptional one, here and there, could be drawn to the religious life, not as a refuge, but with a true vocation. . . ."

"But that there could be enough for a convent!" said Marc. Yes, that the Minister could not believe, "and yet here *are* the convents. There are Béthanies in France and Belgium, Italy, Austria, Switzerland, America—and they are spreading. Of course, all the nuns are not what we call in private 'réhabilitées'; at least half are sisters who come in the natural way—if you can call it natural— And, remember, because nobody knows which are which, they need to have an uncommon call and a special charity.

"Charity?" The Sisters of Béthanie would have said in genuine surprise. "It's a privilege. We're only following Our Lady. Wasn't she the first to do it for love of him? She, the Mother Immaculate with Mary Magdalen."

"Yes. They did hobnob together," said Father Louis.

"Hobnob? That's a strange everyday way to put it."

"But exact. And I expect it was every day—and to the end."

"But the sisters . . . they *must* know which are which," insisted Marc.

"They don't *know*. They may guess, as I have guessed about Soeur Marie Lise, but even so, they do not know what any nun has done or has not done, except the Mother-General. If there is someone who has been an alcoholic or drug addict, for her sake, her first Prioress will be warned—but, of course, the Prioress herself may once have been the same."

"The Prioress!" Marc could not believe his ears.

"They tell me that often the worst criminals make the best nuns." Louis was quite serene. "Because, they have known the depths. 'Out of the depths, I cried to Thee,' " Father Louis repeated softly. " 'Lord, hear my voice'—and he does."

71

"The depths?"

"Go to Cadillac," said Louis, "that terrible once-upon-a-time Maison de Force. Go to Cadillac, and see."

Cadillac was a museum now. It had been a château, almost a fortress, of heavy rough stone, built for the Dukes of Epernon, and had needed hardly any conversion to become, in the nineteenth century, a prison for women. "All that was necessary was conveniently and horribly there," Louis had told Marc and, as Marc came in, he had seen the strong gatehouse which became a guard-house; the high walls; huge rooms that could be divided into twelve or twenty cells—the marks on the floors still showed where they had been. Marc walked through the guard-rooms in the crypt which had been made into workrooms for the task then thought suitable for prisoners, sewing heavy sacks. No wonder hands grew coarse, thought Marc. He walked up the stone stairs, wide enough to take ten in a line of the four hundred prisoners. "There were already grilles at the windows," said Louis, "fortified doors, and the dungeons where the Duke's captives used to be left to die forgotten, were conveniently useful for the prison. Women could be kept chained to the wall down there. Imagine it, Marc," Father Louis' voice had been deep with emotion. "Just some straw thrown on the stone flags for a bed, a bucket seldom emptied, the stink of damp, stale air, their own excretion." Marc could see that, through the high-up slit openings of these "cachots," daylight hardly reached them; the marks of the chains were still on the walls. He came out feeling sick.

To him there was something more poignant still; kept for show in one room were scratchings on the wall where the prisoners had used their nails to get off the whitewash, "To use as face-powder, maquillage," said the curator. How ghastly it must have looked, thought Marc.

He had come with a coach-load of tourists but had lingered behind the guide, imagining corridors lined with locked cell doors along which, Louis had told him, a trolley was pushed twice a day by a prisoner wearing the green girdle of good conduct; at every door, through the shutter—a battered tin bowl would be held out for a ladle of soup—"I can guess it was more skilly than soup," said Father Louis, "and then a hand came out for the piece of prison bread, one piece, no more."

Up on the airy first floor, though, in what had been the most splendid stateroom of all, the Salle des Gardes or King's Room, there were different signs, signs Louis had told Marc to look for. Over the great carved chimneypiece with its white and coloured marble, a shield that had borne the arms of the Duke had been painted over with a cross in gold, and below where the shelf jutted over the hearth, the bust of the King, Henri III, had been taken away and marks on the marble showed where a tabernacle had stood while a table in front made an altar.

"Who did this?" Marc asked the curator, who had come back to him. "Who?"

"It was Père Lataste."

"But . . . who gave him permission?"

"No one. He did it. He wanted this room as a chapel." And what Père Lataste wanted he got, thought Marc.

"You must know the history," Louis had said. "How Béthanie began."

Marc already knew that in 1864 Marie Jean Joseph Lataste, a young priest, had been sent to preach a retreat in this most terrible of all women's prisons. "But you must know it *vividly*," said Louis. It was becoming too vivid now. "Once a woman is sent to Cadillac she is lost," said the tales. "She never comes out."

Some had thrown themselves from the top windows, managing, in their desperation, to force themselves through the bars; some had jumped into the courtyard-well as Soeur Noël, who was to be the first of Père Lataste's "petites soeurs," as he called them, had decided to do on the very day of the retreat. "I don't know what stayed me," she had said, and then, later, "Now I do know."

If only these walls could speak, thought Marc, standing in that improvised chapel, what they could tell. To Marie Jean Joseph Lataste they had spoken in a strange unmistakable way of something no one had ever expected to find in Cadillac—love. But he must have been afraid, thought Marc. "I would have been." The young father had been told, "Few will come," and, "they are brutalised. Take care never to be left alone with any of them." Perhaps he had been teased—"You're so rosy and tender, they will eat you up." The retreat, too, had had to be held in the early hours of the morning or in the evening—"The Governor would not remit one hour of those poor creatures' forced labour," said Louis, but it seemed word had gone round that this retreat was different—and Père Lataste was confronted by nearly four hundred women instead of the twenty or so he had expected. "He described them," said Louis, "as women who were scarcely women any more, dressed in heavy coarse dark clothes. The colour of their fichus showed the length of their sentence." "The French word 'peine'—trouble—is more eloquent than our English word for it, 'sentence,' " Lise had commented to Marc. A handkerchief—head-dress—was bound so low on their foreheads that it gave each a sullen malevolent look. "If they were suspicious of priests, I'm sure it was with reason," said Father Louis. "In those days the church did not spare its brimstone and I expect they had heard those words too often before: retribution, hell-fire, penitence, resignation."

Marc could imagine that scene in the chill of half-past four in the morning: the young Dominican standing waiting in his white habit, black cloak. His hair was tonsured—like mine, thought Marc—his dark eyes watchful—everyone who saw Marie Jean Joseph Lataste had remarked on his eyes.

The women had waited for him to begin. Marc knew from his own talks and preachings, tame though those

74

seemed in comparison, how tense a moment that opening always was. "Be not anxious how you are to speak, or what you are to say," Christ had told his disciples when he sent them out, "for what you are to say will be given you in that hour." Certainly it had been given to Père Lataste. Instead of the customarily distant "Mesdames, Mesdemoiselles," the women's amazed ears had heard the opening that was to ring down the years and mean so much. "Mes soeurs, my sisters, my dear sisters. Yesterday I didn't know you, but today. . . ." Père Lataste had begun. "He did not pretend or soften," said Louis. "You are women disgraced," said Père Lataste, but went on, "We can say these things because we are 'en famille.'" It was true he had found himself at home as never before.

I was astonished at what I saw—he was to write—Not on the surface but in those souls; never has a retreat or mission in the best of parishes given me such joy. I was shown marvels.

He talked to them of Mary Magdalen. "Isn't she the most intimate, tender and surprising person of all in the gospel stories?" asked Father Louis. Père Lataste reminded those poor women of how, when Jesus was invited to the feast of Simon, the rich Pharisee, she made her way to kneel at his feet.

The Pharisee said to himself, "If this man were a prophet, he would have known who and what manner of woman is this who is touching him," and Jesus answered, "Simon, I have something to say to you. . . . A certain creditor had two debtors: one owed five hundred denari, the other fifty. When they could not pay, he forgave them both. Now which of them will love him the more?" Simon answered, "I suppose to whom he forgave more," and Jesus said, "You have judged rightly," and he turned to the woman. "Her sins, which are many, are forgiven for she loved much."

*   *   *

"And Père Lataste saw those handkerchiefed heads—bowed while he spoke, many trying to strangle sobs—begin to lift," said Louis. "He wrote they were like flowers after a storm when the sun touches them. Love . . . forgiveness. We know they were words they had not heard for a long time, perhaps had never heard," said Louis.

The retreat had lasted four days and, on the last night, Père Lataste had suggested they hold an all-night Adoration of the Sacrament exposed in its monstrance on an altar made beautiful with flowers and candles, "Such as I expect they had not seen for years," said Louis. "Some of you might like to come, two-by-two, for half an hour's vigil," Père Lataste had told them. He thought that was quite enough sacrifice of their scanty hours of sleep. He himself spent the night in an improvised confessional, hearing one by one what poured out from hearts more imprisoned, one can guess, than the prisoners themselves, but towards midnight he heard a noise like a tide; the sound of feet on the stairs. He thought it was a riot and came terrified out of the confessional, then stood amazed. "No wonder he was amazed," said Louis. "He saw not two women taking the place of two, but over two hundred. Those women had divided themselves, half watching until midnight, the other half from then till half-past four, when they knew Père Lataste would say the last Mass of the retreat."

Was it then, on that night, Marc wondered, that the idea had come? An idea that must have seemed as impossible when it was first put into words to Père Lataste's superiors, the hierarchy, as it was to Marc when he first heard it; that there could be another Bethany, that house where Mary and Martha had lived as sisters; that among these souls at Cadillac, and other prisons, there might be true Magdalens ready to dedicate the rest of their lives to love of Our Lord;

76

women who had a "call," a vocation to the religious life ... that an Order could be founded where they could follow it without question and in honour. Père Lataste was no optimist. "It's not that many will," he said, "but that they *can*."

"How?" was the inevitable question. At that time he did not know how, only that this would, indeed must be, and, mysteriously, he had found help.

It was the Prioress, Soeur Marie Emmanuel, who had told Marc the story of Mère Henri Dominique. "She belonged to another Order where life was peaceful and safe—you could almost say comfortable—but she left it to join Père Lataste, against the advice—I can guess the scandalised advice—of everyone who knew her." Soeur Marie Emmanuel smiled, "I can guess many of us at Béthanie have had the same since."

Mère Henri Dominique had brought three other nuns with her. "Père Lataste leased a château for them," and Soeur Marie Emmanuel said, "That sounds rich but it was almost tumbling down, and there they established our Rule and the first home of Béthanie."

"They were so poor," she told Marc, "that they didn't have beds, just palliasses stuffed with straw; no tables, but planks on bricks," but at Christmas there came the first of the "petites soeurs." She was that same Soeur Noël who had wanted to kill herself at Cadillac. Marie Jean Joseph Lataste must have had something of the magnetism of Christ who only had to say the words "Follow me," and men, and women, left all that they had to obey; and, "You have a look of Père Lataste," Lise had said to Marc.

"I?" Marc had been startled. "I wish I had."

It was getting towards evening; all around was the light of the Gironde but it did not penetrate the château of Cadillac. Sounds, nostalgic in their homeliness, came up from the little town and, in the silence, Marc could hear the river, the Oeuil, that he had seen by the road, flowing under its old arched bridge; from the top windows of the château it might have been possible to see the vineyards and the hills; did the women, hanging on the bars, strain to see them?

Cadillac was full of echoes; Marc seemed to hear that tide of feet on the empty stairs; they were moving perhaps towards hope, but there were other dreadful sounds: the clack-clack of wooden sabots on the stones of the back court as the prisoners took the prescribed treadmill exercises, "le cirque" as they called it because, like animals in a circus, they were trained to walk round and round in silence, arms crossed on their chests to prevent touching—or punching. He seemed to hear the cries as a prisoner was dragged down to the "cachot" for some trivial offence; there was the sound of that soup trolley.

The rest of the tourists were coming back; the curator shouted and a bell rang. It was closing time.

Marc put out a finger and touched the rough stone of the water stoup.

Chapter
Four

"LISE! AT LAST! WELCOME!" The Prioress of Saint
Etienne, Soeur Marie de la Croix, came forward to
meet Lise, enveloping her in a hug, with a kiss on both
cheeks. The kindliness and warm welcome, after the
strain of the long day, brought tears to Lise's eyes; she
could not stop them running over, but Soeur Marie de
la Croix seemed to understand; she kept Lise's hand in
both of hers.

Saint Etienne was the pre-Béthanie of the Order, "a
sort of clearing house," as eighteen years later Lise
was to tell Marc. "It's where aspirants come, those who
want to try themselves in the life," aspirants, hopefuls.

"In my young day we didn't have them," Soeur Anne
Colombe, the oldest sister in the Belle Source community, chimed in. "We went straight to the novitiate. *We*
knew what we wanted."

"Some of us still do—the lucky ones," said Lise, "but
it isn't so simple for most. For one thing, there is such a
gulf now between family life and the religious one."

"Family life should be religious." Soeur Anne Colombe was as adamant as she was old—"She'll live to be a hundred," said the other sisters. "*We* were brought up to listen to our elders and do what we were told. Now the girls are independent and hoity-toity."

"At least they think for themselves."

"And change their minds."

That was true."Of all my 'set,' " Lise told Marc, "those who were at Saint Etienne with me, only I and Bella, Soeur Marie Isabelle, are left."

That first night of her coming, the Prioress had turned her over to a second white-habited figure. "This is Soeur Théodore who will be your Responsable."

Soeur Théodore, seen in the lamplight, was short, almost squat, a browned face under the black veil, but the eyes were piercing yet kind, as Soeur Marie Alcide's had been. Were these Béthanie eyes, Lise wondered? She knew they had seen the tears but Soeur Théodore ignored them. There was only another kiss as she took Lise's hand from the Prioress. "Come. You must be very tired."

"Yes indeed," said the Prioress. "Soeur Théodore will show you . . ." but Lise felt a small desperate hand thrust into her free one.

Soeur Justine had waited in the car, perhaps from tact, perhaps to take Lucette away.

"Ma Mère," Lise spoke unwillingly. "This is Lucette. She has just been released, like me. I think she had nowhere to go."

"Welcome, Lucette." The deep voice of the Prioress was unfeignedly warm. She isn't pretending, thought Lise as the Prioress called, "Soeur Justine!"

The sister came from the car. "Take Lucette to the hôtellerie—that is our little guest-house—" the Prioress told Lucette. "Very modest, but Soeur Josephine Magdaleine will look after you. Then tomorrow we shall talk, shall we?" There was no response except terror and the words jerked out: "I want to stay with Madame Lise."

80

"Lise has things to do."

More than a hundred years ago when Soeur Noël had come from Cadillac to that first Béthanie, Père Lataste had written to Mère Henri Dominique:

> Reading in the gospel of the welcome the father gave to his prodigal son, wouldn't it be good if each time God lays at your feet, or rather into your arms, one of these prodigal daughters, you, too, made a feast?

"We can only make a little one," Soeur Marie de la Croix, the Prioress, said now, but the tables were ready, laid with nosegays, and a few extras had been added to the supper—the Sub-Prioress herself had gone into the kitchen to make her famous crème brûlée—no one else could make it like Soeur Irène—but first Soeur Théodore had to take Lise to her room, show her the enclosure and, most important of all, spend a few moments in the chapel. All this Lise knew, Soeur Marie Alcide had told her, but there was still the clinging of Lucette's hand.

"Ma Mère, could she . . ." Lise had to say it. "Could she stay and see—just a little? Then she might understand and go away."

Or not go away. If that thought were in the Prioress's mind, she did not say it. "But I have seen providence work in strange ways," she told Lise long afterwards. Now she hesitated. Then, "Ma petite," she said to Lucette. "You have been in a chapel before?"

"No." That will end it, thought Lise, but, "What? Never?" asked Soeur Marie de la Croix.

"When I was small but . . ."

The Prioress made up her mind. "You cannot go with Lise—she has to go into the enclosure—but you can watch. Come with me," and the small cold hand yielded itself up to the Prioress's warm one.

The chapel was empty, for which Lise was grateful,

unlit except for the Sanctuary lamp burning with an amber glow by the tabernacle. She came in with Soeur Théodore and knelt for a few moments before the altar.

The Prioress and Lucette were there sitting quietly side by side, in the benches for guests at the back.

There was nothing for Lucette to see, only a nun kneeling with Madame Lise. Lucette had expected a ceremony, a priest, but there were only themselves, no music, no words until she heard what she thought was Lise speaking to herself:

> *Mon ame exalte le Seigneur;*
> *exulte mon espirit en Dieu, mon Sauveur . . .*

> My soul magnifies the Lord,
> and my spirit has rejoiced in God, my Saviour.
> He has regarded the lowliness of His handmaid
> and He, who is mighty, hath done great things in
> me.

"Who are those nuns?" Five years had gone since Lise had suddenly stopped and asked the wardress that— suddenly, because she must have passed them, "dozens of times" said Lise. There had been nuns at Sevenet, her Maison d'Arrêt, as there were at Vesoul, where they worked as infirmarians and as éducatrices, but they were of a different Order, Soeurs de Marie Joseph, dedicated to prison work; Lise saw them every day but now she was staring as if she had never seen a nun before. "Who are they?" It had been when she and her "division," some twenty prisoners, were on their way to the workrooms and, in the darkness of the January afternoon on that steep prison staircase, Lise saw the two white habits.

"Our angels have come," sneered one of the women. Angels! When Lise came to see them close, she learned that the white tunics were patched and darned, the pinafore-like scapulars worn thin with much washing, and the black veils framed faces that were only too human, often tired and distressed, more distressed than the prisoners, but "One mustn't be emotional, that is the first thing," Soeur Marie Alcide told Lise. She, the elder, was short and plump, but the plumpness was like a rock; she had "gooseberry eyes," as Lise thought when she first saw them, but no matter how plain and circled with tiredness, they were steady, while Soeur Marthe, so much younger, often had difficulty in holding back her tears. "Well, one feels the weight of evil and despair at Vesoul as in all prisons," said Soeur Marie Alcide, "and, still more, the ugly sordidness of some of the stories when at last they are told—or not told, which is perhaps worse,"—but the first sight of the whiteness of those habits seemed to Lise symbolic—"I was blind before. It did seem like light; perhaps that's why Saint Dominic chose it."

"Who are those nuns?"

"The Dominicaines of Béthanie." It was the first time Lise had heard the word Béthanie.

"They come four times a year," said the wardress. "I'm sure you can see them if you like. I will put you on the list," but still Lise had hesitated, "Hesitated for another six months. I missed two visits! I suppose I didn't want to tell. . . ."

"You don't have to tell them anything," one of the other prisoners said. "You can just—chat. It's such a relief to be able to talk to them alone."

"Alone? You mean without a wardress?"

"No wardress. One can be left in peace. That's something—and they don't ask questions."

"They bring peace." Soeur Justine of the Order of Marie Joseph who worked in the infirmary was reverent.

The Sisters of Béthanie brought something else too—not the usual help that came from outside; not just a smile, the comfort of words and encouragement, the sympathy to listen, or a refuge or protection or help in finding work, though they gave those freely; what they really came to offer, for the few who would or could take it, was a whole new life, a place in their own family—one could say "at their own hearth," into their lives and hearts.

At first Lise could not take that in. "You mean someone . . . a criminal, a murderess, a whore like me . . . could become a religieuse, a nun? It seems impossible."

"Why?" asked Soeur Marie Alcide. "Think, Lise. Think of Calvary."

"Calvary? Where our Lord died on the Cross?"

"Yes. Who did he choose to have close to him then, to share it with him, he who could have commanded the whole world? His Mother, Mary Immaculate: another Mary, the Magdalen from whom he had driven seven devils: Saint John, most loved of all his disciples, and two thieves. With him it was more than possible—it happened—and that is the core of Béthanie."

"For more than a year I saw those sisters every three months," Lise was to tell Marc; "they were always two together. We talked of trivial things—I can see now how difficult it was for them. Unlike the others, I had no family they could ask about, no friends, no home; the Rue Duchesne was best forgotten, and yet even there I had had this feeling of groping, searching. Then, one day, when I was with them, the barrier suddenly broke, and I poured it all out at last."

"With the sisters if often happens like that," the other prisoners told Lise. "You see, if you tell anything to the psychiatrist or the doctor, they have to make a report. Those nuns don't. It's as secret as when you go to confession—if you do."

With Lise it was even more secret than usual; against all custom, Soeur Marthe got up and left the room, leaving her alone with Soeur Marie Alcide.

"I see now there was a path that began that night when I ran away from the Rue Duchesne to that unknown church and its presbytery. I wish I could

84

write to Père Silas and tell him," said Lise, "but of course he won't remember me."

"He does remember you," said Soeur Marie Alcide on her next visit, "because of something you didn't tell me. It seems you slipped an envelope into the presbytery letterbox and in it was the ten francs he had given you for the taxi fare."

"But of course I had to return them," Lise had said in astonishment, "especially as I used them for what they weren't given."

"I think I wasn't mistaken in you, Lise," said Soeur Marie Alcide.

"For He that is mighty hath done great things in me," "and me . . . and me . . . and me . . ." How many others had knelt, as Lise was kneeling in the chapel now, and felt those words rise up in them—words that the Dominicaines of Béthanie said every night at Vespers?

Lise did not know she had said them aloud but, "What is she talking about?" Lucette whispered to the Prioress—her whisper was awed.

"She is using the words Our Lady used when she went to see her cousin, after the angel had spoken to her."

"But an angel hasn't spoken to Madame Lise."

"I think in a way. . . ."

"There aren't any angels nowadays."

"No? Well, see what is happening."

Soeur Théodore had waited until Lise was ready, then took her away through a small side door that closed. Lucette started up in panic but the Prioress stopped her.

"Lucette, you love Madame Lise."

"Yes." The eyes that searched everyone for a possible hurt searched the Prioress's face.

"She has gone into the enclosure. Do you love her enough to leave her alone tonight? To let her have her little feast of welcome?"

"If you say so." It was wrung out of Lucette.

"Bien," and it was Soeur Marie de la Croix herself who took Lucette over to the guest-house and called Soeur Joséphine Magdaleine.

"Lucette?" Soeur Joséphine Magdaleine smiled. "Of course. Come, I'll take you to your room."

"You mean—you have a room ready?"

"There is always a room. At times someone has to share but we manage. Here is yours. Simple, I'm afraid, but now, if you like to wash and make yourself comfortable, supper will be in twenty minutes; the dining-room is downstairs."

It wasn't until after Compline, the last Office of the day, that the peace Lise had hoped for, had expected even, came.

She had been shown to her place in choir, the place she would keep as long as she was at Saint Etienne; in front of the double row of white-habited nuns she was only one among several girls and women dressed in skirts and jerseys, even trousers. She had been introduced to them; Julie: Pauline: José: Jeanne—white-haired, perhaps sixty: Micheline and a coloured woman, Bella, much Lise's own age. These might be her companions for the next months, perhaps years, every kind of face from the unafraid and candid to the firmly reserved: from the gentle to the ravaged—but not as ravaged as her own with her scar. There, in choir, it had begun to throb.

"Lucette?" she had asked Soeur Théodore after the delectable supper.

"She is in good hands and there is no more you can do for her tonight," said sensible Soeur Théodore, "so thank God and be happy."

The Sister had marked Lise's book for her and slowly the words, the quiet singing of Compline, began to calm her.

Entre tes mains, Seigneur
Je remets mon esprit.

Into your hands, O Lord
I commend my spirit.

Then,

Let your servant depart in peace
according to thy word
for mine eyes have seen thy salvation . . .

The Prioress came into the centre of the choir and
sprinkled holy water; the candles were put out and, one
by one, nuns, women and girls left to go to their
rooms—they were not called "cells" in Béthanie because of the hurtful connotation.

Outside Lise's window, owls were calling as the
moon sank lower in the sky—a new moon, a good
omen. Her room was high, on the third floor of the wing
built on to the château; the room was as small and
simple as her cell at Vesoul, but utterly different: a bed
with a clean white cover, a small work-table, a chest, a
chair and, behind a screen, a fixed basin with water,
cold, and a small portable bidet. That was all, as at
Vesoul, but Lise was free to open the window, throw
back the shutters; there was no lock on the door and,
"If you don't want to be disturbed for any reason, put a
handkerchief on the handle," Soeur Théodore had said,
and added, "You can put your books here on the shelf,
as well as an ornament or statue, and hang your
pictures up. Don't be afraid of leaving your letters on
the table. I won't come rummaging."

"I have only a few books, no pictures," said Lise, "no
anything, and I don't think there will be any letters. I
have come to you bare."

"That's good. Most of us have too much."

Lise smiled. She had already seen Soeur Théodore's
room, bare of almost everything but papers.

Nine o'clock sounded from the turret, late by prison
hours. At Vesoul, every night, Lise used to try and pace
her cell for an hour to make herself sleep; now she

could kneel in peace and look out of the window. It was too late to see her star. It would have dropped to the horizon by now, but it was a night of stars.

When I look at the heavens,

Lise murmured the psalm,

> the work of Thy fingers,
> at the moon and the stars which Thou hast made.
> What then is man that Thou art mindful of him . . .

and mindful of me, thought Lise, in this extraordinary way.

At this time in the Rue Duchesne the night would not have begun. "As you know, they don't have houses now," Lise was to say to Marc. "It's all call-girls, or girls in cars, pick-ups at clubs and bars. Pity. Ours were looked after; they didn't have to bargain or bother about the fric: a third went to them, two thirds to us—they kept their tips—they were healthy and clean." "You will wash, before and after, each time, every time," she would emphasise. The little squares of towelling, "flannels" Lise's nanny used to call them, were boiled by Eugenia each morning and pegged out to dry. "Marguerite, you should have used eight and there are only seven. Slut!" Eugenia could give a hard slap. "No girl will lend, or allow another girl to use, her soap," Lise had ruled. "Infection can spread." "We never had any," she told Marc. "The doctor came every week, but now it's rampant. As far as possible I saw no girl was abused, though now and again Patrice would be in as vicious a mood as Patagon, his macaw, but only now and again. Our girls were well dressed, ate well; Marcelline was a good cook, bless her." All that, at least, was good, but more and more Lise shrank from the remembrance.

At this time the girls would be having their dinner except those who were going out. Patrice had arranged endless discreet little dinners or suppers in private rooms. Private! thought Lise, when every waiter and chef and door-man in Paris knew about them. It was Lise's task to supply the girls.

"Can't I go?" Vivi had begged.

"You're not old enough."

"If I'm old enough for. . . ."

"Also you have to know what a handkerchief is for, and not use your thumb as a fork," Lise said cruelly, and it was true that Patrice had always insisted, "Send only those who know. None of your trussed little pullets, quivering with nerves."

Vivi certainly would not have been a trussed little pullet but I sent some, "by special request," God forgive me, thought Lise and, as she had so often thought, He may, but I can never forgive myself.

"The past is past," Soeur Marie Alcide had told Lise firmly, "Remember, God does not look at what you were but what you are and, above all, what you want to be," said Soeur Marie Alcide, and, "It has been a long day," Lise told herself. "You can start again tomorrow. Now go to sleep."

Lise had meant that first night to keep vigil, a vigil of thankfulness, as, perhaps, an echo of that long ago Adoration when those poor women of Cadillac kept their watch half the night—but almost at once she was overcome by sleep. "Naturally," said Soeur Théodore. "You had had a long and emotional day," yet Lise had woken almost before dawn.

Soeur Théodore had said nothing about not leaving her room and so Lise dressed, made her bed, set her room in order and, finding a cloak hung on the door— Soeur Théodore must have seen she had no coat—put it on and went silently downstairs. The sound of the key turning in the lock was so loud that she stopped, her heart beating, but nothing stirred. Quietly she opened the door, as quietly closed it and was out. Out! Alone. Free to walk.

It was chilly in the dawn twilight; there were no colours yet; the trees were black shapes, the paths faint glimmers, but everywhere was freshness; freshness in the breeze and the spring dew on hedges and lawns and leaves. As Lise passed, a sense of another freedom came to her, wider than this convent domaine or the forests and vineyards around it; wider than her own release, wide as the paling sky, infinite.

More and more during her years at Béthanie did Lise come to love this sense of space in the empty purity of early morning before anyone or anything were awake to spoil it. Summer and winter, wet or fine, sun or snow, she would be up before the caller's knock and out, pacing the domaine. Marc liked it too; in the days after he came to Belle Source, each would see the other, pacing the empty garden, the kitchen garden and orchard; usually, they turned aside into another path, each wanting to be alone, but once Marc asked her, "Do you always do this?"

"I have, for more years than I like to remember . . . except, there were some years when—I couldn't," and Lise left him abruptly.

That first morning, at Saint Etienne, she stayed out until, in the trees, the birds had finished their first singing; a sister came down to let the hens out and a cow lowed, probably for its calf as it was being milked. Then a bell rang, not a clang but a gentle bell; it was time for Lauds, the first prayer of the day.

The caller must have gone along the corridor, giving the knock from room to room. Perhaps when no answer came from Lise, the sister might have looked in and seen the neatly made bed, the tidy room—perhaps the caller thought she had run away—but there was no comment when Lise joined Soeur Théodore and her flock as they went into chapel. I expect I had "a morning face" thought Lise, and Soeur Théodore knew she had no cause to worry; all the same she quietly told Lise, "Be up and dressed if you like, but don't go out until the knock. Soeur Johanne Magdaleine, our porteress, would be uneasy if the door was opened before the community was up."

"Nowadays," Lise was to tell Marc, "they trust me, but then I had to do as I was told."

She was not "told" to go to the guest-house and see Lucette but, "I think you should," said Soeur Théodore, "if only to say au revoir," but when Lise found Lucette in the little parlour Lucette was surly.

"Didn't they take care of you?" asked Lise. "Wasn't the food good? Ours was, especially after Vesoul. Weren't they kind?"

"Just trying to get hold of me," Lucette mumbled. "Everyone knows nuns do that."

"On the contrary, it's difficult to make them take you but, Lucette," Lise put her hand over the girl's. "They will always help. If you want somewhere to stay, to find work. . . ."

"You want to get rid of me."

"Lucette! I'm only trying to explain."

"Why can't I be what you'll be?"

"You could, but. . . ."

"But?"

"This is not something you choose; in a way you are chosen and often when it seems least likely, almost impossible, as with me. It's as if God put out a finger and said, 'You.' "

Lucette was suddenly angry. "God hasn't got a finger. He can't have because there isn't a God. If there were he wouldn't have let what happened happen to me—or you."

"That's what I used to think, but that wasn't God: it was us."

"Us?" The brown eyes, not angry now but puzzled, searched Lise's face. "Not us, it was them." Then light dawned. "I see, you are going to escape here where there are no men. I don't blame you. Je déteste tous ces mecs. I hate men, all of them. Saligauds. Cons!" The eyes came back to Lise. "Isn't it that?"

91

"No, never, never. For me, when you have loved a man, really loved through everything," Lise spoke painfully, "no matter what he does to you, you can't hate."

"Did you love a man? Like that?"

"Yes. Like that," said Lise.

"Chérie," said Patrice. "I'm going to ask you to move up to the fourth floor."

"But . . . that's where Marcelline sleeps."

"You like Marcelline and, you see, Vivi wants. . . ."

"*Vivi* wants?"

"Yes, I know it's absurd," and Patrice, that accustomed libertine, blushed. "Old fool that I am! But chérie, do you know, I think I should die if I lost that little girl."

" 'Mordu pour une môme?' Don't tell me you are sick with love of a chit," Lise mocked but she could understand. No matter how angry or hard she, Lise, felt, Vivi had only to come sidling up to her with that pretty cajoling: "Madame Lise, it isn't me. It's Monsieur Patrice," and slide her arms round Lise's neck, rubbing her cheek against Lise's, and she would be reduced to helplessness—so that Vivi won again.

It's I, Vivi, who am in the bedroom now. I can sleep all day long if I like in the big bed with the blue satin quilt. Monsieur Patrice says he will buy me a lace cover. I have lace pillows too. Eugenia has to plump them for me. It's I who have the wardrobe full of clothes. I threw out all Madame Lise's in a heap on the landing and got the edge of Marcelline's tongue, but I didn't care. I don't care for anything. I laugh at Monsieur Emile's long face when Monsieur Patrice buys me clothes. He bought me earrings too, and a bracelet. He'll buy me anything, and the funny thing is I can wheedle him in a way she couldn't. I can tease. "No, not tonight," I say. "I don't want to, not tonight." "What, again? All right, if you'll give me . . . buy me . . ." I can guess she never could do that.

"Vivi will forget to feed Patagon," Madame Lise told him.

"Vivi mustn't feed Patagon. He might damage her," and, "Pouponne, don't go near him," Monsieur Patrice told me—as if I would—and, "You can feed him," he told her.

"Then you must banish him too, upstairs."

"I couldn't. He would die without me."

I, Vivi, think Monsieur Patrice needs that horrible bird. He laughs when it pecks him. He likes to be pecked, though it leaves great marks. It's like being whipped. . . .

Vivi wanted to be whipped. Upstairs was a soundproof room which, to her, was an intriguing mystery—"I have seen the whips," said Vivi. "It would be something new, Madame Lise, I'm so bored. I want it."

"Well, you'll have to want. Monsieur Patrice would never allow it." Indeed, when Patrice knew, he was angry—angrier than Lise had seen him.

"Who the devil told her about it—who?" he shouted. "You?"

Lise's only answer was, "Idiot!"

"Who then—tell me." If Patrice ever came near to being cruel to Vivi it was then. "Tell me. Who?"

Vivi opened her eyes wide in innocence. "Zoë—Zoë said she would show me."

He sent for Zoë. "If you put ideas like that into her head, you are out on the street—understand?"

"Ideas into her head!" With Lise standing beside Patrice, Zoë dared to be impudent. "You had better go and learn the alphabet," she told Patrice.

"I'll make him whip me when I want," Vivi said when the dust had died down. "Or I him. For now, I'll let Patagon peck him."

"I'll feed Patagon myself," Patrice announced.

"You're too lazy." Lise had an immediate riposte. "He'll starve."

"You won't let him starve."

93

"I won't come into the flat while she's there."

"She" is me, Vivi, but Monsieur Patrice is right. Madame Lise comes into the flat to feed Patagon with his seed and raw meat, his cuttlefish bone and water; she even cleans out his cage. . . .

Patrice had had the rooms on the fourth floor re-done for Lise. "Milo was fearfully cross but it's beautifully done, isn't it?" he cajoled Lise. "Isn't it?"

"In the servants' quarters. Thanks."

"Nonsense. You have an independent little apartment. Wasn't it nice of me?" Then Patrice was suddenly grave. "No, it wasn't nice of me. I did it because I must keep you close."

"No matter what?" Lise found it difficult to make her voice flippant.

"No matter what. Please," begged Patrice, and he drew her to him. "Chéri, à jamais," he whispered against her hair. "Say it. Please say it."

It was wrung out of Lise. She had to shut her eyes ". . . à jamais."

In a way the fourth floor was a relief, somewhere that Lise could escape into peace and privacy; there was a window where she could stand with Coco in her arms looking. "I suppose that window became my sort of oratory," she told Soeur Marie Alcide. "There was a spire—the man who thought of a spire must have been a genius—and it was over the spire that I first began to notice my star."

The rooms themselves were fresh, emptier than any other rooms in the house—Patrice knew Lise's taste—but in colours she would not have thought of herself, "and done for me with love and care," Lise could tell herself, and, "Yes, I think," she said in the parlour with Lucette, "I think I know a little—I'm sure only a little—about what it is to love. The sisters will teach me the rest."

"Les frangines!" What can they know about it?

94

In the guest-house parlour, the chairs, embroidered in petit point on seats and back, the work of the sisters, were ranged stiffly against the walls, their wood, and the bookcase, table and parquet floor so polished that a breath would dirty them; each ornament and vase had its own spotless crochet mat. Lucette looked even scruffier against the cleanliness.

"I never heard talk like this in my life," said Lucette.

"I hadn't either, but Lucette, as I told you, it wasn't a man, any man, it wasn't even the nuns, that brought me here."

"Then what was it?" Lucette's forehead was knotted, her hands twisted. She was desperate to know. "What *is* it?"

"What I told you; it's like a call."

"That's fancy."

"Is it?" said Lise. "It has been calling me for a long time—only I didn't listen. I may be too late. I can only try—with all my might," Lise added under her breath.

Lucette was surly again. "You'll be put upon."

"Over and over again." Lise said it with satisfaction.

"I *don't* understand." It was a cry.

"Hush, Lucette. It's just that . . . well, you know this as well as I do—you can't have something for nothing. Here you pay with all you have."

"Suppose you haven't any money."

"You don't pay with money."

"Then with what?"

"I suppose—with yourself—and you don't ask anything in return."

"That's a funny business."

"It can be because 'you can be repaid an hundred-fold,' " said Lise softly. "That may, or may not, happen, but one of the rules seems to be that you don't keep anything back"—"which is why I am in the parlour talking to you," Lise could have added, but refrained—instead she looked at her watch; miraculously it was going, but then it was a watch among watches: Patrice had paid a small fortune for it. "I must go; I have a class."

"A class! Are you going back to school?"

"In a way—yes."

"You mean, *you* have things to learn!"

"Of course. It may take years, as the Prioress, Soeur Marie de la Croix, told you. Besides, I expect there will be quite a few little battles to be fought."

"Battles!" Lucette bristled. "With them?"

"No, with myself." Lise rose. "The Prioress is coming over to see you."

"I don't want to see her."

Lise did not answer that but, "Lucette, talking of money—how much have you?" she asked. "You took a room for the night and that train fare was expensive."

Lucette was silent.

"If I were you," Lise said gently, "I should see the Prioress."

"I don't need to stay here," Lucette boasted to Soeur Marie de la Croix. "There's a house in Marseilles where they would be glad to have me."

"But would you be glad to go?"

Lucette's head came down on the table and sobs shook the shoulders that were so thin and so queerly hunched. "I don't know where to go. I don't know what to do. I only want. . . ."

"Want?" The Prioress was patient.

"Want what Madame Lise wants."

"What is that?"

"I don't know. I don't know, but whatever it is that makes her—shine when she talks. I want it."

"If you really want it, wouldn't the best idea be to find out what it is?"

"You are turning her into one of you—I know *that*. She'll be a nun."

"Perhaps."

"Perhaps." The head lifted with a glare from the

96

eyes. "You ought to be down on your knees to have her."

"We are, but it doesn't rest with us."

"Who then?"

"With Lise herself—and God. Listen, Lucette." Soeur Marie de la Croix had a calmness, a dignity and authority that acted as balm on Lucette. "Of the hundreds of girls and women who have come to Saint Etienne down the years—and they are only a few hundred of the thousands who don't—only a few, perhaps three or four out of each hundred, sometimes five or six if we're blessed, go all the way and become Sisters of Béthanie. That's no fault of the rest; it simply means God has other ways for them, and there are many many ways. I think He has sent you here to find yours."

"Then—I can come straight away?"

"That would be too fast."

"You took Madame Lise."

"Lise has been working, studying and praying for the last five years—yes, while she was in prison—and still she is only here on trial. She has a long way to go."

"How long?"

"Before she can make her final vows? Probably nine or ten years."

"Ten years! Then, for me, it should be fift.y"

The Prioress laughed. "Or it could be very quick. You can only learn what you can—and we shall help you all we can—but first you must find out about it. What you have to do now is to go away and think—and learn. There is a foyer in our town. . . ."

"A foyer?" Lucette was at once suspicious.

"It's what we call a halfway house where you can rest and get strong—I think you are not very strong, Lucette—so that is the first thing you must do. Meanwhile, they will find you work suited to you that will keep you until you decide if you really want to try and follow Lise—without her—it would have to be on

97

your own—or whether you would like to find permanent work or want to marry."

"*Marry!*" Lucette was scornful. "I have seen a skinful of that!" and she demanded, "What if I want to go back to the old life?"

"We can't stop you; only you can do that but, no matter what you decide," said Soeur Marie de la Croix, "you can come to our guest-house any time you want."

"You would let me come?" Lucette marvelled.

"Of course. We don't shut our doors."

"And see Lise?"

"When she is settled herself and if she is still here; even if she is sent to another of our houses you could go and see her, but now you must leave her," said the Prioress, "to have her chance."

Chapter Five

"EVERYONE SAID I WOULD find it hard," Lise was to tell Marc. "I never did. From the first hour I only felt privileged."

The convent day began at six with the caller's knock; then came half an hour's silent meditation, for most of the nuns in chapel, but Lise made hers in the garden unless the rain was too hard. "It rains so much in the Gironde," said Soeur Théodore. "That's why the grapes from our vines are so good." Not all the aspirants got up as early: some slept on, even through Lauds, until Mass at half-past seven. They had to get up then. "After all, they are here to take things seriously," and then the sacristan, having cleared the altar, brought in the monstrance, the priest put in the Host and the Adoration began. No one could open the doors except when the clock chimed the quarters, or at the half-hours on which the watch was relieved, and

Lise had never known anything as still and as fulfilling as those half-hours.

> The Lord passed by and a great and strong wind rent the mountains and broke in pieces the rocks but the Lord was not in the wind; and after the wind an earthquake but the Lord was not in the earthquake; and after the earthquake a fire but the Lord was not in the fire; and after the fire a still small voice—and it was so. . . .

Over and over again Lise thought of that passage.

It was in this quiet that she learned the meaning of forgetting, or transcending, as she could call it now, in which, or what, she could lose herself, surrender.

Not always; sometimes she would be earthbound, as if held deliberately low, and the minutes would pass slowly—she could hear the clock ticking and would be conscious of faint sounds; a ring at the gate for the porteress: the telephone: footsteps: seldom voices because silence was the rule. She could hear birds, a workman's hammer, the convent's car starting out, even a lorry on the road. Then the only hope was in words; almost every nun laid a book on the prie-dieu; and some of them said the rosary which each nun wore at her belt, but the wooden beads were large and slid softly through the fingers without a click. Sometimes they remembered psalms, prayers, poems.

> As a dare-gale skylark scanted in a dull cage
> Man's mounting spirit in his bone-house mean-house, dwells . . .

"Can I say that in chapel?" Lise asked Soeur Théodore.

"Why not? Everything beautiful belongs in chapel. It would be a good place for a poet to write his poems in."

Another day there would be no need for a word; there was no sound, no sense of time and the nun or aspirant coming to relieve Lise had to tap her on the shoulder so that she could give up her place. For Lise, as an aspirant, her half-hour usually came late in the day, "Though, as you know, you can slip into chapel whenever you have time," but duties had to be done, times kept.

After Mass came breakfast and the hot coffee was welcome, as was the bread with, sometimes, a little allowance of butter made from their own cows' milk and, sometimes, there was jam, homemade cherry jam or gooseberry jelly or any fruit the domaine could grow, but never the marmalade made of expensive imported oranges Lise had introduced at the Rue Duchesne.

Then there were classes: "Going back to school," as Lucette had said. In those days there was Latin, and Lise was carried back to Greenhurst and Aunt Millicent. "Aunt, do I have to learn Latin?"

"You will do as you're told," said Aunt Millicent, but had added more gently, "You'll never regret it, Elizabeth. Try." But who would have thought I should be needing it now, thought Lise and, "I'm terribly rusty," she told the nun who took the classes.

"At least you have a smattering. Some have never even heard of Latin."

The sisters had a difficult task; in the old days, many of the "petites soeurs" were illiterate, "and there are still good aspirants who are semi-illiterate now," Soeur Théodore told Lise, "and yet we have a Doctor of Philosophy. I don't know which are the hardest to teach."

Then there were what the nuns called "personalités" —discussions that helped each aspirant to build up her confidence—"to find herself," said Soeur Théodore. There were classes on the Bible, too, Old and New Testaments, and on one day a week each aspirant chose her own text in the gospels and talked of it. Every week, too, there were lessons in the liturgy, in singing, the meaning of the feast days, a talk on the work of Père Lataste and, always, on the Sacraments. Every aspirant had to try and write, as best as she could, an essay on a subject set by the Responsable, and these were dissected and discussed, sometimes in private, sometimes in a group. In fact, all morning, every morning, the aspirants wrote, read, listened. "I never dreamed there would be all this to learn," said Lise.

Lise had begun studying long ago at Vesoul under Soeur Marie Alcide, helped by the prison aumônier and the éducatrice, but she was years older than Julie or José and most of the other aspirants and it was a shock to discover how difficult she found it to learn by heart, even to remember. I suppose, thought Lise, for years and years I had not used that part of my brain. There had been few books in the Rue Duchesne; the girls read magazines if they read at all, but Lise still treasured the books she had brought from England; she had asked Marcelline to bring them to Sevenet, "and I took them to Vesoul and was allowed to keep them," said Lise. Among them was the *Oxford Book of French Verse* given to that far-away Elizabeth Fanshawe as a prize at school. "Elizabeth Fanshawe. First Prize for Senior French," and Lise thought, as she had thought of the Latin, How surprised they would have been if they had known how I should use my French!

These were poems she had loved as a schoolgirl and still knew by heart, though some she could not bear to say now.

> *Quand vous serez bien vieille, au soir a la chandelle*
> *Assise aupres du feu, devidant et filant,*
> *Direz chantant mes vers, en vous esmerveillant*
> *Ronsard me celebroit du temps que j'estois belle.*
>
> *Je seray sous la terre, et fantôme sans os*
> *Par les ombres myrteux je prendray mon repos . . .*

We, Patrice and I, could have been two people growing old in the candlelight by the fire, thought Lise, then, No, we wouldn't, she contradicted herself. It could never have been like that.

"If Monsieur Patrice were alive, when you come out of Vesoul would you feel compelled to go to him instead of to us?" Soeur Marie Alcide had asked her with accustomed directness, and Lise had stared at her in genuine astonishment. "But—I couldn't—with what I know now."

"What do you know now?" and Lise could only answer, "Le Seigneur, Our Lord," but, she added, "Poor Patrice."

Mordu pour une môme—lovesick for a chit. Poor poor Patrice.

Vivi was seventeen when she first saw Luigi—and Luigi saw her.

"Who is Luigi?" Lise asked Marcelline.

He was the big gentle lorry driver who delivered the ice. "In those days of course we didn't have a freezer," and the ice came twice a week in great blocks wrapped in sacks and sawdust; Luigi carried them in on his shoulder down to the trays in the cellar as easily as if they were sacks of feathers. He must have been twenty or twenty-one, thought Lise, and his Italian good looks, the dark curly hair, skin, dark already from his Italian birth, made richer by sun and health, filled the kitchen with colour and life. He often whistled and sang as he went between the lorry and the cellar:

> *Come prima, più di prima t'amero*
> *Per la vita la mia vita ti darò*

> More than ever, more than ever ev'ry day,
> I will love you more than ever, come what may.

It was Marcelline who saw to him, "and saw him off," said Marcelline, because to Luigi the house in the Rue Duchesne was a palace of marvels. "How much do they cost?" he whispered to Marcelline.

"Far too much for the likes of you," said Marcelline. "Besides, I thought you were a good boy."

The kitchen at the Rue Duchesne was the most neglected part of the house, stone-flagged, its only window barred, "against burglars," said Eugenia. "As if there were not enough burglars in the house," said Marcelline. Its walls had not been painted for "a hundred years at least," Lise often reproached Emile, who shrugged, yet Marcelline's kitchen was like herself, cheerful and wholesome in that strange house. It was warm; her rocking-chair with its old red cushion stood by the stove for the rare occasions when she sat down. On the shelf above was a statue of the Mother and Child with a vase of pink paper roses. Clusters of onions, smoked hams, great sausages and bunches of herbs hung from the beams; there were always good pungent smells and good simple work. Coco, if Lise were busy, liked to come down and lie on the rag rug, rather than be petted by the girls. Marcelline would not call him Coco. "That's not a dog's name." She called him "Trésor"—treasure.

After her morning prowls, when Lise met Marcelline just come back from her marketing at Les Halles, Gaston behind her carrying the baskets, they would have coffee together at the kitchen table. Marcelline made Gaston take his into the shed or the empty bar: she would no more have thought of sitting down at table with him than with Patrice. It was she who alerted Lise about Vivi and Luigi.

"I was chopping onions at the table and my eyes were streaming, so I didn't see her at once. If I had, that little minx would soon have been sent packing," and after the trial Marcelline was in tears. "To think, if it hadn't been for those onions, all this might not have happened."

"I think it would," said Lise. "If it hadn't been Luigi it would have been someone else," but, "I'll never look at an onion again," vowed Marcelline.

It had been a Saturday morning; Luigi had just delivered his ice and was waiting for Marcelline to sign "and hoping for that bowl of hot chocolate I was soft enough to give him," when Vivi came into the kitchen.

Vivi was greedy and when she woke towards noon— "She lies in bed most of the day," said Marcelline. "*She* doesn't have to work, oh no!"—Vivi could not wait for lunch but came down and raided the larder and took what she wanted back to bed. "She'll eat a gigot with her fingers, gnawing it to the bone, or steal all my tartelines." Already she was putting on weight, a plumpness, Lise guessed, that would seem adorable to Luigi's Italian eyes.

"She was barefoot, Madame, the little gutter cat, and not only that—there was nothing, absolutely nothing under her negligée, and that you could see through, chiffon edged with lace," said Marcelline derisively, "open to her legs and more than her legs. 'And who is this Monsieur?' she asked, saucy as the princess she thinks she is.

"The onions were out of my eyes and I said, 'Upstairs, Mademoiselle, where you belong,' but do you think she would budge? 'There's nothing for you here,' I said, and 'I think there is,' she said and came round the table to that big owl of a boy.

" 'What's your name?'

" 'Luigi.'

" 'Luigi!' You know how she can make her voice soft, Madame," said Marcelline.

" 'Luigi what?'

" 'Luigi Branzano—, Mademoiselle.' The poor fool could hardly stammer it.

" 'Luigi Branzano—you are very very handsome,' and that brazen slut was giving him the look as she went into my larder. I yelled at her to come out: there were my beautiful mousses au chocolat à l'orange there, just setting, and terrines ready for tonight, but do you think she would take any notice? She came out munching, with the end of a baguette filled with butter and ham. 'Have a bite,' she said, holding it out to him. 'Here where my little teeth have been.'

"I told her I would call you, Madame Lise, and she only laughed. 'La pauvre Balafrée—she can't do anything to me. He wouldn't let her.' 'He' was Monsieur Patrice and I said indeed he would if he caught her making eyes at Luigi and, 'Anyway, Luigi's going,' I said.

" 'He isn't—he's coming upstairs with me.'

" '*Upstairs!* Think, Madame! A lorry driver!

" 'You would like to come, wouldn't you, Luigi?' and she went close to him—you know that scent she has. I thought he would fall down in a swoon; then he looked at her, not with greed, Madame, but as if she were a vision.

" 'Upstairs,' and, believe me, she actually gave him the little jerk of her thumb.

"I ran across from my stove. 'Mademoiselle Vivi! You can't.'

" 'Why can't I? Anyone can come—if they have the money.'

" 'That settles it then,' I said. 'He hasn't any money.'

" 'Mademoiselle . . .' and still Luigi could only stammer. 'It's true—I haven't. In any case. . . .'

"And that little strumpet," said Marcelline, "with the tips of her fingers, took a wad of notes out of her sash, right there in front of us and peeled off three and held them out to Luigi.

"I was paralysed, Madame, but that dear boy—he didn't take them. He backed away and his big face was full of blushes, and he said, 'I couldn't. I couldn't possibly—not here.' Then, 'I have my lorry waiting. The flies . . .' He ducked his head and was gone.

"I burst out laughing, but Vivi . . . she put the notes back and, 'You'll laugh the other side of your face,' she said to me like the vicious little vixen she is, and then, 'He comes on Wednesdays and Saturdays, doesn't he?' said my lady. And Madame," said Marcelline, "when I went into the larder I found—from spite, *spite*, Madame—she had put her fingers into every mousse and flattened each terrine!"

Luigi is like Stefan—only he isn't gone in the head—and yet in a funny way he reminds me of Pom-Pom, only he isn't a poor little ugly like Pom. Luigi's beautiful.

Lying in her bed, licking butter and ham off her fingers, Vivi thought about Luigi, Stefan and Pom-Pom.

Why should I remember Pom? Perhaps because he was the first one—no, the only one—I loved. I called him my little dog. Madame Lise's Coco has a look of him, that crinkled-up face and little puzzled eyes. It was because of Pom-Pom that I didn't do what I thought I would—to get even with Madame. I thought I would ask to take Coco for a walk, then take him down the métro and, in the crowd, lift him off the platform with my foot just as the train came in. "Hue! Hue! my little dog—he jumped." They would have taken me home in tears, hysterics, and Madame Lise could not have said a thing . . . but I couldn't do it because of Pom. . . .

Oh, I'm so tired of old men. . . .. Monsieur Patrice, when he's undressed, with that big white belly he wants me to stroke. He looks all right when he's dressed and he smiles, but ugh! Oh, I want to do it for fun. Luigi's so handsome and fresh and firm I could bite him, bite him all over. That would be fun because he would be s usurprised—he's so shy. I could tease him. Perhaps we could run away and have a room where we could do what we liked. I cu ld go with him in the lorry.

"You can't," said Luigi. I had waited for him in the cellar where there's no Marcelline. He was so surprised, he almost dropped the ice. "Of course you can't. It's not allowed."

"I could sit on the floor."

"You! On the floor of a lorry," and he wouldn't. If I were with Luigi I might be a good girl—like with Monsieur Grebel.

"Never," Marcelline would have said. "You're bad to

the bone." Perhaps I am, but I want Luigi. I want him and I'm going to have him.

"But Mademoiselle Vivi had a surprise," Marcelline told Lise. "She took to waiting for him in the cellar and he wouldn't stay there with her, not for five minutes. He marched her up to me. I think it was the first time in her life our Vivi had met with that. She was furious. 'What do you think I'm here for!' she said to him as if she spat, and he . . . Madame, that great big young man was almost in tears. 'Tell her why I can't,' he said to me. 'Make her understand. To me,' he said, 'she's like her . . .' and he pointed to my Virgin Mary. 'Our Lady!' " Marcelline was shocked.

"Vivi couldn't only wheedle—she could diddle me," Lise told Soeur Marie Alcide.

"Madame Lise, will you help me—us?"

"Us? Lise was alert. "Who do you mean by 'us'?"

"Luigi and me."

"Luigi?"

"Luigi Branzano, the ice delivery man."

"The *ice delivery* man?"

"Yes. He has been courting me all summer. Ask Marcelline."

"It's true, Madame," Marcelline said when Lise asked her. "Nothing will turn him from it, but it's been proper courting. I can answer for that."

As a matter of fact Marcelline could not; between four in the afternoon, when Luigi finished his round, and six o'clock was a dead time in the Rue Duchesne: there was often quite a trade at lunchtime but now everyone was asleep; even Marcelline rocked herself off in her chair with the red cushion. Lise had seen the dressed head sink back with its combs and curls and Marcelline snored almost as loudly as Coco who lay at her feet. If the courtship was "proper," that was due to Luigi. "We sit in the lorry and hold hands; he won't do any more." Vivi was virtuous. "Sometimes we go to a café but he won't let me have anything stronger than a grenadine—usually it's a citron—and he won't let me smoke. He brings me back to the corner just with a kiss and that not on the mouth."

"And he wants to marry you."

"He's been asking me all summer." Vivi knew how to be demure. "He wants to take me to his home in Italy, but we have to be married first. It's the only way I can get him, Madame." That, at least, was honest, but Lise had been too perturbed to listen.

"But," said Lise, "he's a *respectable* boy."

That sounded such a strange objection from someone older to a young girl. "What will his family say to you?"

"They won't know. Luigi says they won't know. He says they could never imagine a place like this."

"I'm not so sure. I think he's a peasant and peasant mothers are shrewd."

"He'll tell them I have been in service in Paris; so in a way I have," and Vivi pleaded. "Madame Lise, please, please. You have always wanted me to be good. I could be, with Luigi."

"And I, like a fool, believed her," Lise told Soeur Marie Alcide.

"Do you love him?" she had asked Vivi.

"I'm mad for him."

"Which perhaps was the right answer," said Lise. "Luigi has arranged it. We can't be married in a church because I haven't been baptised."

"But you must have been baptised; you have a rosary."

"Then I don't know where it happened." Vivi had turned taciturn. "So we must be married in a register office. Luigi says he can get a licence."

"Vivi, you will have to tell your proper name. You can't be married as Vivi Ambard."

"Why not? Luigi says I have to have a tuteur— guardian—because I'm under age, and if anyone's my tuteur, it's you."

"I thought you had changed me for Monsieur Patrice. Besides, Ambard is not my name either," said Lise.

109

"You use it."

"Not on documents."

"Why do there have to be documents?"

"Because marriage is a contract between two people and it must be true. Who are you, Vivi?"

Vivi was sullenly silent. What stories she had told the other girls about herself, Lise could imagine; indeed, some she knew: "My mother was a duchess."

"Where did you get those manners from then?"

"My mother was a well-known concert singer."

"Odd that you have a voice like a crow and can't tell one note from another," or, more dramatically, "I was born in the street at night, under a lamp post and on a gendarme's cloak spread on the pavement." "That's Edith Piaf, not you." Vivi told these tales to the girls, perhaps to Eugenia, never to Marcelline or Patrice or Lise and now, "I'll tell Luigi," said Vivi, "but I won't tell you."

"Vivi. Why not?"

"Because you're clever and will want to rescue me and pry and probe. Luigi won't. He doesn't even dream he should do that."

"And even then," Lise told Soeur Marie Alcide, "it didn't dawn on me that she hated me," but Marcelline knew. "Madame, don't ever let that street arab take Coco for a walk."

"Vivi? But she dotes on Coco."

"Does she? And, if I were you, I wouldn't let her into your room."

It had been Marcelline Lise had been curt with then and, as usual, she gave way under Vivi's cajoling.

"It was you who found me, you who tried to take me out of this place," Vivi pleaded. "I know because he told me—Monsieur Patrice. You said I was to go to school and I laughed but now I wish I had gone—only I wouldn't have met Luigi. Luigi doesn't mind if I don't know much—he doesn't know much either. We'll be so happy—if you let us, Madame Lise. It's only you who can do that. You could tell Monsieur Patrice I have the

110

toothache and you have to take me to the dentist. Tell him anyti ng. By the time he finds out I shall have gone."

"But I shan't," said Lise.

"He doesn't do things to you."

He does—at times. But Lise would not say that.

"We won't tell you where we're going, so he can't make you tell. Luigi and I will be grateful all our lives long. I'll write to you sometimes—through Madame Chabot at the little tabac on the corner. Madame Lise, it's my only chance. Please. Please."

It was an oddly touching wedding—because of Luigi—and dismaying—because of Vivi.

Had Luigi, Lise wondered, ever worn shoes before? She thought it would have been boots, heavy boots, or else barefoot, as he would have been as a child. Now he had smart patent-leather shoes which obviously drew his feet so that he walked as if he were on hot coals; instead of the dark blue peasant Sunday suit Lise had expected, he was in pale grey checks, his big muscles bulging under the cloth, unexpectedly light, and Lise realised with a shock that Vivi had made him dress in imitation of Patrice; Luigi's tie, purple and grey, was a foulard Lise recognised; Vivi must have filched it from Patrice's drawer. Some things, though, were Luigi's own idea—the white carnation in his buttonhole and the hair oil that shone on his dark curls and filled the office with overpowering scent; and he looked at Vivi with such adoration in his eyes that Lise had to turn her own away.

Vivi had wheedled a new dress—from Patrice, "of all people!" Lise exploded.

"Why not?"

"It's cheating."

"Tant pis! He's had plenty out of me, so why shouldn't I have what I can out of him?" It was in her favourite pink and she had bought a pink veil, "That's even more cheating," but, fastened with rosebuds, it looked rav-

111

ishing. Luigi had bought her a bouquet of roses too, stiffly wired, and offered Lise a camellia. Round Vivi's wrist was the pale pink rosary. "I must have my beads," "Yes, her chapelet," Luigi said it tenderly, and "I shall take her to our priest," he assured Lise. "As soon as she's baptised we'll have a proper wedding."

Lise took them to a little restaurant for a wedding breakfast where Marcelline joined them. Vivi ate like an eager piglet, Luigi scarcely at all. Then Lise saw them off on the express to Milan. Luigi wrung her hand so that she thought she would lose it; Vivi flung her arms round her and showered her with kisses. The train pulled out and Lise went back to the Rue Duchesne to face Patrice.

"It was a good thing they didn't tell you where they were going," said Marcelline as she applied the famous steak. "Those bruises! Madame, he has tortured you!"

And Patrice knew how to torture, thought Lise, but she remembered that it was he who had collapsed in her arms weeping, not she in his.

No one else was taken into the apartment after Vivi. "I came in and out but only to feed Patagon and the fire seemed to have gone from the big bird too." He grew dull, no longer stabbed and scolded; presently he died—and Patrice began to look old; he hardly mentioned Vivi's name and avoided the other girls. "I had not known you would grieve like that," Lise could have cried and, now, "Patrice! Patrice! If only you could know that I shall never stop loving you; all I can do now is pray for you, as I do for Vivi too, while this new love grows in me. . . ."

"I'm afraid I'm not at all that sure that I want to stay at Saint Etienne." Lise heard aspirant after aspirant say that.

"My fear is that they won't let me stay," was her only answer.

After studies came the chief meal of the day when

aspirants and nuns sat down together. Formal grace was said: "Donne, Seigneur, du pain à qui a faim," "Give, O Lord, bread to anyone who is hungry. Give, Lord to *all* who are hungry," then a reader read to them during the dinner.

The aspirants took it in turn to serve, putting the tureens of soup on the tables. In the old days, each nun carried her knife in her pocket, so there was only a fork and spoon at her place; between courses she wiped these with bread and when dinner was over washed them and her plate and bowl herself—there were bowls and jugs of hot water on the tables. The food was simple but good. "Well, most of it comes from our own growing, our own poultry or beasts," said Soeur Théodore. Every day there was soup, mostly vegetable, then meat or fish served in the French way that still, after all these years, Lise found trying, with the vegetables coming after the meat as a separate course. There were exquisitely fresh salads; cheese, sometimes goat cheese; on feast days a special dessert. The nuns and girls, too, were hungry, which is the best sauce, "And doesn't God give us our food? So it's our duty to enjoy it," old Soeur Anne Colombe at Belle Source used always to say. At Saint Etienne Lise, remembering her jaded appetite in Paris and Vesoul, was amazed at what she could eat. It's because the days here are so busy, she thought. On some, instead of studying, the aspirants were recruited to help in the house or garden, orchard or farm, "planting, picking, *plucking*," said Lise in dismay when she and Bella, the coloured woman with whom she had made friends, were first shown how to pluck poultry. Sometimes it was sorting potatoes, smelly, disgusting work; some might help in the laundry—the big wash that took place once a week. There might be lorries to unload, hay to make, bonfires to stoke, "anything, everything, no matter if it's pouring rain, the heavy rain of the Gironde," and, too, they ate in silence, "so that you really taste what you eat," as Lise said to Bella, while the voice of the reader went on—the book,

113

not necessarily spiritual, sometimes on current interests, even a novel—until the Prioress gave the knock; then there was a scraping of chairs and another grace was said: "Lord, for our faith, you have given us these things to eat; we beg you, in your justice, to give the same to others. Amen."

At recreation Soeur Théodore let them do as they liked, walk, talk, chatter, play games—badminton was popular. Bella did gymnastics: José ran like a young gazelle and climbed trees: Jeanne stayed in a chair and knitted. Others sat around Soeur Théodore, in summer on the grass or, if it were raining, on the floor of the recreation room, when they played records and idled—no one at Saint Etienne thought it a disgrace to idle at recreation. "When you can enjoy yourself do just that," said Soeur Théodore. Indeed now and again they spent the whole day at the sea, or in the forests.

The bell rang at three o'clock for "Lectures," readings from the Old and New Testament, prayers and perhaps a talk from the Prioress or one of the other senior nuns. Then came handwork: sewing, knitting, embroidery, painting, "I can't do any of that," Lise had said aghast, but it was found she could do something—make scrapbooks for children in hospital. "People send us old Christmas cards and catalogues," said Soeur Théodore. "It seems a pity not to use them." Everything was used, one way or another, at Béthanie. The collage was soothing work and Lise found she had a gift for it. "It's a kind of paper patchwork." She began a screen and, "We could sell that," said Soeur Théodore with satisfaction.

The Sisters of Béthanie lived on what they earned and on what was given to them. "But it's astonishing how the money comes," said Soeur Théodore: some came by the occasional dowry, "but no one with a real vocation is turned away for want of money any more than we would accept anyone who would bring us riches if she hadn't the 'call.' " It was astonishing, too, how from that poverty the nuns managed to give alms—"Well, people give things to us and we give them away"—as they had given them to Lucette—and how they managed to pay for the aspirants, "feed, keep and clothe them," said Lise. Her black dress was a hand-down from "I don't know how many postulants." It was clean and neat, but Lise had had to ask for underclothes and nightdresses. "Take what you need and don't worry," said Soeur Théodore.

While they did their handwork, the aspirants listened to more reading, perhaps to a discussion: sometimes one or another would be called apart for special instruction; they all pretended not to know when Cécile, a newcomer, had to be taught to read. Perhaps one of them would have a private talk with a nun, or slip away for a vigil in chapel; but time wore on until all work was put away and they stood in the corridor, waiting for Vespers, and told their faults.

"I wouldn't help somebody who asked me."

"I answered a sister unkindly."

"I contradicted Soeur Prieure."

And, most often, "I used bad language."

That, for most of the newcomers, was one of the big difficulties—to suppress what rolled so easily off the tongue and was so expressive, from the casual swearing and colloquialism of universities, its fashionable argot, to the argot peculiar to the streets and prisons where it was needed as self-protection.

"It's all very well for you," Bella told Lise. "I'm just a ragbag, but anyone can see you have come from a gentle home." Lise felt her mouth drop open. "Why, I don't suppose," said Bella, "you have ever heard a proper downright filthy word in your life."

"Salope: enculée: putain: tu me fais chier!" said Lise, and it was Bella who was left open-mouthed.

It was a revelation to the aspirants that the sisters, some of them elderly impressive nuns, filled with quiet holiness, should publicly admit their faults. Could Soeur Imelda de Notre Dame, that calm saintly person, really have snapped sharply at anyone? Could Soeur Marie

115

Dominique have lost her temper? "Then do you go on being you till the very end?" they could have moaned. "Even after all this trying and training?" "Always," Soeur Théodore would have told them. It was a good thing Compline finished with a prayer of Mary Magdalen: "Intercede and pray without ceasing for us, Marie Magdaleine, you who are so close to our Lord Jesus."

After Vespers, supper: soup again, a simple dish of pasta, or vegetables—potatoes in cheese or courgettes and tomatoes baked together or hot chestnuts still in their skins—then fruit or salad. After, there was another short recreation and, finally, Compline that ended with the "asperges," the Prioress or the hebdomadarian —leader of the choir for the week—sprinkling her whole family with the blessing of holy water; then each went quietly to her room and at ten the lights were put out.

"Of course it's easier for me, after the discipline . . ." Lise told Soeur Théodore, but broke off. One did not talk about the past. "I mean I have been drilled to discipline but for those who have come straight from home, and independence, cut off from so many things they had taken as a matter of course—comforts: entertainments: drinks"—though there was always wine on the table it was understood no one took more than one glass. "Cigarettes." "We don't make anyone give them up all at once," said Soeur Théodore. "You can always have a cigarette in the garden. . . . But they have to be denied in the end." There is no chatter and also to have only the company of women. Women! Women! The need to curb speech and eyes and feelings. The monotony. . . ."

"But it isn't monotonous," Soeur Théodore defended. "How can it be when, within its frame, every day is different. For instance, you'll see how you will learn to welcome the feast days and saints' days, each with a different story, another aspect. The Communion of Saints is real, a living thing."

"But intercession. There's nothing in the Bible about that," argued Bella who always argued.

"No?" asked Soeur Théodore gently. "When the Greeks wanted to see Jesus they came to Philip and asked him if, and how, they could reach him. Philip went to Andrew who perhaps had more authority and together they brought those men to Jesus. What is that but intercession? Think, too, in a worldly way, how sensible it is; if you are trying to do something with all your might, heart, body and soul," said Soeur Théodore, "and are lucky enough to know an expert in that very thing, isn't it wise and natural to ask his, or her, help?"

"I don't feel I know them as well as that," Lise said doubtfully.

"You will."

The saints were certainly a vivid certainty at Béthanie. Especially dear was Saint Joseph. "Saint Joseph will help you with everything from your work to your dying." Soeur Théodore spoke as if he were a friend just round the corner, as indeed he was. One of the favourite places in the domaine for prayer was in the small enclosure round his statue; the statue was sentimental and cheap but that made no difference; it evoked Saint Joseph and many were the little bunches of wild flowers, thank-offerings, laid at his feet—garden flowers were for the chapel.

Then there was Saint Dominic, visionary, founder of the great Order of Preachers of which Béthanie was a humble branch. "I tell you we're proud to put O.P. after our names. Think," Soeur Théodore said to Bella, "in a few years you may be Soeur Isabella de Notre Dame, O.P."

"Sister Bella of Belzébub, more like," said Bella, but not altogether flippantly.

And there was Mary Magdalen. "Have you noticed," Père Lataste had asked those women at Cadillac, "that the very things she used before as enticements for men, she used to show her sorrow and love for Christ? Her scent, her kisses, long hair?"

"Our Lord did not speak of the Magdalen's faults," said Soeur Théodore. "He only spoke of her love. It was Mary he defended against excellent Martha whom he also loved, but not as deeply. Mary stood at the foot of the cross: Mary who came early to the sepulchre and, above all, she was the first to see, and recognise him risen. Risen!" said Soeur Théodore.

Lise never forgot her first Christmas at Saint Etienne. I suppose I had never had a real one, she thought. In England with Aunt Millicent it had been almost a dreary day. "You're too old for a Christmas stocking," Aunt Millicent had decided when Lise was seven years old. There had been the long service in the parish church, then Aunt Millicent's friends, all elderly, for an equally long luncheon which Lise had to help wash up. "I usually spent the afternoon by myself while everyone slept." She did not remember ever making a crib or having a Christmas tree; "there was one in the church, but the presents on it were for poor children—not me."

She had heard of the pageantry and beauty of the Christmas Eve Mass in some of the Paris churches but she had never been able to go—ironically the great religious feasts, Christmas and Easter, were the busiest and hardest times for the girls in the Rue Duchesne. Men seemed to want a relief from too much family and the days of Christmas were, for them, simply a holiday in which they had nothing to do. The girls were exhausted, Patrice at his hardest, Emile gloating because the money poured in—patrons were absurdly generous at Christmas—"And I couldn't get away even for an hour" said Lise, "though I could hear the church bells ringing."

There had been no midnight Mass at Sevenet or Vesoul; it would have meant extra work for the wardresses who were already taxed enough. Christmas in prison was always an emotional time; a time of tears and nostalgia, when even parcels from home caused heartache, more tears. The day itself had never been as bad—not even the worst grumblers could deride the Christmas dinner and there were attempts at gaiety and decorations, often carols or a concert, but religion was limited to a crib in the chapel and daytime services. But now, "It all seems new—so new," said Lise.

"It is new. Every time a child, any child, is born, it is new—and different; that is the wonder," said Soeur Théodore.

Christmas at Béthanie was homely, the only word Lise could find for it—home-like, and simple, as suited the infant Christ. The house was decorated with holly and mistletoe, a crib made in the cloister.

Christmas Eve was a day of prayer with a vigil in the afternoon and, at Vespers, the martyrology was sung: "Even in the joy of the Nativity, we mustn't forget the faith and endurance of the church," but just before midnight the Prioress took the statue of the holy child in her arms and went to the end of the cloister where she held him out as the nuns and all the household came in procession with lighted candles to kiss him and take him to be laid in the manger in the crib; then Mass began, the long beautiful solemnity of the Christmas Mass. "It's words will stay in your heart," Soeur Théodore said rightly.

Afterwards, at the, to the convent, strange hour of one o'clock in the morning, came Réveillon, the Christmas wakening feast with hot chocolate, cake, crystallised fruit, strawberry jam eaten with a small spoon from saucers—Lise never ceased to wonder at the Sisters' appetite for sweet things—and when they went to their rooms, on every pillow was a small package from the Prioress. "Like children!" Lise could imagine an outsider's patronising tone. But how refreshing it is, she thought, now and then to become a child again with a child's sense of joy and wonder.

On Christmas Day, Lauds was not until eight o'clock so that, for everyone, there was the luxury of an extra hour in bed. There was sung Mass to which many of the villagers came, most of them with gifts, provender, a carefully potted flower or cut chrysanthemums for the chapel, "And there was a true Christmas dinner," said Lise. "Turkey, hot chestnuts, the Bûche de Noël—a cake shaped like a log and iced with chocolate—and wine. No wonder we needed a siesta after it,"—and they slept until they met in the chapel to sing the Vespers for Christmas Day.

Lise was almost at the end of her second year at Saint Etienne when the Prioress sent for her. Twice the year had come round; twice Lise had seen the long rows of vines, so dead-looking after they had been pruned, quicken all along their black branches into bud; first, pale nodules showed on the twisted black stems, then, as the leaves unfolded, there were beginnings of grapes, clusters so tiny they looked like elves' fingers, until the knots grew and swelled. As the sun grew hotter, men with cans on their backs sprayed the vines with copper sulphate that turned the leaves to turquoise, a blue sheen that shimmered over the hills.

The grapes ripened and, through the long hot days when the girls longed for the sea and Bella ran under the sprinklers on the lawns soaking her clothes so that they clung to her big brown body, the clusters grew heavy with fruit.

Then came the vintage, and all day on the roads the lorries came and went as the pickers toiled. "I wish the Catholic church had the Harvest Festival," said Lise, "when everyone brings their ripe vegetables and fruit and crops to decorate the church." She could see herself toiling behind Aunt Millicent, the skirt of her overall held up to carry apples, a marrow, carrots from the kitchen garden—but this vintage was no church gathering; brought up in England, then city-bound, Lise had not seen anything like it. There were shoutings and laughter and songs and, in the evenings, the sound of music came up to the convent with something disturbingly restless in the air. The vintage was always a difficult time for Soeur Théodore and for the aspirants.

"Ma Mère," José announced. "I think I have fallen in love with Pierre." Pierre was the gardener's son. Perhaps José expected or hoped the Responsable would be shocked but, "That's natural at your age," said Soeur Théodore. "The only thing is to ask yourself, do you love Our Lord more?"

"Blood will be blood," said Soeur Théodore. "It wouldn't be surprising if they ran away," but there was no need to run. Each was free to go. "Our gate is made to open," said Soeur Théodore.

It was not only the girls. "People think," said Soeur Théodore, "that we nuns have a mysterious power that lets us sublimate ourselves. Yes, sometimes we are given that but it doesn't mean we don't feel desire. It's odd how it assails one suddenly. I am sure there are sisters who, at one time or another, have had times of longing—almost burning. Then the ony thing to do is work, physically hard work.—And you can always pour it all out to Our Lord. He was human too."

Bella's rages too were at their worst, the unaccountable outbursts of temper that shook not only Bella but the convent. "Don't they want you to send her away?" Lise was tempted enough to ask, "The other nuns . . . don't they advise?"

"If I listened to all they advised," said Soeur Théodore, "we should have lost some valuable nuns," and, "Try counting ten before you speak," she urged Bella.

"Ten! When it's on me like a flash."

"Try counting one . . . then perhaps it will become two . . ." and slowly, "It's working," said Bella. "I do believe it works."

"What have I done wrong?" Lise asked herself when the summons to the Prioress came. Soeur Théodore was there too and both nuns looked so grave that Lise's heart seemed to beat quickly while she waited for them to speak.

"Lise," said Soeur Marie de la Croix. "If you are still of the same mind. . . ."

121

"Yes, ma Mère." There, Lise was sure.

"Then—we are going to send you next week to the novitiate to start your training as a 'petite soeur tertiaire,' and soon, I hope, your postulancy. This is earlier than is usual but there is a reason for it which you will be the first to see. We have decided to admit Lucette."

"Admit Lucette! But. . . ."

To Lise, Lucette was a perpetual irritant. She had settled well in the "foyer" or waiting-place the sisters had found for her and was working as an auxiliary in a hospital and seemed content except that she was forever coming out to Saint Etienne, asking to see Lise. And, every time, "I think you should see her," said Soeur Théodore.

"Why—why do I have to be the confidante of young girls?" asked Lise.

There had been the awkwardness of those letters sent by Vivi for delivery to Madame Chabot at the tabac: little, badly written, badly spelled missives with the stamps set crooked, often without enough stamps so that a fee had to be paid; the envelopes were often soiled, and there was really nothing in the scrawls. Vivi was well. Luigi was well. They were living with his Mamma. One day they would have a place of their own, Vivi hoped, and always in them was "thank you for the money," and usually, "but could you let me have another hundred francs? Three hundred . . . five . . . you see Luigi can't . . . I can't ask Luigi. . . ." But what if Madame Chabot had handed one of those letters to Patrice or to one of the girls?

There came a day when there was real news. "You will never guess," Vivi had written—as if I didn't guess at once—"we have a baby, a son, Luigi and I. You might think a baby had never been born before. Luigi thinks him so wonderful. It's to en called Giovanni-Battista Giuliano, I can't spell it"—which was obvious —"and you are to be godmother. . . ."

That softened Lise but she had had to write: "I can't

122

be godmother. You must get a Catholic." The answer came back: "No one but you."

Lise had been tempted to go but, of course, could not. She imagined herself saying, "Patrice, I'm going to Italy."

"Oh—where?"

"Milan." The Branzanos' village was near Milan.

"And why?"

"That's my private business."

"You have no private business."

That was true and to go would have been too risky.

Every now and then, Patrice would still assail her. "You have heard from Vivi?"

"How could I? You see every letter, every note that comes here."

"Telephone calls?"

"I have no calls except on your business."

"Yes, but I still think you know where she is," and he would break out in an agony of blows and arm wrenchings. Suppose I went, and he traced me, thought Lise. It would be the end of Luigi, and she had to content herself with sending extra money for the baby. She bought what she thought Vivi would admire—a fleecy white topcoat and a minuscule pair of white kid boots—"The first time in my life and probably the last that I have ever been in a baby-shop and bought baby things." She would have liked to keep them for a day or two to look at and fondle, just for the novelty—but novelty was not the right word for something so new and wonderful—but she did not dare to take them back to the Rue Duchesne.

"Would you have liked a child?" Soeur Marie Alcide asked her, which had startled Lise. "Even as a thought, it never came my way," she had said, "but I suppose in most women somewhere deep down is a wistfulness, perhaps an innate unfulfilment," and it was true that even now Lise felt a pang when she remembered Luigi's pride in his son, and Vivi must be like a child with her first doll, Lise had thought fondly.

123

*   *   *

I know more about dolls than Madame Lise.

"I'm not going to," I said. "I'm not going to—I won't." I lay face downwards on the bed so that Mamma—Luigi's precious Mamma, "Mamma mamma mia"—couldn't turn me over; I couldn't bear to look . . . my two little "lemons," as Patrice used to call them, are big and swollen ugly. But that will go away if I don't. . . .

"But this is Luigi's son," the older woman was dumbfounded. "And yours!"

"All right. Feed him yourself."

Mamma had on one of those black cotton blouses peasant women wear, high-necked, long-sleeved, like Marcelline's; Mamma's was patterned with small white flowers with tucks down the front so firmly stitched they would last a lifetime and probably had. "Open it. Feed him yourself. You're always telling me you fed eight. Go on."

Luigi's mamma hasn't Luigi's patience. She slapped my face hard. "Mamma, don't! don't!" It was Luigi who wept. "Please mamma, she's only a child. She's frightened."

That was true. No one knows how frightened I was. I don't want that brat near me, but I wasn't going to let them know and I called out, "I'm not frightened. I don't want to, that's all."

"Mamma, don't be angry," begged Luigi. "She's little and a Parisienne—different."

"Yes, different! Trash!"

Luigi tried to coax me himself. "That's what it's there for."

"What is?"

"The beautiful milk. Try and understand, cara. None of our babies has been fed from bottles and he's crying. . . ."

"Let him cry," and I lie back on the bed against that uncomfortable bolster and polish my nails. I have put a tight bandage round my chest and the doctor—they

124

called him in for quite the opposite reason, I'm sure—has given me pills to take the milk away.

"She got round him, the minx!"

"Yes, I got round him—easily," and I laughed.

The doctor didn't come when it—I can't call it "he"—was born because, though I thought it would hurt me, it didn't. It was funny when it just slithered out, wet and warm, still tied to me. For the first—and the last time if I have anything to do with it—Mamma was pleased with me. "As easy as a ewe with a lamb." But it wasn't easy. Suddenly I was back in the shed with Claudine; the baby, still wet and warm, tied to her—I dried its slime with an old towel and Claudine cut its string with a penknife we found on the window sill. We put it under the corn in the dark end of the shed; the corn fell on to its face, into its eyes and mouth. I still wake up in the night and I could shriek again because of that baby under the corn. There were sacks of corn and corn falling . . . and suddenly in that big bed of Mamma's and Luigi's I began to shriek, like in the Maison Dieu. I shrieked and shrieked. "Why? Why—when it's all over?" Mamma and the midwife couldn't understand, nor could Luigi. "Cara, don't, don't, cara mia." In the end they had to take the baby away and Luigi held me till I went to sleep.

"The first son of my first son, the eldest of the eldest," said Mamma. The eldest—and the only—I'm not going to let anyone do this to me again, ever.

The funny thing is that if it, "he," I suppose I must call it that, had been helpless like Rico, even a hunchback like Renée or a dwarf like my Pom-Pom, I would have loved it, but this Giovanni-Battista Giuliano—yes, I suppose I must say "him"—was beautiful from the beginning, as beautiful as Luigi with the same black curly hair. "It'll fall off," said the midwife. "It won't," said Mamma. His eyes were blue. "But they'll soon be black," and his creased face was already rosy.

I looked at him once. That was enough. "You're not going to hold your son!"

"Ugh!"

Mamma showed him round the whole village. "Giovanni-Battista Giuliano—eldest of my eldest."

"Vivi—he's crying, Vivi." Poor Luigi, he's so puzzled. I shrug. "She'll find someone to feed him," and she has; that great tub Angelina, bursting out of her bodice. "And you! Good for nothing," Mamma, Mamma spits at me.

"You don't know what I'm good for," and I go on polishing my nails.

"Lying there like a princess, you lazy slut. I was always up cooking dinner, making pasta, the next day."

"Which is why you look seventy, not forty." I said it sweetly, which made her angrier. "No thank you. I'll get up when I'm ready"—and only when I'm ready—only I don't say this aloud—I shall take Luigi away. As for that morpion—that crab-louse—Angelina can have him.

For Lise, the thought of Vivi, Luigi and Giovanni-Battista Giuliano had been like a little flame of warmth, of reassurance in those days. I don't expect I have ever done any good to anyone but at least I did that, she used to think.

"Yes. *You* did that!" the inexorable voice came back.

Put it behind you, Lise was able now to command herself and succeeded now and then. There had been enough—too much—of Vivi, Lise had thought there had been enough of Lucette too, Lucette and her endless questions.

"It's like a boarding-school here, isn't it?"

"Yes, if it's a school where no one puts you—you put yourself; and from most schools you can't go away the moment you want. Here you can."

"Why do you have to stay so long before they make you proper?"

"Because it takes a long time to see if it endures. The life might come to bore you if you haven't a vocation; there is nothing more boring than trying to live a contemplative life unless you are a contemplative—which means prayer, by yourself, Lucette."

"But if I can't pray, there are other things. You pick gooseberries. I have seen you. I can pick gooseberries. I can do that as well as anyone."

"I'm sure you can. But we don't just pick gooseberries. It sounds impertinent, but we pick them to help in the work of God."

"Merde!" But when Lise came to think of it, the questions had ceased lately. Talking to Lucette had suddenly become like talking to an ordinary person on an ordinary level and, "I thought she had given up the idea," Lise told the Prioress. "On her last two visits, she hasn't mentioned it."

"Which is the very time when it has possibly taken root."

"But Lucette! That funny little thing."

"God often likes funny little things. They tell me at the hostel, and the hospital, that she loves, no, venerates responsibility, and when she is given any, carries it out as gravely and carefully as a child."

"If only she can stay like that," said Soeur Théodore and sighed.

"I think you may have been privileged, Lise," said the Prioress. "You may have been the instrument of a vocation."

"I can't believe I had anything to do with it."

"No? How many people accept what it means to be an instrument? Have the patience? Particularly," added the Prioress with her direct gaze, "when you did it against your will."

"Ma Mère . . . I don't know what to say or do!"

"You do. Keep out of her way—and pray."

"Nuns are always trying to get hold of you." It was not only Lucette who said that "everyone knows it."

"I wish," Lise said to Bella, "that mythical 'everyone' could know what you have to go through before you are accepted, even as a postulant."

There was a rule in the Constitutions that applied to every stage in the religious life, "every rung of the ladder," as Bella said. She used to sing to her guitar in her deep warm voice the old spiritual:

> We are climbin' Jacob's ladder, ladder
> We are climbin' Jacob's ladder
> We are climbin' Jacob's ladder
> For glory of the Lord.

The ladder was steep to climb, "and it gets stiffer and stiffer," moaned Bella.

To become a postulant, each of them had first to provide some worldly things— "we are still *in* the world, though people talk as if we weren't," said the Prioress. Birth certificates if possible—some of those street births were never registered, nor was baptism or confirmation—and a medical one was needed "to show you are strong enough in every way to stand the life."

There was a questionnaire to be answered, in writing again if possible, and each woman or girl had to sign an assurance that she would not expect any payment for the work she would do in the House. "We come here to give, not get." She had to make an inventory of all her possessions, usually they were meagre enough, which was signed by her Responsable, and she herself had to write, or dictate and sign, a formal letter asking for entry. Then everything was sent to the Mother-General, head of the Congregation, who would lay the matter before her Council so that they could vote. "That is on the worldly side," Lise was to tell Marc "and, on the spiritual, if the answer is 'Yes,' you make a three-day retreat, so that you can be quite, quite sure you want to go on. You see we are thoroughly sieved, and have to sieve ourselves, which is more difficult."

She, with Bella and José, journeyed to the mother house away in the French Alps. "Right across France," said Bella. "Funny," she was to say, "I never travelled

128

so much until I tried to be a nun." Bella did not know it but she was to go to an American house one day. When they arrived, José went straight to the novitiate proper while Lise and Bella joined the petites soeurs.

"There used to be two ways, two paths," Lise told Marc. "One for the réhabilitées, another for the sisters who came in the ordinary way—ordinary for nuns, that is."

"So there was a difference."

"For a time," said Lise, "but of course no réhabilitée knew what another had done, nor did the sisters. For the réhabilitées it was longer, that was all—and in those days, I think they needed that; there were not the opportunities, the care there is now in prisons, nor for prostitutes if they wanted to get away. In those days they could come to Béthanie as aspirants, then become a petite soeur as they were called. A petite soeur probably had an easier time than those in the novitiate proper but, though they wore the habit—it was black— they were set apart. Yet, even then, they could eventually merge with the others, going up to become a postulant." Lise did not mention that she had spent three years as a petite soeur tertiaire before she and Bella went up. "We called it 'going up' because then the novitiate was on the top floor of that huge building and as the would-be postulant came up the staircase we used to sing the *Magnificat*."

"It was a big jump," said Lise, "exchanging Soeur Théodore who had come with the petites soeurs for Soeur Raymonde, Responsable of the Novitiate."

No two nuns could have been greater contrasts: Soeur Théodore was small and as round as the round horn spectacles she wore, behind which the eyes often had a kindly twinkle. There was something comfortable about Soeur Théodore; Soeur Raymonde, far younger, was statuesque, austere and exacting, yet once they grew to know her, she cast something like a spell. "She makes you taller than you are," said one of the other girls. Soeur Raymonde had, in particular, a curious influence on Bella, not curbing her but somehow teaching her respect. She never flinches, thought Lise, and is never ruffled; perhaps that's why we're half afraid of her. It was no light thing to go through the hands of Soeur Raymonde.

"But she brings you up and up," said Bella, "higher than you think you could go."

After six months, perhaps even a year, as a postulant, came noviceship, an even more serious step: a vote would be taken from every professed nun in the house after a private report was made by each to the Prioress. "I'm terrified," and Bella rolled her eyes.

Though José failed the test and left, Lise and Bella were accepted to their own surprise. "There was a ceremony," Lise told Marc, "not as ceremonial as it was in other Orders at that time, when the postulant was dressed as a bride, but it was held in the chapel and we knelt before the aumônier, then went to the back of the chapel where the habit was laid out on a table—at last a white tunic, scapular, white stockings, brown belt and shoes."

"Either you feel you're wearing fancy dress," Soeur Raymonde had said, "or it fits you so comfortably you think you have been wearing it always, which is a good sign." For Lise it felt as if these were the clothes she had been looking for all her life, "and the veil should hide my scar for ever. Deo Gratias," said Lise.

They changed in a side room and Soeur Raymonde cut Lise's hair. "You can't wear that heavy coil under a veil," and at once her head felt lighter. "You'll have to shave mine," said Bella, "or my veil will stand up as if it were on springs," but with a species of crew-cut she looked like a strong boy.

"Nowadays the ceremony is utterly simple, held in a room in the novitiate and, thank heaven," said Lise, "there is only one path now, one way. The name 'Petites Soeurs' has been abolished, as has the black dress; aspirants and postulants alike wear their own clothes and when, as novices, they are given the habit, it is

130

identical with that of a fully professed nun. White veils didn't suit some of the older, sometimes ravaged, faces," Lise did not add, "like mine," "but we are still given new names—our names in religion."

Bella became Soeur Marie Isabelle. "Lise will be the second name I have discarded," said Lise.

"Why not go back to Elizabeth? Be Soeur Elizabeth or Marie Elizabeth?" But Elizabeth seemed a phantom. "How strange names are," said Lise. "You would think any name would do—when you are going to efface yourself," but it still seemed of the utmost importance. "Could I be Soeur Marie Lise de la Croix?" That was what Lise had meant to say. How then did it come out as "Marie Lise du Rosaire?"—of the Rosary?

"It seems I am never to get away from it," said Lise.

> *Luigi and I have come back to France with our baby—I can't spell all his fancy names,* wrote Viv. *Lise, you would love him with his big eyes. His eyes are like Luigi's, dark brown and trusting,* she could have added, *except when he sees me, then he cried. It's funny how babies know far more than grown ups. The Morpion knows perfectly well I don't like him. Luigi hates me to call him Morpion. "Cara, that's a disgusting thing! It's horrible to call him that!"* but I think he's horrible, so I do, but she wrote,
> *How glad I am, Madame, to get away from Luigi's Mamma with her nag, nag, nag. Isn't this my baby, not hers? Luigi can't bear to let him out of his sight, but he has to—Luigi is a long-distance lorry driver now. . . .*

When she read that, the first apprehension had stirred in Lise; it meant that Luigi was away two or three days at a time, two or three nights. Vivi seemed content but. . . .

The house was at Ecommoy, in the Sarthe, a good centre as it was near Le Mans where Luigi picked up plenty of work. In that hot summer Luigi came to the Rue Duchesne whenever his lorry happened to be anywhere near Paris. From the breast pocket of his shirt he would take a new snapshot of the baby. "Not another picture," said Marcelline, but she herself had put a photograph of Giovanni-Battista Giuliano, naked but for his vest, at the foot of her Madonna. Luigi kept his photographs in a heart-shaped frame; on the reverse side was Vivi. He always had to show them, too, something he had bought for the house. "It's one in a row but there's an upstairs and a downstairs," Luigi boasted. "It has a shower and the kitchen has butane gas, but it's so small I can hardly turn round in it."

"*You* turn round in it." Marcelline was shocked. "Vivi should do that when you work so hard."

"Oh well," said Luigi.

Once he brought in a box of geranium seedlings from the market. "I'm going to plant them in our front garden," and the next time he came: "You know those geraniums? They've turned out so fine I'm going to put them in for the flower-show they're holding at the château. They might win a first prize."

Another time it was a toy tricycle. "But Luigi, it will be two or three years before Giovanni-Battista Giuliano can ride that! He's only nine months old."

Luigi was downcast. Then he brightened. "At least he can hear the bell," and then he asked anxiously, "Do you think Vivi will laugh at me?"

"He's besotted," said Marcelline after he had gone.

"Only happy and proud," but Marcelline shook her head. "She doesn't look after him. Did you see that great rent in his shirt, and I swear it had never been ironed—and I bet our Mademoiselle Vivi doesn't look after that child."

"Madame, your baby was crying and crying last night."

"Oh?" It was snooping old Madame Robert from next door.

"Crying and crying."

132

"So what?"

"So I think . . . you don't by any chance go out and leave him alone?"

"You don't by any chance have the money to lend me for a baby-sitter? Or perhaps you would like to baby-sit yourself?" and I went closer and closer until Madame Robert backed away and I slammed the door. Then I sat down at the table and cried.

Luigi was cross because I forgot to water the geraniums. Some of them died. I hadn't washed the Morpion's napkins either, so they ran out and I let him go without them and the mess was worse. His bottom's all red; I put my face cream on it but it must have stung because he screamed. I nearly put the pillow over his face. If only Luigi had let me leave him with Mamma.

And I? Do they expect me to stay here in this hot mingy common little room these summer evenings? Down in the square the little tables outside the cafés are full; the people walk up and down. I can hear talking and laughing and singing. I lean on the window sill and look out but nobody comes up this hole of a street. There are soldiers in the barracks at the end. I go out, down the path and lean on the gate. One of them looks out and waves.

With the money Madame Lise sent the Morpion last week I have bought myself a new suit. I'm wearing it now. Luigi won't be back till Friday. The Morpion's crying, but I can't hear. Let Madame Robert hear. I'm going out.

Next time Luigi came Lise had asked him, "Do you have to go so far?" He was bound for Hamburg.

"I have to go where I'm sent." Lise thought she saw a shadow of worry on that ingenuously happy face. "I don't like it, Madame. Vivi's so young—but I'm not my own master."

"If you had your own lorry. . . ."

"Ah! If I had that. . . ."

"I sold my mother's diamond brooch," Lise told Soeur

Marie Alcide, "the only valuable thing of my own I had, and gave Luigi a lorry. They used that little fact at the trial."

The sisters said the rosary in chapel after Vespers but in silence, each making her own interpretation, thinking her own thoughts. Lise knelt with the others but never touched the beads at her girdle; she kept her hands under her scapular.

"I think that's downright rude," said Bella.

They were in the last year of their noviceship; for the final six months they would go to one of the other houses of Béthanie to try community life; they would be separated and Bella obviously thought she should speak now.

"Rude?" Lise was dumbfounded. "I have been rude? When? To whom?"

"To Our Lady. Every day."

"Soeur Marie Isabelle!" But Bella was not abashed.

"Yes—every day. *She* didn't set herself up. . . ."

"You mean I do," Lise interrupted. "Just because I choose to make a private prayer."

"Private—at that time—as if you didn't need her. Oh Lise!" Bella used the single name, familiar between them. "What you miss! It's a wonderful prayer; it holds everything. Think, it's for an ignoramus like me and for someone as learned as—as the Pope. Our Lady makes everything plain, which is marvellous, because she didn't say much. In all the Gospels she says less than two hundred words. I have counted them."

"Saint Joseph said none at all."

"Saint Joseph was a great saint but she is the saint of saints, and when she did speak, what words." Bella's eyes were brimming. "Think! 'They have no wine,' she told him. It wasn't a matter of life or death—it was just a party—but she knew the shame you feel if the food or drink runs out, and she dared to ask him, who could stop a storm, make waves still, raise people from the dead, to do that little little thing. That's what she does

134

for all of us when we don't dare, are too frightened, bewildered, to ask for ourselves. Even when he seemed to put her down, she knew he didn't mean it. 'Do whatever he tells you,' she told the servants—and that's what she has taught me," said Bella. " 'Do whatever he tells you.' I say that to myself twenty times a day."

"But Bella, one can still honour her without the rosary."

"Seems to me like saying you honour a poet and can't read his poetry," said blunt Bella.

Lise went to Soeur Raymonde. "Ma Mère, is it valid?"

If the Responsable had noticed Lise during those evening fifteen minutes, she had not commented. "Bella only said it for my sake," said Lise.

"Of that I'm sure. Dear Bella, she's like a cornucopia, overflowing with love and concern. One day she'll make a great nun. It can be a little like Niagara at present, but sometimes we need a Bella. She's right—and she's wrong," said Soeur Raymonde. "It isn't a question of the rosary; for some people it holds the whole teaching of God, of the Gospels and the church and meditation; for others it seems a part of what they call 'Catholic treacle.' "

"There's none of that here," said Lise, which was true. What statues there were at Béthanie were placed in the garden, "as reminders in our work." The chapels were refreshingly bare; only the light burned before the tabernacle, or candles by the monstrance. "The saints are in our hearts and minds where Our Lady surely has a special place. It does us good to remember her faith, long suffering and patience." Lise winced as she thought of how she had answered Bella.

"And her compassion," added Soeur Raymonde. "Simeon was right when he said a sword would pierce her soul. There are plenty of swords," said Soeur Raymonde, and, "I can guess, Soeur Marie Lise, some have stabbed you, but. . . ."

"But what?"

135

"Just 'but,'" Soeur Raymonde was doing what she always does, thought Lise, putting you back on your own feet.

"Just 'but,'" and Soeur Raymonde said, "Think about it, Sister. Think about Bella too," and Lise was silent, remembering something Bella had told her; Bella had always had battles, fierce ones, against herself. "But there was one that was worst of all," Bella had told Lise. "I don't know about you, but I had to wait two years before they took me at Saint Etienne; they sent me back into the world though I spent weekends with them; if I hadn't I should have gone out of my mind. They had found me work as help in the house of a doctor's family. I was lucky to have it, but I had been in college—no, it wasn't what you think," said Bella. "I didn't mind what work I did, but we black college girls and boys had sworn we would never work for whites, no matter how good and kind, and I was breaking that promise. Béthanie taught me I had to, because it was a wrong promise. There is no difference between colours," said Bella firmly. "Of course not—it's we who make the difference, not God."

Then is there a stumbling block for everyone? thought Lise and, "I'm not as big as Bella," she said aloud. "Ma Mère, what am I to do?"

"Be as big as Bella," said Soeur Raymonde and, in Bella's parlance, "give over."

"What if I can't?" said Lise.

Lise had had a custom, "a superstition you could call it," since she was a girl; if she were in a dilemma and did not know what to do, she took a book—it must be a classic, but preferably the Bible—and shutting her eyes, opened it and put her finger on the page. "It's probably superstitious, but I still do it," she told Soeur Raymonde afterwards. She did it now and, "O, ye stiff neck!" read Lise.

That serves you right, she told herself and could not help laughing and, in chapel, kneeling by Bella, she

136

kept her eyes open, her hands down, and said the decades. She still did not touch her beads but one early morning, walking in the domaine, she found herself saying the first of the "joyful mysteries" on her fingers. After all, I have ten fingers—how useful, and, "Fiat," whispered Lise.

In this last novice year, little by little, the discipline tightened: permissions, excuses, the indulgence towards faults, were slowly withdrawn. More was expected, And we can give more, thought Lise, as if the very deprivations gave strength. After all, we have to stand on our own feet, discipline ourselves. One can't have a Responsable for ever.

There were, of course, days, weeks even, that could only be described as glum, when the weather was dismal and nothing seemed any good, only hollow and purposeless. What am I doing here, Lise would ask herself, treading round and round? I might as well be taking exercise in the prison courtyard. "Well, you did that to get fresh air and health," she answered herself. "It wasn't purposeless." A sensible answer but it did not make her feel better; sometimes, indeed, there was almost rebellion. I can't help feeling I'm not as humble as this, doing a servant's work.

"Here we are all servants," Soeur Raymonde would have said.

It was in such times that Lise learnt the meaning of community. "Ours is not a silence of separation but of communion." Working alongside Bella in the turnip plot, seeing her stop and wipe the sweat from her forehead under the handkerchief they wore for manual work—the drops of sweat stood out pale on the dark skin—and hearing Bella swear to herself: "How did I ever damn think I should come to this!" and then look up at Lise with a broad smile, had an odd power, "If our sisters can, we can," said Bella, Soeur Marie Isabelle—not at all Soeur Bella de Belzébub—and we could, thought Lise.

It was on the evening of one such hopeless day that Lise escaped to walk in the garden—to walk and pace, even in the confine of the domaine, helped her mood of helplessness, as it always had—"Oh, your long legs!" Patrice would moan—and on this summer evening, Lise, already soothed, had stopped to pull a stalk of lavender and rub it between her fingers, lavender with its sensible earth-and-spice smell. How blessed I am, she thought, to come before I get too old and live in the country!

There was a butterfly hovering over the bushes, an ordinary cabbage white, but, watching the fluttering wings, the antennae searching, Lise was struck as if by a miracle, the everyday miracle of a butterfly that has gone through its stages of growth. Isn't that happening to us? thought Lise. We are getting a power we didn't know we had, any more than a grub knows, when it spins its chrysalis, that one day it will come out with wings. How can a grub know it has wings?

No wonder, thought Lise, standing in the summer evening light, that the old-time Chinese sages thought a butterfly the symbol of the soul. Slowly, and she was sure of it now, she was coming from the chrysalis; her wings, still creased and crumpled, were unfolding imperceptibly, but unfolding.

One day they might even fly.

Chapter
Six

"I, SOEUR MARIE LISE DU ROSAIRE, now vow and promise Poverty, Chastity and Obedience to God, the blessed Virgin Mary, to our holy Father Dominic and to you, Very Reverend Mother, Soeur Marie Emmanuel, Mother-General of the Congregation of Dominican Sisters, called Béthanie, and to those who will succeed you in this same charge, according to the Rule of Saint Augustine and the Constitutions of the Congregation of the Third Order of Saint Dominic for three years."

Lise knelt before Soeur Marie Emmanuel, Mother-General, one hand in hers, the other laid on the book of the Constitutions, which Soeur Marie Emmanuel held open on her lap. These were what mattered: the hand in hers for loyalty and absolute submission—and the Constitutions; Lise had read them from cover to cover—they held the whole vision and rule of life at Béthanie. These were the bastions on which the Congregation was built. "As Christ . . . is called the corner stone, so also are his members called stones," ". . .

lively stones." And now two new stones—pebbles, thought Lise—she and Bella, were being added in this quiet ceremony in which they took their temporary vows in the chapel before the priest and the community.

"It seems queer—when you reach your heart's desire," said Lise, "that it should seem so simple, steady, almost logical."

"I have heard of girlsfoainting with relief when they were accepted," said Bella with fellow feeling.

"I don't think there's need for that," said calm Soeur Raymonde. "As Soeur Marie Lise said, it is logical. After all, you have been tested for a long time."

"Seven years," said Lise.

"It's hardly likely you would get as far as that, or that we should let you, without it being more than a hope and, in any case, if God has chosen you, he will admit you."

"If not?" Bella was still apprehensive.

"Not." There was no doubt about that. "But I don't believe he would let a handful of nuns, however wise, turn him from his purpose. It might not be just yet," Soeur Raymonde had said, "but I'm sure it will happen," and, mercifully, it had.

"Of course you may not be ready at the end of three years to take the next step, Profession, your final vows, the vow until death," said Soeur Raymonde, "though you can renew these simple vows for another three years, and again and again, but you are nuns now. God bless you."

"I think he has," said Lise.

They had not met the new Mother-General, Soeur Marie Emmanuel, until two months ago when they had been called to the office she kept in the novitiate to be told whether they were admitted to take these vows or no. Lise had expected someone elderly, slightly grand and dignified, though she knew Soeur Marie Emmanuel had only been elected last year. The dignity was there, but here was a slight woman, hardly older than herself, with a soft creamy skin set off by a black veil and brown eyes that could be amused as well as penetrating. They were amused when Bella, getting up, clumsy in her emotion, caught her heel in the hem of her habit and, "Merde!" the Bella word came out, though she clapped her hand over her mouth in consternation.

Not to be with Bella! From now on they would be, in truth, what they had been by courtesy, Soeur Marie Isabelle, Soeur Marie Lise. Not to have Soeur Raymonde! But once it had been, Not to have Soeur Théodore. "I'm sure we shall meet again," said Soeur Raymonde. "It's remarkable how in Béthanie our paths separate, then suddenly cross or meet again."

And so Lise came to Belle Source.

This house of Béthanie was in Normandy, standing inland among apple orchards that spread in a basin of low hills. Part of the convent was once a château, the Château de Lanvay; workrooms, two floors of bedrooms and a chapel had been built on, but it still had its gatehouse, now used as a modest hôtellerie and its spreading domaine, part of it a moat where ducks and geese swam; in the garden was an enchanting small pavilion, where once the Comte de Lanvay had held his notorious midnight suppers. The sisters used it if any of them needed a day retreat and, if one of them died, it became a chapel of rest where she could lie in dignity on a candle-lit bier until her burial. "Yes, it's a holy place now," said the Prioress as she showed it to Lise.

"So it's places as well as people you convert," said Lise.

"God converts," corrected the Prioress.

It seemed to Lise that a blessing lay on the whole of Belle Source. "It's odd," she told the Prioress, "This is the kind of house I have wanted to live in all my life, and never thought I could." Everywhere the eye looked was beauty, something she had not expected. Saint Etienne and the novitiate, though well designed, were

functional buildings. Here the stucco walls of the château had faded to a warm cream-yellow while the
slates of the mansarded roof were dove-grey. The walls
of the whole domaine were of old French brick, rosy
behind the espaliered fruit trees; not a foot of space was
wasted. The once-upon-a-time gardener's cottage where,
now, the garden tools were kept, was inset in the walls
and matched them as did another cottage, hidden behind a yew hedge, the aumônier's house to which, one
day, in that Year of the Rabbit, 1976, Marc was to
come.

The big vegetable garden was set out in orderly
rows. Soeur Fiacre, fittingly named, because Saint
Fiacre was patron of gardeners, would not permit a
single weed. Separated from the orchards by a pond,
there was a paddock for the cows, pens for the pheasants, while rabbits were bred for sale. "We make pen-
nies where we can and breeders pay handsome prices
for our pheasant eggs and plump rabbits as they do for
our Jersey calves," Soeur Thecla, who was the farmer,
told Lise. The cows were Bienvenue, Bibiche, Blanchette,
and Joyeuse, born on the Feast of the Annunciation.
"We have a better strain even than the famous herd at
Solesmes," Soeur Thecla said with satisfaction. "The
monks come to us to buy their calves."

As in every house of Béthanie, besides the nuns'
individual skills there was always a general employ-
ment for the outside commercial world "so as to bring in
a modicum of money we can at least count on," said the
Prioress. One house sent out circulars for an insurance
company; another supplied a Paris shop with hand-
worked tapestries and petit-point for upholstering chairs
and stools. At Belle Source, First Communion robes
were made for boys and girls in fine white linen or
muslin.

Belle Source, too, made cider, a specially sought-
after cider from a recipe handed down by a certain
Soeur Marie Dominique who got it from her father, a

Normandy farmer; she had been one of the few sisters of Béthanie whose ancestry was known.

Lise helped in the cider presses, the tending of the trees, the picking of the apples. She helped too in the laundry and in the kitchen. "Marcelline's work," Patrice would have answered.

"Then I like Marcelline's work," and yet, wasn't it not so long ago, thought Lise, that she too had thought servant's work degrading?

"What has happened to those elegant hands?" Patrice would have asked, shocked.

"Well, never mind if sometimes they are chapped red with cold from getting up to help with the cows, or covered with mud from planting out potatoes," Lise would have retorted, "They are happy hands now," and, as with all the sisters, ready to turn themselves to anything. There was no sense of rank at Béthanie. "Take Soeur Agnès de la Trinité," Lise was to tell Marc. "It was Soeur Agnès who was sent as Prioress to found our new Béthanie in America, a high position; she also happens to be one of Belle Source's delegates to the General Council, but it's she who does the laundry for the whole house—all those white tunics, scapulars, black veils, blue aprons, not to mention sheets and towels and dishcloths."

Soeur Thecla, who had been at university and was the community's best scholar, was up at five to milk the cows and, with her sturdy strength, did the work of two men on the farm, ploughing, mowing, carting hay, straw, crops, manure. By evening she was so tired that she could not stay up for Compline but still she had translations to do, Latin to transcribe and, often, letters to write for sisters who could not write or spell. "Well, what of it?" Soeur Thecla would have asked. "Any of us do anything—*within* the bounds of our capability," she added severely, which meant no one else could milk her cows.

There were endless needs, few of them ordinary and, "I had thought a convent would be a peaceful place!"

said Lise. Now she knew the reason for those long years of training in self-denial, instant obedience—and adaptability. "When we get up in the morning we get through our daily chores as quickly as possible," the Prioress told Lise, "because we never know what will fall on us or what the day may bring." The day or night. It was nothing for the telephone or the gate-bell to ring at midnight or two o'clock in the morning. "Nor, when the gate is opened," said the Prioress, "do we know what we shall find."

Once it was a woman with three small children standing in the road, shivering in their nightclothes. They had escaped through a window from a drunken battering father and fled to the gendarmerie and the gendarmes, uncertain what to do, brought them to Belle Source. The woman was pregnant, beaten and bruised, the children numb with terror. Of course they were taken in and, as they could not stay long in the guest-house, the Prioress, with the help of the Mairie, found them a flat, but it was the sisters who furnished it—or compelled people to furnish it, as they clothed mother and children and, eventually, provided a layette. Soeur Elizabeth, the porteress, was a conjurer on the telephone and had factories, shops, rich people on that conjuring line. "Yes, I'm a bully," she often said laughing. "I'm sure they must dread hearing my voice," but soon mother and children became another Béthanie family established and protected. "The baby, when he arrived, was called Dominic, for us."

It was not always tragedy. One midnight it was two poachers who had been caught and the gendarmes did not know what to do with their catch of hares, pheasants and trout. "They should be eaten *fresh*," they said with all a Frenchman's respect for food. It was the poachers themselves who suggested the loot should be given to Béthanie. "We lived like gourmets for a week."

The provender, though, was not often as delectable as that or was given in such easy ways. "I sometimes

144

think we are the world's refuse-bins," said the Cellarer, and added, "fortunately."

A fruit farm might have a glut of apples. "We have some cases of 'seconds,' some are going rotten but you could pick them over—if you like to come and get them. . . ." "Twenty kilometres!" said Lise, "and the picking took us hours."

A pâtisserie offered éclairs. "We can't sell them; they're yesterday's. The cream may have gone off a little, but still. . . ."

A farmer gave a ton of sub-standard potatoes, "which had to be sorted," groaned the nuns—some for the compost heap, some for the table, some for the pig, "but be careful of those," Soeur Thecla instructed. "*He* mustn't have a tummy upset."

Lise, as one of the two convent car-drivers, soon learnt of Béthanie's innumerable errands. As well as what she called "foraging," there were the sisters' normal needs—visits to dentists, doctors, opticians, visits, almost every day, to the hospital. There was marketing, though as little as possible was bought, and there was "rescuing," chiefly by the senior prison visitor, Soeur Marie Mercédes who, just as Soeur Marie Alcide had gone once a quarter to Vesoul, made, every three months, the long journey to France's other Maison Centrale for women, the prison of Le Fouest.

Soeur Marie Mercédes's bones had a defect which made them so brittle they broke if she stumbled or knocked herself; often she had to walk with a caliper or had an arm in a sling, yet still she climbed the prison stairs and managed to sit through the long hours of the week on a hard wooden chair, listening, counselling, encouraging. She had surprising influence; lawyers, even judges came to consult her and she had endless . protégées, especially girls to whom she was a mother. "I'll die if she dies," said one. They had to be fetched and taken, to the guest-house, the station, a foyer, or places where Soeur Marie Mercédes had found them work. She interviewed each employer remorselessly;

sometimes Lise drove her to châteaux, sometimes to slums—there seemed no bounds to Soeur Marie Mercédes's network. "You see, Denise has a child and if she works for Madame X, Madame will let her keep it." No matter that Madame X happened to live forty kilometres away. . . . Or, "No, no. This will not do. They are exploiting Thèrése. We must take her away at once."

"The car will wear out," said Lise.

"It does."

"How can we replace it?"

"I don't know, but it will be replaced," said Soeur Marie Mercédes.

Lise remembered an evening when she had been in and out all day with innumerable calls: the Prioress to visit one of her flock in a hospital several towns off; an urgent call to another battered family—"The police think the husband has found out where they are and we must act"; finally an interminable thirty kilometres through confusing country lanes to pick up a gift of pullets, "two heavy crates of them." Then, just before Vespers, Soeur Marie Mercédes was called to the telephone.

"Soeur Marie Lise, we must go. It's Jacky. She has tried to throw herself in the river."

"Well, why not?" Lise felt like saying. This was at least the tenth time she had taken or fetched Jacky, but the Prioress laid a hand on her shoulder.

"Jacky is a nuisance, I know, but Sister—I can tell you this because she isn't one of us—Jacky was raped by sixteen boys one after the other while the others stood by and laughed. Then, to stop her telling, they smashed her teeth in with a brick, which is why she has such difficulty in talking and that adds to her problems."

"I'll go at once," said Lise, but the Prioress shook her head and smiled, an indulgent smile which meant that, while liking her spirit, she saw that Lise had not learned to temper herself. "After Vespers and supper will do." The Prioress could have added, "Even Jacky is

146

not extraordinary; remember it's day in, day out; and, remember too, that important as all this is, it's still not the most important." Lise knew that. The first work of every house of Béthanie, of every nun, was prayer; five times a day the community gathered in choir, "and if you have been working outside in an overall or boiler-suit, it's a real penance to get out of them and heavy wet boots and change back into our white—then back again . . . five times, dear Mother of God!" Soeur Fiacre sighed. And if some of those set times had to be missed it was made up in private prayer, in meditation or vigil before the Sacrament. "Of course. How else would we get strength?" asked Soeur Marie Mercédes.

Lise had never known anything like the strength of this fiery little nun; the way she fought for her proté-gées and, particularly, how she kept the distress and hideousness of all she heard, saw—and endured—entirely to herself being, in the community, friendly, witty and invariably unruffled. "I don't think you'll find this matter-of-course acceptance anywhere but than in Béthanie," Lise was to tell Marc.

What other convent, she wondered, would not have been put in a flutter by, for instance, the episode of the drugs, and how many of their Prioresses would not have condemned? It was not for nothing that the word most used at Béthanie was "miséricorde"—mercy.

The "day of the drugs," as she called it, had hap-pened not long after she had come to Belle Source when as Soeur Doyenne, the oldest of the newly professed—Lise was just three months older than Bella—she was sent to the new novitiate, Saint Xavier, to help Soeur Raymonde who had an unusually large number of postulants and novices. "But . . . I thought I was to stay at Belle Source," Lise had not been able to help voicing her dismay.

"When you are needed at Saint Xavier?" The Prior-ess's rebuke made Lise flush. "It won't be for long, three months or so; a Sous-Maîtresse will soon be appointed and you are too junior for that. Meanwhile you can take charge on occasions, sometimes oversee work. Soeur Raymonde asked for you," the Prioress added quietly. "That, ma Soeur, is a compliment."

The novitiate had been moved now from that far-away great house Lise and Bella had known in the French Alps, "where we were put through the mill," as Lise said, to the new building of Saint Xavier outside Paris—modern, totally different yet still Béthanie, as Lise found. Saint Xavier was beautiful in its new fashion, one that did not please many of the sisters but that the young took to at once and, above all, it was at the centre of things. "We must *know*," Soeur Marie Emmanuel had said, "not doze and dream in our rut."

Once again Lise saw a new range of girls and women new to her, not Bella, Julie, José, Pauline, Jeanne; now it was Yolande, Gilberte, Sophie, Stéphanie, Germaine. Again there was every kind of face from young to middle-aged, open or baffling in secretiveness, pretty, even beautiful, or plain to ugliness. At that first time Lise had had to keep custody of her eyes, but now it was her duty to look, be watchful, and she had immediately noticed the girl, Sophie, seen her thinness, the pallor of her skin, the dark grey shadows like stains under her eyes; long sleeves hiding arms that Lise guessed carried telltale prick marks. Sophie would suddenly break into agitated talk, was excitable and couldn't concentrate for more than ten minutes; Lise was certain she had been on drugs. Had Sophie been in prison too where, unless the doctor and matron were sympathetic, she probably had to go "cold turkey"— endure the withdrawal without help, driven almost to dementia by the pain?—Lise had seen it often; but perhaps Sophie had not been in prison, just one of the girls, of all classes, who left home and . . . Lise pulled herself back; Sophie was here to forget, "And so are you," Lise reminded herself and, indeed, watching the girl in chapel, Lise could see how, at times, Sophie could be illumined by happiness; at others, Lise found her sobbing there.

"What is the matter, Sophie?"

"Nothing."

"Are you sure? Nothing I can help with?"

"Nothing. Nothing."

Poor waif, thought Lise. Waif in another way from Lucette.

Lucette had gone to Saint Etienne; she should have been at Saint Xavier by now. Lise had expected and half dreaded to find her there but, "Haven't you heard?" asked Soeur Raymonde.

"I haven't had a letter, or a note, for almost five years," Lise said, "not since she went to Saint Etienne. I was pleased about that, thinking she was so content and busy she had no need to write."

"I'm afraid no. Lucette has had a blow that most of us wouldn't have been able to take. It was kept hushed-up for her sake, poor child."

"But . . . where is she?" Lise was filled with consternation and contrition. "Where?"

"Back at Saint Etienne—miraculously. As I say, we kept it hushed, absolutely secret, but I think Soeur Théodore might tell you."

Soeur Théodore, now Prioress at Saint Etienne, was at Saint Xavier for a conference. "To have you and Soeur Raymonde both here at the same time," Lise had said. "That's a bounty I never even hoped for," and Lise went to her old Responsable now. "Ma Mère"—she still gave Soeur Théodore that title. "Can you tell me about Lucette?"

"It was terrible. Terrible." Soeur Théodore gave a shiver. "As you know, she came to us from the foyer and from her work at the hospital and was admitted as aspirant, and I have never seen anyone as happy. She went about her work sensibly and thoroughly, but as if it were in heaven. We found she had a sweet voice and Soeur Philomena was teaching her to play the cithare—just by ear, but her ear was true. Then, one evening, just before Vespers, a police van arrived with two gendarmes who had papers. It appeared that by a clerical error, Lucette had been released from Vesoul too soon. She had ten more months to serve; they had come to take her away."

"Away? Not—back to prison?"

"Yes. Back to Vesoul."

"But—when she had been released—after all that time."

"She still had to pay in full."

"How cruel. How abominably heartlessly cruel."

"It was. Even the gendarmes could hardly bring themselves to do it. We managed to get a stay of twenty-four hours—our Prioress even dared to telephone the Minister of Justice—but the gendarmes had to come again next day.

"Lucette had, of course, been given her black dress and was so pleased and proud—and she had to take it off. I remember I folded it and said, 'It will be waiting for you,' yet, as I did that, I couldn't believe after a knock like this she would want it again, but I didn't know Lucette. Ma Soeur, that little thing went without a cry or a tear, just held my hand tightly for a minute and then submitted. They couldn't let one of us go with her. God knows what it must have been like to drive in through those gates again and hear them shut. Soeur Marie Alcide saw her, of course, every time she went to Vesoul and in all those months there was not a murmur or complaint—only that Lucette was counting the days.

"When she came out, I had permission to fetch her, but she wasn't to put on the black dress for a long time; as soon as that horror was over, Lucette was seriously ill and for six months we thought she might go out of her mind. We kept her at Saint Etienne and one of us was with her day and night; the girls, too, helped, and gradually, slowly. . . ."

"But—why wasn't I told?" asked Lise.

"She asked for you not to be."

"*Not to be!*"

"I confess I was surprised," Soeur Théodore admitted. "I had thought she would have fled to you for help, but not this Lucette. She knows you have your way to make and that you should keep to that. This would have cut across it."

"Indeed it would, but it makes me selfish, selfish." In her distress Lise was crumpling her handkerchief almost to shredding it. Soeur Théodore took it from her, shook it out and folded it again.

"Put that in your pocket. It isn't selfish at all," Soeur Théodore went on. "You and Lucette are both trying to do the same thing—she knows that. She wouldn't let even such an ordeal—one of the most searing I have ever known," said this downright Sister, "wouldn't let it interrupt her; even when she was ill, not in command of herself, somehow she didn't swerve. Nor, Soeur, should you. Lucette is not your responsibility, but I know she would treasure a letter. She is back with the others now and she will come here to Saint Xavier, but in her own time, which is God's time. I think He has a special plan for our little Job."

There was one thought that comforted Lise; no matter what Lucette had suffered, she was no longer a waif.

Next to Sophie, in date of coming to Béthanie, was Gilberte. Both girls were in Lise's group and could not have been more different—Sophie a problem, stretched to tension with her scruples and fears which seemed to be growing more rather than less. She had a bad limp—was she born like that or did something happen? —and for all the care at Saint Xavier could not put on weight. "Will she ever be strong enough?" Lise asked Soeur Raymonde.

"We'll see. She's strong in love, which is what matters, isn't it?" Gilberte was apple-cheeked, open-looking and merry, surely one of the "makeweights," as Lise secretly called them.

Lise had, wistfully perhaps, invented a family for Gilberte; a solid kind father: a mother of the same rose complexion: plenty of brothers and sisters and a noisy, friendly, hospitable and comfortable home. Lise sometimes tried to imagine what the father and mother, the whole family, thought about the coming of this cherished daughter to Béthanie and the company she kept, but nothing seemed to disturb Gilberte's calm, her lazy insouciance and, "Gilberte's a delight," she said.

"H'm," was Soeur Raymonde's only reply which surprised Lise but, as the days passed, she had to admit that often Gilberte was lazy, almost to sleepiness. Perhaps she's a little stupid, Lise had to admit that too, but I like her independence. Gilberte did not cling to her in the way Sophie was already doing. "It seems inevitable with me and young girls," Lise said hopelessly to Soeur Raymonde.

One day in her third week at Saint Xavier Lise went up to her room to fetch a book; her room was at the end of the long row of cells and as she reached the corridor, she saw the Prioress coming down it with two gendarmes and a dog; the dog, an alsatian, was sniffing.

Lise stepped quickly back out of sight. As they passed, the Prioress's face gave no hint of agitation; she walked without hurry and her hands were under her scapular as they usually were. The three were making for the rooms at the end of the corridor where the postulants slept.

When they had passed Lise slipped into her room, found the book and would have gone swiftly downstairs when she heard a sound. It was a stifled sob coming from behind the screen in the corner and there, crouched down in terror, was Sophie.

"Sophie!"

"Ma Soeur, don't send me out. Don't, Soeur Marie Lise, don't. They won't look in here. Ma Soeur, please, please."

"Look for what?" Lise tried to unclench the clutching hands and hold them.

"It's under the floorboards in her room," Sophie was gabbling. "They'll find it. The dog will find it. They always do. I wouldn't keep it for her."

152

"Keep what?"

"Stuff—for Gilberte."

"*Gilberte!*" Lise was truly astonished. What a myth—my happy family! but Sophie was saying:

"She has only just begun. She hadn't tried before."

"But how?" asked Lise. "How could she—here?"

"Easily," said Sophie. Lise had succeeded in taking her hands, pulling her up to sit on the bed. "You don't know, ma Soeur, I don't think anybody does . . . except Soeur Théodore, and she has gone back to Saint Etienne. Oh, if only she hadn't." There was a fresh bout of tears. "I'm afraid of Soeur Raymonde."

"You needn't be—but go on, Sophie, tell me."

"It creeps in everywhere." Sophie gave a terrified look over her shoulders as if the menace were here. "There was a girl at Saint Etienne. She knew my Uncle. She didn't stay more than a month, but that was enough—she told him. If he hadn't traced me like that, he would have somehow else. They're so clever. Of course, he isn't my Uncle, that's just what we called him. I was never a 'pusher,' but that's what he wanted me for—I soon knew that. I wanted to be clean but I didn't know how, or how to get away from him or it; I couldn't go home—my mother and father would never have understood, so I did the only thing I could think of to do. . . ."

"Go on," Lise was holding her.

"I cut off everything, every label, every tag that could show who I was, and took nothing with me and I burned everything in my bag and all my letters. . . . I couldn't do this—this—in my lodging so I went to a shop. It was one of those big shops with departments on all floors. It had stairs as well as lifts and on the second floor I jumped down the well of the stairs."

"Sophie! *Sophie!*"

"I know, but I thought if I hurt myself badly enough they would have to put me in hospital, perhaps for a long long time, and they might help me. If it was more than hurt, well, it didn't matter, did it? I broke my hip

153

and leg—that's why I limp—and hurt my head, but then the wonderful thing happened." The tears dried and Sophie's face lifted.

"The hospital was near Saint Etienne and one of your nuns was there, a sister of Béthanie. I think she was very ill—she had a room to herself and the others came in and out, every day, sometimes twice a day to visit her, sometimes in the night, and they began to visit me. One of them, Soeur Marie Lise, was Soeur Théodore." At that name the tears burst out again. "Oh ma Mère, ma Mère! if only you were here."

Lise held her closer. "We are here. We'll help you. But, Sophie—how long ago was this?"

"Nearly five years." Sophie sat up dabbing her eyes. "I was almost a year in the hospital, then I went to the clinic and then Soeur Théodore took me to Saint Etienne straight away—she got permission. There I could always stay inside if I needed to. I never went alone into the garden all those years. I thought I was safe, then . . . then. . . ."

"Then?"

"Uncle found me. Though he didn't come to Saint Etienne he followed me here at Saint Xavier; he found Gilberte too. There's a place in the domaine where the hedge is broken and you can get through. He spoke to Gilberte first, gave her a message for me and I had to go. She said she would tell if I didn't."

"*You* should have told," but Sophie shrank.

"No, I couldn't—I couldn't. Here it's not like Saint Etienne; it's all new, and Gilberte, she was soon hooked. She makes me help her do it—she's frightened of the 'fix,' of using the syringe, so the works are in my room." Sophie was again so convulsed with terror that Lise could hardly understand her. "The dog will smell them and no one will believe it wasn't me, but I swear to you I never took even a pinch—I swear—but they won't believe me. They won't believe me."

"I believe you. Hush! Hush!" but, "Gilberte said she would tell," Sophie gabbled again. "At first she was just curious, but Uncle has a kind of power"—like Patrice, thought Lise—"Once you have started, Uncle can make you do anything—anything." Sophie shivered.

"No, he can't," said Lise. "He couldn't make you."

"Why—no! He couldn't." Sophie lifted her face from Lise's shoulder in amazement. "He couldn't. Ma Soeur, I never thought of that." Then the helplessness came back. "They'll never believe me. Gilberte looks so. . . ."

"Innocent and open," said Lise, "Yes."

"She took you in."

"She did," Lise admitted it, "but I don't think she took in the others—certainly not Soeur Raymonde. I see now Soeur Raymonde had her suspicions and I can guess that's why the police have come; they have probably been watching this Uncle, trying to catch him. Listen to me, Sophie. Go now to Soeur Raymonde and tell her what you have just told me."

"But they'll put me out. I can't bear it. I can't. It's my whole life."

"Yes, Sophie—your whole life." Soeur Raymonde was standing with the Prioress in the doorway and she put out her hands to the distracted girl. "Ma petite, come with me and we'll explain to the police."

"Gilberte? She'll be found out. . . ."

"We know about Gilberte, poor child, and so do they. The dog found it."

"But what will happen to her? Poor Gilberte. Look! She didn't sell it." Sophie's voice grew shrill. "Just taking it yourself isn't. . . ."

"We know that too." The Prioress, still calm, made way for Soeur Raymonde who lifted Sophie to her feet and kept a strong arm round her. "Now come with us, with Mother and me," said Soeur Raymonde.

"But . . . you'll keep Sophie?" Lise asked Soeur Raymonde in astonishment.

"Doesn't it say much for Sophie that, in the midst of

155

such temptation, she never fell? Of course we'll keep her."

"And Gilberte?"

Soeur Raymonde gave a sigh. "Gilberte's very sorry now. We'll have to see."

"I wish I had your imperturbability," said Lise.

It was not just a shell; Lise herself could keep her face and voice in control when in reality she was in turmoil; this was deeper—the nuns were not perturbed over things like this. "When you have seen as much of God's providence as I have," said Soeur Raymonde, as any of the nuns would have said, "seen the unfathomable ways in which he works, if you have any sense at all, you learn not to question or to judge—only to trust. Think of Lucette's story. . . ."

And Lise thought, "Think of my own."

The oddest things brought it back, turning them to the macabre; on one of her first mornings at Belle Source when, utterly happy, she was peeling parsnips in the kitchen, it suddenly came. There had been all the homely things of a quiet domestic busy-ness around her—one blue-aproned sister working at the stove, another, the baker, kneading dough; a good smell of soup from the outsize pans and of onions and herbs hung from the ceiling—it was much like Marcelline's kitchen; perhaps it was the thought of Marcelline that brought it—but suddenly the wrinkled yellowish outer skin of the parsnip looked like the skin of someone grown old because he was dead—had been dead for five days.

At first, remembered Lise, in my dazed state, stupefied, I had thought Patrice would be in the Rue Duchesne, laid out on his own bed, candles burning each side of it, flowers perhaps, or else he would be in a chapel, then, slowly, I realised he would be in a drawer in the morgue, a drawer slid out as if from a filing cabinet. I had had to go there once to identify a client, a German who had fallen dead on the pavement outside the house; he had been with us just before and no one else seemed to know who he was. Emile made me go; the man had been dead three days, but Patrice would have been worse—they keep them just as they are until after the inquest. He would have been as I last saw him, as he lay in the geranium bed of that little front garden but, like the German, he would have yellowed, wrinkled, shrunk. . . .

"Is anything the matter, Soeur Marie Lise?"

"I . . . I'm going to be sick."

"Madame Lise," said Marcelline, "Monsieur Patrice has gone out."

"Oh?" It was a stifling hot August afternoon but Lise had taken Coco for his usual walk, though a little later than usual, and was bending down to unfasten his lead when Marcelline had come running up to the hall from the kitchen; she was twisting her apron in her fingers, even the coiffure was slightly dishevelled and her blue eyes were distressed.

"Madame, go—go quickly. I think he has gone after Vivi."

"*Vivi?* But . . . how?"

"I don't know how but he took me by the throat and shook me. 'So that was your dirty trick! You and that . . .' I won't tell you what he called you, Madame. I thought that he would strangle me."

"You told him where they are?"

"I didn't have to. He knew."

"How could he know?"

"Perhaps she wrote to one of the girls. Perhaps Madame Chabot. . . ."

"She wouldn't."

"Someone has, Madame. He has taken the car to Ecommoy. Oh Madame, Luigi and the baby! That little family! Be quick."

Lise was looking at her watch. "I think there's an express to Le Mans some time about now. He won't be able to drive very fast, it's the rush-hour. With luck, I'll get there first. Fetch a taxi, Marcelline, while I get some money."

I didn't only get some money; from the drawer in Patrice's desk in the office I took his gun. It was a small 6.35 automatic.

Lise made sure it was loaded: a calm efficiency had come on her in which she felt nothing, yet knew she would not make a mistake, not this time, thought Lise. What I have to do I shall do. The gun was small enough to go in her handbag.

She remembered how, in the hall, Coco, his lead still on him, had waited anxious at the foot of the stairs. "No, mon trésor, you must stay here." I gave him a swift pat. I didn't know it was the last time I should see him.

Lise had made the taxi-driver go like the wind from Le Mans—only in that stifling August there was no wind; the roads were white with dust, the trees, as they passed, looked tinder-dry: they were as dusty as the roads and Lise felt dust in her nostrils and in her hair. They tore through villages bright with flowers where old women in overalls, flowered too, sat in open door-ways knitting; the men were still in the fields, finishing the harvest with the younger women and children. Then the taxi swept into a little town—Lise had the impression of a sunlit square, the centre filled with cars, awnings over the shop fronts, an oversize church with a clock face. They drove to a street beyond and another leading off it, and "Stop!" cried Lise.

Patrice had left his car at the end of the street—probably he did not want to attract attention. Lise left the taxi there too, threw the driver some notes and ran.

Patrice was standing on the doorstep of a small two-storeyed house, one of a row; Lise recognised it by Luigi's geraniums, brilliant in a bed below the windows where the curtains were tightly drawn though it was so hot, the sun still blazing as it moved towards evening; they were crooked too, which gave the house a slatternly look. Mercifully it seemed that Vivi had not

158

heard Patrice; probably she was asleep in one of her lazy kitten sleeps in which she liked to lie most of the day. Lise could hear a baby crying—Giovanni-Battista Giuliano—and she saw a woman's head looking out from the window of the house next door, a watchful neighbour.

"She didn't have to look long," said Lise. "It only took two minutes."

"Patrice."

"You!" He had stopped, astonished. "You."

"Yes, me. Don't knock. Don't dare to knock."

He had turned. "What are you talking about? What are you doing here?"

"You know very well what I'm doing here. Come away from that door."

"Don't be silly, chérie, and don't be so theatrical." He was laughing. "Just keep out of the way."

Lise stood on the garden path, her hand was steady. "This is something you're not to interfere with. You can't have her, Patrice."

"No?"

"No. Come away from that door."

"And if I won't?"

"I shall shoot you."

"Shoot then." He turned his back and, "I shot." Lise's voice was dulled as she told it, first to Jacques Jouvin, then Soeur Marie Alcide—because she still could not believe it. "I shot twice; one shot hit the back of his neck, the other between his shoulders. For a moment he staggered, lurched against the door and fell sideways into the flower-bed.

"I turned him face upwards; blood was beginning to come up over his collar but he knew me as I knelt in the flower-bed bending over him."

"*You!*" As if he could not believe that she, Lise, had done this to him—at last.

"I heard the door open as he began to choke. 'You—wouldn't even let me see her.'" His eyes were beginning to glaze, the red welling faster. "I bent closer, then. . . ."

"Then?"

"Then there was no more breath. It was over.

"I got to my feet, the automatic still in my hand. The front door was open a crack. Vivi had come down, I thought the shots must have woken her. I pushed open the door to go to her, hold her, tell her she was safe, but she was standing at the foot of the stairs like a furious little girl. 'Why? Why? Why?' she screamed. 'Why did you come?' and she wailed, 'You have spoilt it all.'

" 'Spoilt it?' I must have stammered because she mocked me.

" 'Yes, s-sp-spoilt it. Don't you see we were going away? He had come to fetch me.'

" 'Fetch you? But who told him? I never gave anything away, nor did Marcelline. How did he know?'

" 'Because I told him.' Vivi stamped her foot.

"Neither of us heard the lorry that drew up at the gate among the crowd that was gathering; we didn't hear the voices either and I had forgotten I had the gun still smoking in my hand."

"Told him!" Lise could not believe it. "But . . . you knew what he would do."

"That's what I wanted. Did you think I was going to stay here in this hole of a place all my life?"

"But Luigi. . . ."

"That oaf!"

"And your baby—Giovanni. . . ."

Vivi shuddered. "Squalling, messing, driving me mad . . . and everyone talking, talking, scolding. Monsieur Patrice was going to take me away and I need never have come back, never, never. Now. . . ." She began to sob. "I hate you. I hate Luigi. I hate his brat."

There was a sound like a whimper, the last whimper that comes after the screams of a tiny animal in mortal hurt, but it came from big Luigi as he stood at the open door. Then he looked at what was lying in his prize geraniums. Luigi moved slowly closer to it and bent down.

"Is he . . . ?" The crowd had come into the garden. It was the woman from next door who spoke over the fence.

"Mort." Luigi said it, stood up and ground the heel of his boot into Patrice's face. The crowd gasped.

Vivi screamed and put her hands over her face. It was only then that Lise saw she was wearing a smart new suit and had a small suitcase.

Luigi had already seen. There was a babel now outside—voices, shouts. Luigi took no notice. He took no notice either of Vivi or of Lise but went straight up the stairs. He came down carrying a bundle, Giovanni-Battista Giuliano, wrapped in a blanket.

Luigi strode through the crowd and, with the bundle, got into his lorry.

The next moment they heard it drive away.

Chapter
Seven

"JUREZ-VOUS DE DIRE la vérité, toute la vérité, et rien que la vérite?"

"Je le jure."

"Will you tell the truth, the whole truth, and nothing but the truth?"

I suppose that is how hundreds of novels about crime begin, thought Lise, but this isn't a book. It's real.

". . . rien que la vérité."

"Je le jure." I swear.

Vivi said that. Vivi who did, and meant to do, just the opposite.

Lise had been brought into the big courtroom of the Cour d'Assises in handcuffs between two gendarmes, who took them off when she reached the "box": she sat down chafing her wrists.

Below her was Maître Jacques Jouvin in his robes and wig, his junior beside him. They were sideways to the Court and Lise could see in its well twenty or so men and women waiting to be chosen as the jury;

ordinary men and women, some stolid, some nervous, none speaking, or even whispering, but all of them were staring at her. The raised benches at the top of the court where they would presently sit, with the tall chairs of the Président and his two assistant magistrates, were still empty. On one side was the box like a pulpit for the Public Prosecutor; opposite was the slanted desk of the Greffier, the Clerk of the Court, while facing Lise was the press gallery, crowded to overflowing and from which rose an excited hum. There, every line of Lise's face with its scar—deep red, she was sure—her dress, her handbag, her least movement and word would be noted—and twisted and exaggerated, thought Lise in despair.

"What are you going to wear?" Maître Jouvin had asked.

"I have only the Chanel suit Marcelline brought to me at Sevenet."

"Not Chanel. That might prejudice the jury."

"Well, I have nothing else," and, "What does it matter?" asked Lise.

"It matters a great deal. You must make a good impression. Oh, Lise, do please try and help yourself a little."

"Dear Jacquot." Lise had smiled. "I promise you I'll be clean and tidy.

"But not too soignée, Lise. I know it's part of your courage, but it can look like arrogance."

The far end of the room, the public gallery, was in turbulence as the police fought to control the crowd; there was, Lise knew, an enormous crowd outside. "This is something after their own hearts," Jouvin had said in disgust, "and Vivi has become notorious."

"Vivi?"

They'll all be there to see me—me, Vivi.

When, that day, Emile came to Ecommoy to fetch me, I thought everything was over. Silly little me.

Emile came very quickly. I don't have to call him

163

"Monsieur" as I had to call Monsieur Patrice. We are on a very different footing—he has to do as I like.

After the police had taken Madame Lise away someone—a woman but I don't know who—helped me into her house. They left the body a long time in our garden until the doctor and the photographers had finished. I watched them through the window. They were police photographers—they hadn't let the newspaper ones in yet. I was glad when Emile came. Till then the woman who took me in wouldn't open the door; I don't think she took me from curiosity—it was pity. The neighbours were shouting and spitting, especially Madame Robert, but this woman was kind; she helped me to the bathroom and gave me some cognac and told me not to look—but of course I looked all the time. That's how I saw Emile.

Funny none of us at the Rue Duchesne had taken much notice of Milo before; he was just the one who looked after the money and had his office off the bar, but now I come to think of it he took notice of everything. If our tips were not enough, *"Do you think you're here for flea-bites?"* and he used to fine the girls for every little thing. It's a pity he's so small and pale and almost bald, but he's clever. He had come to take me back at once to the Rue Duchesne.

"But—we'll be ruined," I said.

"We shall be made," said Emile. *"There's nothing like a scandal. I'm very much obliged to our Balafrée. Where we had one client asking for you now and then, we shall have hundreds. They'll all come, if only to look at you, but we won't let them—not without at least four hundred dollars."*

"Four hundred dollars a time! Me?"

"That's what you'll charge. I'll have Patrice's flat done over for you."

And last week he had said, *"At the trial you'll wear...."*

"Can I go to Balenciaga?"

"No! No!" Emile was horrified. *"Don't you see, you must be simple, a young young girl; an artful simple*

164

little dress, black perhaps, white collar and cuffs—yes,
that will show up your skin. No jewellery. Your hair
brushed simply. Let her go to Balenciaga—much good
will it do her." But she didn't. Madame Lise was in her
old red suit, the suit I used to envy but it looks passé now
. . . and she has grown so thin it hung on her. I could see
her shoulder bones, her wrists like sticks and her face;
only her eyes looked big, too big but the blue had gone
dark, and her hair was pulled back in a knot. She was
deathly pale—it was she who needed the maquillage
Emile wouldn't let me have—the scar showed horribly.
The photograph showed it too, but most were of me.

I was in all the papers. I shall be the one to write my
memoirs. I—not Madame Lise.

In the court Lise had hardly looked at anyone except
the Président when he was speaking, the Avocat Général, Monsieur Turland, and Maître Jouvin. She had
only smiled twice, once reassuringly at Marcelline,
once at Zoë, but she did not even glance at the journalists or public. "It would help if you did," and Jouvin
had cautioned, "You are not playing poker, you know."

"I can't help it," said Lise. "At Sevenet I had forgotten there were people outside."

Everyone stood while the Président and his two assistant magistrates came in with a display of scarlet
robes; Monsieur Turland was stoled in ermine. The
jurors were elected; it seemed to Lise that Maître
Jouvin objected to over-many. They went to their places
behind the Président and their roll was called.

On the panelled wall behind and above their array
was a bust of Marianne, symbol of the republic, with a
wreath of laurel and a star; below her a gilded relief of
the scales of justice and behind Lise, in the "box" a
great tapestry showed the child-king Louis XIII half-
lying, half-sitting on his throne and wearily holding
his sceptre as he was offered the crown of France by his
mother, Marie de Medici, flanked by nobles, cardinals

and men-at-arms. It must have seemed to the tired little boy as wearisome a pantomime as Lise's dossier, read aloud by the Greffier, seemed to her. The only thing vivid to her was in a small glass case in the well of the Court—Patrice's gun. . . .

First to be called was the ballistic expert. The automatic was taken out of its case; he showed how to pull the trigger. Lise shut her eyes, her hands clenched in her lap. She could feel that smooth little butt in her hand. Next the police doctor described the wounds. . . . "He was dead when you arrived. . . . Can you say how long?"

"Twenty minutes—half an hour. Not more. There was nothing I could do."

Next Luigi. "I don't know anything," said Luigi. "I wasn't there."

They had traced him, of course; he had gone where Lise knew he would go—straight to Mamma to hand over Giovanni-Battista Giuliano; he had told Maître Jouvin that he had ordered the old woman, "You will not ask me one word; you will not say one word to anyone, and you will not say *her* name." "Her" was Vivi—but in the Court, Luigi still looked bewildered and, "He was useless," said Jacques Jouvin, "almost a puppet in the hands of Monsieur Turland," especially, it seemed to Lise, of the Président—almost, not quite; the Président, for all his acumen and experience, did not understand the depth of Luigi's hurt.

"You saw Madame Lise with the gun in her hand?" but Luigi had shaken his head.

"No . . . I suppose I was only looking at her. . . . "

"Your wife?"

"At Mademoiselle Vivi—and him. I . . . didn't see anything else," but most of what Luigi said made it easy for the prosecution.

"Did Madame Lise encourage you to marry Mademoiselle Vivi?"

"She did everything." Luigi, with his great calf eyes, was innocently trying to pay tribute to Lise. "She made

166

it possible. Hid it from him . . ." He would not name Patrice.

"And she sent your wife, Vivi, money?"

"She isn't my wife . . . but Madame was generous."

"She sent Vivi money—to keep her quiet."

"But . . ." Luigi was genuinely astonished. "But it was for Giovanni-Battista Giuliano, the baby."

The crowd laughed and the Président called, "Silence or I shall have to clear the court." Then he turned to Luigi.

"The money came regularly long before you had the baby . . . Madame gave you a lorry."

Luigi nodded miserably. "Yes or no? Answer."

"Yes, Monsieur le Président."

"Why?"

"So that I could keep an eye on that . . . that . . ." He could not go on.

"So Madame Lise was aware. . . ." A ripple ran though the court. "Very well aware. . . . "

Jacques tried to mitigate the effect. "Each time you came to the Rue Duchesne, you gave the impression both to Madame Marcelline, the cook, and to Madame Lise, that you were happy."

"I was, but . . ." Luigi hesitated and Lise remembered how once he had asked her in a whisper, "Excuse that I should mention it, but Marcelline has such a sharp tongue. Madame Lise, do babies have to . . . have to smell?" It had come with a rush and he blushed.

"Were happy then until . . . ?"

Luigi looked at the Président. "I had begun to wonder," and he added, "I told Madame Lise. . . ."

"He only meant he told me about Giovanni's smelliness." Lise tried afterwards to exonerate Luigi to Jouvin.

"*Only* . . ." groaned Jouvin in despair.

Most of the girls from the Rue Duchesne were called and almost all were favourable. "Madame was good. She seldom interfered."

"Except if you attracted, shall we say, notice, from Monsieur Patrice?" suggested Monsieur Turland. It was Zoë who once again innocently, said, "Oh, that was only over Vivi."

In the Rue Duchesne Zoë, next to Lise, was the senior by presence and experience, a dark girl but buxomly built and a favourite with many clients. She was also one of the few who was not really afraid of Patrice—in fact she scorned him—and she was fond of Lise.

"Madame Lise was jealous of Vivi?"

"Well, it's not very nice to be put out of your room, is it?" asked Zoë, "pushed up to the servants' quarters, have somebody else in your bed? He even gave Madame's furs to Vivi, and most of her jewellery. That skunk!"

"Oh Zoë! Zoë! Dear Zoë!" Jacques Jouvin bowed his head.

"And Madame Lise said nothing?" The Président seemed to intervene with relish.

"No, but she felt. One could see how she felt."

"Felt—and did nothing, or seemed to do nothing—very dangerous."

Jouvin was on his feet. "Pardon, Monsieur le Président, but I really must object . . ." and indeed the Président interfered. "Monsieur Turland, you must not lead the witness."

"Pardon. I withdraw the question." But the suggestion had taken root.

Zoë, perspicacious, tried to retrieve it. "I just meant that Madame Lise was reserved. She kept her place, we kept ours—even when she was toppled. . . ."

"Toppled?"

"I mean with Monsieur Patrice. She kept her head high but we knew by her eyes," and Zoë lost her temper. "Why are you asking such things? You men! Men like you!" Intrepid Zoë dared to hurl that at the Président. "You think girls like us have no feelings. We do. We do. We do."

The court had to be cleared before the hearing could go on.

Marcelline's evidence was as sterling as Zoë's, "and

168

did nearly as much damage," said poor Maître Jouvin, "if not more."

"I put it to you that you are talking like a faithful old servant—deliberately blind."

"I may be faithful, Monsieur, but I am not blind." Marcelline was sturdy. "And I tell you, the moment Vivi came down those stairs and saw Luigi, Madame did everything she could to bring them together."

"Exactly," and the Avocat Général hitched up the robe on his shoulders with complete satisfaction. Marcelline glared.

"And afterwards, every week faithfully, she sent Vivi the money she had promised." Marcelline heard Jouvin's groan and turned on the Président. "I tell you, for Madame that young father and mother and baby were like the Holy Family."

To her bewilderment titters ran round the court.

"The Holy Family! I should say a marriage of convenience, if ever there were one."

"No. No. You had only to see Vivi's letters."

"If only we could—but not one can be produced. Pity."

The sarcasm was lost. "Madame burnt them—for Vivi's sake."

"You say she burnt them."

"I don't say it. She did."

"Madame Marcelline!" The Président was astute. "It's clear you are a good woman—and devoted," he said again, "but you cannot deny that Madame Lise was in love with Monsieur Patrice."

It was then that Marcelline came near, for the first time, to engaging the sympathy of the Court for Lise. "And if she was," demanded Marcelline. Not to be downed, and forgetting the august bench she faced, she set her arms akimbo as she did in her own kitchen. "She loved Monsieur Patrice, so what? She loved that worthless garbage Vivi too. She loved Luigi and the baby, perhaps him most of all, but she made no claims—indeed she never saw him. She loved the girls;

at least she was kind to all; she loved Coco her dog. She even loved me. What is wrong with love?" and Marcelline broke down.

For a moment there was silence in court. Then, "No questions," said Maître Jouvin and the Président said gently to Marcelline, "Madame, you may stand down."

Lise had expected no quarter from Emile, and got none.

"You see, I would never have anything to do with him," she told Maître Jouvin.

Emile took his revenge, or tried to; this was one witness Maître Jouvin could dispose of with ease. After the routine questions about police, the Rue Duchesne, Ecommoy, Patrice's body, Jouvin said, "You were never on intimate terms with Madame Lise and knew little about her. On your own admission you had few dealings with the girls and none at all with young Mademoiselle Vivi. You didn't even know about her marriage with Luigi Branzano until the police called you, and we have evidence that you were not in your brother's confidence."

"I handled all the money."

"Not Madame Lise's. It seems she almost ignored you."

"He tried to step into Patrice's shoes," Lise had said. Emile had once come to her: "We could work together, Lise, you and I," and, "We could not," Lise had answered him clearly, "but it was always Emile's ambition to be another Patrice, so he couldn't forgive me. Now he has his weapon in Vivi."

"The evidence that really counts, God help us," said Jouvin.

"But she's under oath. She *cannot* tell lies here."

"Lise, for a woman of your age and experience, you are curiously naïve."

"But . . . I believe, deep down, Vivi is good. She . . ."

"Sent for Patrice." Jacques Jouvin had no illusions.

"She was tempted," said Lise. "Luigi left her too much alone. I had only just given him the lorry and he

170

was still under contract to his firm. Vivi was too young and thoughtless to have a baby. I know that now, but she *is* affectionate," Lise insisted.

"Affectionate! Did she come to see you at Sevenet, in more than two years of detention?"

"N-no. Probably Emile wouldn't let her. Marcelline says he runs everything now. He has made Vivi a sort of queen and she's easily spoiled, but you'll see in the end: she'll corroborate everything I say."

"Humph!" said Maître Jouvin.

"Madame Branzano—no, you are so young, I shall say Vivi. We shall have to ask you a few questions. They are, as I know and the Court knows, painful questions." The Président was dulcet in his sympathy. "Try and answer like a brave girl," and Monsieur Turland asked gently, "Is it true that Madame Lise, shall we say, *advised* you to marry Luigi Branzano?"

"Advised?" The grey eyes opened wide, as wide as they were capable of going, thought Lise. "She said she would buy me a wedding dress, a trousseau, give me a dot. I would have a ring and a house. I . . . God forgive me, Monsieur le Président, I had never had, or dreamed of, anything like that. I asked about Monsieur Patrice. He had been kind to me and there is loyalty . . . but she . . ." Vivi looked down and fluttered her lashes.

"She?"

"Told me Monsieur Patrice would get tired of me; that he was growing old and capricious; he often changed his mind. Then I would soon be out of the Rue Duchesne—he always turned against his favourites. Oh, poor Monsieur Patrice!" and Vivi broke into sobs.

"So she frightened you—and bribed you."

Maître Jouvin again jumped up: "Pardon. Mais, Monsieur le Président, permettez-moi d'objecter," and the Président had to say again, "You must not put suggestions."

"Then let us say she helped you with the marriage?"

"She helped us both—Luigi and me, and she—

171

Madame Lise—dressed me for the wedding; we had to take a room in a hotel so no one from the house would see. She took me to the register office. She gave us a wedding breakfast afterwards and put us on the train. She sent the money. . . ."

"Why did you send the money?" Monsieur Jouvin had asked Lise in his questioning for the defence.

"To make it possible for them," Lise had said truthfully. "Luigi earned well but someone like Vivi was out of his means. He was used to peasant women—his family are peasants—and I guessed his mother and sisters did not need much. I don't suppose any of them had ever seen cosmetics. Vivi had been pampered and she would never have been content—and I so longed for her to be happy. Then . . ." and Lise's voice softened, "I made it a little more to help get ready for the baby."

They were coming to him now—Giovanni-Battista Giuliano. "I think Madame Lise wanted a baby of her own." As Vivi put in her poisoned darts, Lise shut her eyes: that fleecy coat, the little boots. "Monsieur le Président," said Vivi, turning towards him in his high seat. "She couldn't leave us alone. From the moment my baby was born, she and Luigi. . . ."

"So the marriage wasn't a happy one?"

"No." It was a sorrowful whisper.

"And yet those letters? What were these famous letters?"

Vivi answered in clever astonishment. "Letters? They were receipts. Madame Lise is a good business woman. She always wanted a receipt."

"The horrible part," Lise told Maître Jouvin in the midday break, "is that everything Vivi said is true—in a different light. In a way those letters were receipts, endorsements that I was getting what I hoped I was paying for."

"What I cannot understand is the spite," said Maître Jouvin.

"Nor do I, but . . . in English, if you change one letter in the word 'spite,' make the 't' a 'c,' it becomes 'spice,'

172

and I'm beginning to see that spite is the spice of Vivi's life—a kind of irresistible naughtiness.

"Naughtiness! Deliberate wickedness!"

"Tell us, Vivi," the Président was still all sympathy. "Did Luigi Branzano ever beat you?"

"No, never, but . . ."

"But?"

"It hurt. He was so—big." There were no titters; the court was hushed. "Monsieur, they said I lay in bed all day because I was lazy, but sometimes I couldn't get up. The poor little baby was crying but I couldn't, I couldn't."

Some of the women in the gallery began to weep.

Maître Jouvin did his best. "If you couldn't get up, what about the soldiers?"—he had called Madame Robert—but "Soldiers?" asked Vivi, as if she could not remember.

"Yes, soldiers in the café."

"You wouldn't understand—you, or her. I went to them for someone who wouldn't scold, who would be copains—comrades. They were young too, a little drunk, I know, but we were friends."

"That's not their testimony."

"And if I did go with them? Les pauvres gars! Remember what she had taught me," Vivi flung a look at Lise. "Most of them, too, had no one. Luigi was gone two, three, four days at a time and I was so lonely, so homesick for Monsieur."

"Monsieur Patrice?"

"Monsieur Patrice." Vivi bowed her head. "He was a gentleman. I wasn't used to soldiers, or Luigi, no matter what she told you. Everyone was so unkind, and at last I dared to write. . . ."

"To Monsieur Patrice?"

"To Monsieur Patrice. He was the only one strong enough to stand against her."

"Against Madame Lise?"

"Yes, and you see she followed him. He must have told Marcelline where he was going. Marcelline was her spy. He was coming to help me but rather than let him, she . . ." Vivi covered her eyes with her hands but Lise knew she was peeping through her fingers.

"She? Courage, ma petite."

"She." The whisper filled the court. "She shot him, Monsieur Patrice, my benefactor, my best friend."

Again Maître Jouvin tried. "You say Monsieur Patrice was your benefactor. Wasn't it rather Madame Lise? She always did the best for you. Isn't it true she rescued you, took you from the streets, saved you from being taken up by the police for being drunk?"

"It was her job, wasn't it, picking up young girls? And I was put straight to work. I was only fourteen."

"But the servants, Madame Marcelline, the barman Jock, Gaston, the doorman and Mademoiselle Zoë all say Madame Lise wanted to send you to school."

"Yes, when Monsieur Patrice took a shine to me."

"And you really expect us to believe, Madame Lise," said the Président when it came to Lise's turn, she being the last for cross-examination in the case, "you expect us to believe that you acted as you did towards this young girl, Vivi, entirely for her good?"

"From the beginning to the end—yes."

"You expect us to believe that?"

"Yes, because it is the truth."

"And that she was happy in her marriage with Luigi Branzano?"

"She said so, over and over again."

"In letters you are unable to produce."

"Marcelline has read them. She has told you."

"An old devoted servant."

"And I have told you too that I dared not keep the letters. Patrice—Monsieur Ambard—would have thought nothing of searching my drawers and desk. He was suspicious. Over and over again, he tried to force me to tell. . . ."

"How force you?"

Lise was silent.

"How force you? Answer the question, Madame."

"I would rather not," and she said angrily, "He is dead, Monsieur. Isn't that enough for you?"

"Lise," Jacques Jouvin pleaded after the first session. "You must be more explicit, more courteous with the Président and the Court. It's as if you were deliberately trying to antagonise them. Why?"

"I suppose because I no longer care. What have I to live for now?"

"Then why are you letting me defend you?"

"Because, willy-nilly, I shall have to live—in prison," said Lise. "And perhaps you might make the time shorter, poor Jacquot. It's not being shut away, it's being shut in. At Sevenet there was a gipsy woman who was on remand with me. She was in the next cell. Someone had been printing counterfeit hundred-franc notes and when she took her things to market, clothes pegs, twig brooms and baskets, she was paid in some of them. She couldn't even read so how could she tell they were counterfeit? She was caught passing one—buying food for her family. The police found others on her but she couldn't tell who had given them to her. How could she with so many customers? But she was arrested and had been seven months at Sevenet waiting for trial—she who had always lived in the open air, never in a house. She used to bang her head against the cell wall. I could have banged mine."

"You are banging it against a wall now, partly of your own making. Lise, I don't want to shock you, but there is not much sympathy nowdays for the 'crime passionel,' especially when, as it must be beginning to seem, there is the victimisation of a young girl," and for a moment he laid his hand on hers. "I'm afraid."

"It's going badly for us?"

"We shall be defeated," said Maître Jouvin. "The last part of that little gamine's evidence was deadly."

"Vivi," the Avocat Général had said, "tell the Court why you think Madame Lise came to Ecommoy that day."

"So that I shouldn't have Monsieur Patrice."

"But it was the other way round." Lise sank back and gave a little gasp. "It was so he shouldn't have her and break up that happiness," but Vivi was saying, "I can prove it."

"How prove it?"

"When I heard the shots I flew of course to the door and opened it. He . . . he was lying in the flower-bed. She was kneeling beside him and he spoke. . . ." Tears overcame Vivi.

"Courage. Courage. Tell the Court what he said."

"He said, 'You!' to Madame Lise and then I heard . . . heard. . . ."

"Come, try and tell us."

"He said, 'So you wouldn't even let me see her,' then he died. Ask Madame Lise if he didn't say it. Ask her," said Vivi.

"Madame, did he say that?" the Président asked Lise. "Did he say that?"

"Yes," said Lise.

"No wonder the President thought I was furiously jealous," said Lise. "But Jacquot, that wasn't all Patrice said."

At the last moment Patrice had opened his eyes again and smiled at Lise, the slow sweet smile that always smote her. "Chérie. . . ."

"Patrice."

She had to bend low to catch that last whispered word.

"Cherie," and his hand had groped for hers.

"A jamais," Lise said it close to him, "and I think, I hope he heard."

"But why didn't you *tell* me?" almost shouted Jacques. "It might have made all the difference."

"I didn't want anyone to know."

"Didn't want. . . . Good God, Lise!" and he said with conviction, "It *would* have made all the difference."

"It was private, a signal between Patrice and me."

"Private! When we might—we might have won."

176

Three questions had been asked of the jury:

"Guilty?" "Yes."

"Premeditated?" "Yes."

"Extenuating circumstances?" "Some."

That startled Maître Jouvin. "One or two of the jury must have had a doubt . . ." he told Lise.

"Why? They had heard it made plain enough," she said bitterly.

"Perhaps it was you yourself, or Marcelline's honesty. Perhaps someone saw through Vivi," and he leaned forward to hear the verdict. "I was sure it would be twenty years but, 'Quinze ans de réclusion criminelle —fifteen years.' "

"Fifteen years!" The scream was not from Lise but Vivi. "No! Oh no! No!" Emile was struggling to hold her. "What I said did that! No! No!" The sound of her sobs filled the court, reducing its pandemonium to sudden silence. Lise stood absolutely still.

"Have you anything to say?" the Président asked her.

"Rien. Nothing." The handcuffs were put on and the gendarmes took her away. Lise had a last glimpse of Marcelline, bowed down, broken, of Zoë trying to comfort her. She did not look at Vivi or Emile.

"She sent you this." Maître Jouvin was allowed a few moments with Lise before the police van came to take her back to Sevenet for the night; she would go to Vesoul next day. "She asked me to give it you—in the midst of those theatrical tears." Jacquot said it in distaste. " 'For Madame Lise,' she said. 'Tell her I want her to have it.' "

Lise opened the small parcel—it was just a twist of paper—and recoiled from the chain of pink mother-of-pearl beads; and silver cross.

"A rosary!" Jacques was completely mystified. "Vivi had a rosary!"

"Yes." The way Lise said it was savage and, to Maître Jouvin's amazement, she took the little chain of beads and, in her strong hands, broke it into pieces, then put them back into the paper again. "Give those back to her," said Lise.

"I wish—I wish I hadn't done that," she was to tell Soeur Marie Alcide, although, "I'm delighted you did," Jacques Jouvin had said.

"I wish I hadn't," said Lise and, "I shall never see Vivi again. I can't tell her I am sorry."

Chapter
Eight

LISE'S THREE MONTHS at Saint Xavier's had extended to two years. "It seems you have a way with young girls," said Soeur Raymonde.

"I'm popularly supposed to have victimised them," or, "It comes of long training," but Lise did not say either of those bitter things and, "I'm glad now I stayed," she was to tell Marc.

"Béthanie has had to come into the world—our houses can't all be isolated in far-away villages, though we need that too. Our 'spring'—I like to think of it as that—must be at the centre of things; our young be trained in the outside world as well as in our own." Thinking of her own novitiate, Lise often wondered at the freedom given now to the young postulants and novices; their easy confidence and capability; how they would perch on the edge of the Responsable's desk and swing one trousered leg as they talked to her. "We used to have to kneel down," Lise told Marc. They talked, too, openly, freely, and the Responsable listened. "As a

179

novice, it was I who had to do all the listening. There was no exchange." These new ones sat on the floor in chapel, cross-legged or against the wall, completely at home, "which is what one should be. We just learned Latin and the Bible and singing—now they take courses in Paris. Of course it's far more tiring for the Responsable. I must say we sometimes longed for the old 'instant obedience.' "

"The ironic part is that I have never liked young girls," but Lise could not tell that, nor "but I loved . . ." She knew she had to try and love all with the same undifferentiating love as Soeurs Théodore or Raymonde, but, one more of those trips on the métro! thought Lise—but, of course, there would be dozens of trips. She must not flag, no matter how tired she was.

"We are sending you back to Belle Source," Soeur Marie Emmanuel told Lise at the end of those two years.

"Belle Source!" Lise knew a light had leapt into her eyes. "But, ma Mère. . . ."

"If you want something badly, that is no reason against your having it." Soeur Marie Emmanuel said it with her warm smile. "Besides, they need you. They have many old sisters. You are one of the few who can drive a car, and when you are not so tired you are strong, and I think clear-headed."

Sometimes indeed it seemed to Lise that she was clear, clear of herself, as if the old self had dropped away, and, As if I hadn't been given enough! thought Lise, she's sending me to beloved Belle Source.

It was January when she came back, the turn of the year with a powdering of snow over the domaine and bitter cold, so cold that the big moat was frozen and the ducks had had to be taken in. The big vegetable garden was bare except for a few carrots and cabbages and Soeur Thecla's procession of cows only went out for an hour or two and then were brought in to the warmth of the pig-house for the night—it was too big to be called

a sty. Soeur Thecla had been ploughing the empty
fields, the fruit trees were being cut back; everything
was dormant, sap and life low—except in the chapel.

Lise was in time for Epiphany, the feast that celebrated the coming of the Magi—Wise men? Astrono-
mers? Kings? No one knows, but the feast kept the day
or night on which the infant child was recognised as
Christ.

> Arise, shine for thy light is come and the glory of
> the Lord is risen . . . and his glory shall be seen . . .
> And the Gentiles shall come to thy light and
> kings to the brightness of thy rising. . . .

Not just the few familiars in Bethlehem, carpenters,
innkeepers, shepherds, but men from far away, paying
homage and bringing gifts from a far bigger world, the
world of courts and kings, governors, counsellors, all
titles that presently would be given to this humble
Child; and it was only the first homage paid by men of
vision, men who had eyes that could read the stars,
tongues that could tell the Word which, as the prophets
had foreseen, would spread from land to land, nation to
nation.

> Lift up thine eyes and see roundabout: the multi-
> tude of camels . . . the dromedaries of Midian and
> Ephah; all they that came from Sheba . . . They
> shall bring gold and incense. . . .
> . . . the isles shall wait for thee and the ships . . . to
> bring thy sons from afar . . . thy gates shall not be
> shut day or night.

How did Isaiah know all these things fifteen centuries
before Christ? wondered Lise. The foreseeing of the
prophets never ceased to astonish her.

In the refectory after Vespers the galette was brought
in, the traditional huge flat round cake of the three
kings; somewhere in it was hidden a midget plaster

figure of a king. The sister who found it in her slice would be crowned with a gold paper crown and be King for the day. Lise found herself hoping, even praying, it would be Lucette who would get it.

"You will find Lucette at Belle Source," Soeur Marie Emmanuel had warned her. "She wasn't strong enough for Saint Xavier. In fact it alarmed her, so we are allowing her to finish her novitiate at Belle Source." The Mother-General gave Lise a penetrating look. "Will you mind?"

"Only ... if ..." Lise hesitated. ". . . I could upset her."

"I don't think you could. This is a new Lucette."

"New and not new." Lise had, of course, not contradicted Soeur Marie Emmanuel and indeed she saw little of Lucette who was almost always with her Responsable, Soeur Marguerite, to whom Lise had hoped the trust and love would be transferred; but not; though Lucette scrupulously followed every word Soeur Marguerite said, when she met or saw Lise, there was still the same mute appeal in the brown eyes, the appeal Lise found as touching as it was irritating—and hated herself for being irritated; that "old self" she had thought wiped out had not gone after all. Lucette, too, had the power to make Lise long for Vivi—with all the spite and wounding and cheating—for Vivi's tough beauty and independence. "Why do I like them wicked so much better than good?" Lise asked herself despairingly. Was it because Patrice and Vivi called out something good in her, Lise, while Lucette brought out what was bad? I must be very vain, thought Lise, vain and selfish and she prayed: "Finding the King is only play, a tiny thing but it would give Lucette such confidence. Please, please," prayed Lise, and Lucette got the King.

Perhaps it was a good omen, thought Lise; that year she took her final vows.

Again it seemed as natural and logical as when she had made her Promise, only this time it was after

Mass, and a vow to God in the presence of the priest as well as to the Mother-General.

After the Solemn Mass, Lise prostrated before the altar.

"What do you ask?" It was the priest's deep voice which seemed—and was—the voice of the whole church.

"God's mercy and yours." Lise had lifted her head.

"Rise up."

After he had spoken to her of the life, the loyalty and steadfastness it would need, the faith and trust, Lise knelt as before in front of Soeur Marie Emmanuel who was holding the book of Constitutions; again Lise laid one hand on it, the other in the Mother-General's hand and again said the same words: "I, Soeur Marie Lise du Rosaire, vow and promise . . ." but this time the vow was far deeper, ending with the words: "jusqu'á la mort"—until death.

The nuns sang the psalm:

Eructavit cor meum verbum bonum . . .
Dico ego opera mia regi . . .

Joyful the thoughts that well up from my heart,
the king's honour for my theme . . .
the blessings God has granted can never fail
Gird on the sword.

Lise was blessed; then came the blessings of her veil "in the hope," Soeur Marie Emmanuel had explained, "that when you wear it you may be pure in soul and body."

"I!" thought Lise, and then, "Why, perhaps I am now—not pure but purified . . ." purged in another sense; every paper or form that showed she had once been convicted and in prison was destroyed . . . every proof; it was as if a weight of lead had dropped off her.

And what a pilgrimage of strange milestones, or little monuments, if you could call them that, had led to this day; a fountain lit with red, white and blue lights playing on it to the sound of singing and shouting: a silk dressing-gown and a huge blue and yellow macaw: the grey and white of a pseudo-Rockingham tea set: a little French bulldog in a rhinestone-studded collar: a gold lamé dress: a ten-franc note given her by Père Silas: the broken end of a bottle: a hand clutching a string of mother-of-pearl beads with a little silver cross—"Don't," Lise interrupted herself. "Don't. Don't." But they went on: her clothes thrown out on the landing: a warm cheek rubbed against hers: a wedding dress that must be pink too—"Please, please, Madame Lise,"—a raw steak held by Marcelline to a throbbing black eye: several steaks, several black eyes: letters printed in writing like a child's on cheap paper: a pair of white kid baby boots: a bed of geraniums and blood oozing into the earth: interviews in the visiting room at Sevenet: and papers, papers, papers: scarlet and ermine robes and the sea of faces. La Balafrée, condamnée. The courtyard at the Division d'Accueil where you were put out to walk round and round, up and down . . . the sound of the judas—the spyhole in the cell door—as it was lifted and an eye looked through: the star through the window pane.

"Searching is finding." Lise knew that now. The pilgrim had come home.

> Give me my scallop shell of quiet,
> My staff of faith to lean upon,
> My scrip of joy, immortal diet,
> My bottle of salvation.

The words of Walter a leigh's poem, forgotten until now, seemed to come of themselves into Lise's mind over the nuns' singing.

> Over the silver mountains
> Where spring the nectar fountains . . .

*   *   *

Nectar. Belle Source. At last she could settle down, and the last trace of me blotted out, thought Lise.

The Normandy February was usually wet and cold but there were days of clear sunshine that reminded Lise of her childhood in England when there might be catkins; the willows turned red and the first snowdrops were out. There were no catkins at Belle Source but she found an early primrose in the bank below the aumônier's house and a scattering of snowdrops. "Soon the lawns will be a sheet of crocus," said Soeur Fiacre. "If they're not soaked," said Lise.

André Foucan from the village pruned the vines and lettuce was sown in the frames. "Crops are beginning," said Soeur Fiacre.

Candlemas came, the last lit feast till Easter, with a procession in the cloister, the candlelight moving in slow rhythm to the chapel which was filled with light for the Purification of May and the Presentation of the Child in the Temple at Jerusalem and, soon after, in contrast, was the sombreness of Ash Wednesday; those who could, fasted on bread and coffee; for the rest there were vegetable and soup, and so the days of Lent began.

"Like the weather, Lent is nice or nasty," the Prioress said in her address, "but remember, unlike the weather, it is what you make it." Breaking the austerity there were still feast days: on March the tenth, the anniversary of Père Lataste's death, when his picture hung in the cloister, "and we remember how Béthanie started and why"—the first violets were always for Père Lataste. On the nineteenth came Saint Joseph's day; if it were fine enough, tables were set in the cloister for goûter, the mid-afternoon break, with drinks—"children's drinks," Lise would have said in the old days—fruit juice, syrupy grenadine, but to the nuns a treat; there were cakes too, just as there had been a special dessert at lunch.

Then came the Annunciation, but this was a solemn

day when the Martyrology was sung, the long list of the men and women who had died for the faith, died willingly. Those of the nuns who were able prostrated themselves in the choir as a tribute to the courage, steadiness and fidelity, not only of the martyrs, but of that young girl, Mary, who said "Fiat" to the angel's message knowing, part at least, what that would bring her.

And meanwhile, in typical Saint Joseph fashion, the work of the house went on. Spring cleaning was done, whitewashing, and in the garden much was being sown, more carrots, spinach, tomatoes in the frames, more lettuce for the invaluable salads, onions and shallots planted; and it was not only food for humans; there was lucerne, oats and mangolds for the cows. The farm was busy too; chicks were bought and pullets: the first brood of ducklings hatched out, and Bienvenue was heavy with her calf. The plum trees were in blossom. "The plums are always the first," said Soeur Fiacre. There were daffodils, narcissi. . . .

Most of the sisters were out of doors, "so we are hungry," said Lise. "Yet we have to fast on Wednesdays as well as Fridays. But we manage—strength comes." "I was given some roots of white violets," said Soeur Fiacre. "I thought them rare so some I planted in the shelter of a cold frame and some under cloches, but there wasn't room for them all, so some had to go outside and face the cold and wind and wet; the ones inside died, or were sickly and pale, the outside ones flourished," and it was true that the nuns looked much better, more fresh and clear-skinned than the guests in the guest-house, always busy for Easter, where no one was asked to fast or work.

On Maundy Thursday, Béthanie kept the traditional washing of the feet, the Prioress taking the role of Christ and kneeling before her daughters, and, after an evening Mass, just as Christ went from the Upper Room, the Cenacle, to the Garden of Gethsemane, so the Host was taken from the altar's tabernacle and borne in procession to an altar in the ante-room made welcoming with flowers and candles; the chapel itself was left stark, with the tabernacle door open, showing the emptiness inside. The nuns watched at the altar of Repose until midnight, taking it in turn, coming quietly in and out, as their work or strength dictated.

On Good Friday, the "big service," as the sisters called it, was held; it took all afternoon, with the reading of the Passion, the prayers of intercession for the whole world and Veneration of the Cross and the singing of the *Improperia* with its poignant refrain:

> My people what have I done to you?
> How have I offended you? Answer me.
>
> I led you on your way, in a pillar of cloud
> but you led me into Pilate's Court . . .
>
> I gave you manna in the desert
> but you struck me down and scourged me.
>
> I gave you saving water from the rock
> but you gave me gall and vinegar to drink.
>
> I gave you a royal sceptre
> but you gave me a crown of thorns.
>
> I raised you to the height of majesty
> but you raised me high on a cross.
>
> My people what have I done to you?
> How have I offended you? Answer me.

The Cross was left exposed on the stripped altar. It was a day of silence; most of the sisters were wrapped in their own thoughts as they still were on the curiously blank day of Holy Saturday, blank as it must have seemed to the apostles and disciples and for Mary and the other women; for them it was the Jewish holy day, the Sabbath, on which all movement and work were forbidden: their own hope of holiness was sealed silent in a tomb. What did they do, wondered Lise, what think? Could they keep their faith and trust? Peter had already denied him. Mary had been warned from the beginning and never lost hope, but Mary Magdalen? She must have known despair. True, she had seen the raising of Lazarus, but could Christ raise himself? It must have seemed impossible and she surely believed him dead. Why else did she bring spices to the sepulchre and ask, "Who will roll away the stone for us?" That Saturday of waiting, when she was held helpless by custom and respect, must have been most terrible of all—or was she stunned by the disillusionment? At Béthanie's five o'clock Vespers, some of the sisters looked as if they had been weeping; all were pale, but Easter was to come when hope comes back to the church as, long ago, hope came back to the apostles.

There has never been on earth, thought Lise, anything more beautiful than the Easter Vigil, herald of the first Mass of Easter Sunday; "But it's not of earth," said Soeur Thecla. "It's a glimpse of heaven."

The new fire was kindled outside the chapel; the big paschal candle was lit from that new fire and the aumônier took the first step into the empty dark church; he raised the candle "*Lumen Christi*—The light of Christ." Three times the cry echoed as the new light was passed from candle to candle held by the nuns, then to the villagers gathered in the externe chapel. As the candles caught, one from another Lise had a vision of the flame running in the same way from one church to another through all Christendom, far around the world: new light, new joy, new hope.

This is the night on which heaven was wedded to earth.
On this night Christ broke the bonds of death,

and, the night shall be as light as day,
the night shall light up my joy.

188

On Easter morning, very early, Bienvenue's calf was born; "I heard lowing in the pig-house," said Sister Thecla, "got up and went out, and there she was in the straw, a little heifer." She was called Aurore, in honour of the dawn and was to be sold a year later down to the South of France. "It seems the fame of our cows has gone far and wide," said Soeur Thecla. "But the papers that poor little thing had to have! The arrangements, more than for an orphan child!" On that Easter Sunday she had called Lise to see and, after the marvel of the little creature, with its velvet coat, small black muzzle and big wondering eyes, standing upright on its legs, had been admired enough for Soeur Thecla, Lise had come out into the first daylight of the domaine as, long ago, day must have come in its freshness to Joseph of Arimathea's garden; that was far away from France, yet Lise seemed to smell freshly-watered dust paths, hear the movement of long-stemmed olive leaves, see pink and white rosettes of oleander flowers.

"You have been to the Holy Land!" Soeur Marguerite's exclamation of astonishment and wonder brought Lise up short. They had been talking of the Holy Sepulchre at recreation and, remembering her thoughts of the morning, Lise had said without thinking, "No one knows where it was, but I should rather it was there, in that garden, which possibly was Joseph of Arimathea's, than where people have been taught to believe it is, in the Church of the Holy Sepulchre. That seemed to me a dreadful place. But in the garden," said Lise, "among the olive trees you seem really near—they can't be the same olives, of course, but they might be from slips of the old. . . ."

"And you have been there?"

"Yes." The whole circle of faces watching Soeur Marie Lise was eager.

"To have been there!"

"How wonderful!"

"Were you on a pilgrimage?"

"No." Anything but, Lise could have added. Every other year or so Patrice or Emile had gone out to the Middle East, Algeria, Morocco, Cairo, "to ... to recruit," Lise had said finally, trying to find the exact word for Soeur Marie Alcide. "Don't let imagination run away with you; it was not white slave traffic, but they found girls, often in poor circumstances, and offered them 'an opportunity,'" she did not know what else to call it. "We had beautiful girls at the Rue Duchesne, and many of them were foreign. Patrice also controlled 'centres' or houses—I don't know how many, but there was one in Cairo and he had heard there would be a coming city in Tel Aviv; in those days it was just growing. He was an astute business man in spite of his laziness, Emile more so, and we spent some time in what was to be Israel. I don't know why he took me—perhaps he was not feeling well and needed ballasting; perhaps Emile was bullying him which, surprisingly, he often did—but most of the time I was at a loose end and I hired a car and drove; perhaps, though I didn't know it, that was part of the searching. I went to Nazareth and Galilee. We. . . ."

Lise choked and the Prioress came forward to rescue her. "Sister, this was long ago," but Lise took breath and went on. "If you have seen the stars over Gethsemane, those same stars that shone on the agony in the garden. . . . As I said, no one knows where the sepulchre really was, but at five o'clock in the morning, in Jerusalem, the air is fresh, dew lies on the paths, or they water them early, and the olive leaves stir as they did then; and there are already gardeners going about their work—no wonder Mary Magdalen mistook him for the gardener. . . ."

In April the apple trees flowered; the orchards all round Belle Source and in the orchard of the domaine were a dream of beauty, but there was no time to dream; all the sisters who could were planting potatoes, dirty, wet work—"Try bending double in the rain,
190

wet soaking down your neck, your hands so wet and mud-caked they are frozen." A notice appeared on the board of the cloister:

> *On Wednesday Lectures will be at two o'clock, not three; the pig is being killed. On Thursday Midday Prayer will be an hour earlier; we are cutting up the pig.*

"I never thought," said Lise, "that making boudins could be part of my trying to serve God!" The boudins, blood puddings, were laid out in black glistening rows to dry. "Ugh!"

"But they are delicious." Soeur Fiacre was surprised. "I look forward to this time all the year."

Ugh!" said Lise again, taking off, at last and thankfully, her red-spattered apron.

Soeur Fiacre laughed as she went back to her sowings of haricots. "If you have ever lived in a convent you never want to see haricot beans again," said Lise; tomatoes were put out, more lettuce, and the garden was a mass of flowers, lilac, tulips, pansies.

There was the same pattern of festival for Ascension Day; then June was hay-making month—always anxious because rain might ruin the hay—then strawberry time with strawberry picking—more back-breaking than the planting of potatoes; there was picking of currants and gooseberries too, and those nuns who were not outside toiling in blue aprons and with great straw hats over their veils to keep off the sun, were in the kitchen making jam and bottling fruit; the shelves in the stillroom were gradually filling. "We're like squirrels, working against the winter." Some of the sisters dried rose petals for the pot-pourri they sold: the roses were in full bloom, with lilies, the pinks Lise loved for their clove scent, sweet-peas and, for Corpus Christi, one of the great feasts of June, there were enough flowers to decorate the small altars that were set up around the domaine as "stations" where the monstrance, with its precious burden, was set down for a few minutes and the sisters knelt to sing, while, when they reached the paddocks and pens, the cows, chickens, rabbits and pheasants watched this strange invasion of their territory. "But they know that it is holy," Soeur Thecla declared. "If you notice, the cows watch and do not graze until we have gone."

"They chew their cud though," said Lucette.

"That means they're thinking."

One of the "stations" was by Belle Su1rce's small cemetery, a fenced enclosure with crosses made from rough apple branches, still with their bark, and marked only with a name and date, sometimes two or three names because more than one nun could be buried in the same grave. Here were other Soeur Irènes or Henri Dominiques or Lucie Magdaleines, row after row lying undisturbed except by the rustling of the trees or by a new burial and, every year, by Corpus Christi with its procession of new candles and singing. "I like to think they are visited by him each year," said Soeur Thecla.

Before Corpus Christi, though, was Pentecost when the workrooms were at their busiest because this was the time in the world of First Communions and the robes for boys, the long dresses for girls, all in white, hand-stitched and pleated or tucked and embroidered, were made ready, the white and silver boxes were piled high. Family cars drew up to fetch them, other boxes went by post and, typical of Béthanie, thought Lise, in every box was a paper cornet of white sugared almonds sent without payment to sweeten the day and its demands for some young Pierre or Michel or Jeanne or Solange. Prayers were said for them too.

It was often penalising to have to wear a habit and veil in July; sweat streamed down Soeur Fiacre's and Soeur Thecla's faces—they were the two most outside. It was unbearably hot in the sun and often thunder gave Lise a headache, but no sooner was the picking of soft fruit done than the plums were ripe and there was the added burden of watering and hoeing; the weeds

192

seemed as plentiful as the vegetables and flowers. "They must be sinful or they wouldn't multiply so fast," said Soeur Fiacre in unwonted irritation; more irritating were the gnats and flies: "We're so mosquito bitten we look as if we had measles," said the Prioress; and, with all the crops, the garnering, the constant work of visiting, rescuing, organising, the unexpected requests and important errands, went on, and the guest-house was crammed. Because of the heat it was a danger time for quarrels; tempers were quick and patience wore thin. "If I bottle any more haricots I think I shall go mad," said Soeur Monique, and Soeur Anne Colombe, obsessed with cleaning, disturbed even recreation with her mop and bucket. "This is rest time, Sister."

"Maybe, but this floor hasn't been washed for a week."

"You washed it yesterday."

"I certainly did not."

"Leave her, leave her," said the Prioress. "She is old."

"So she, above all, should rest." Soeur Irène was the infirmarian.

"To try and make her would only tire her more. Let her go her own way," which, in any case, Soeur Anne Colombe would have done.

Now the harvest was beginning to reach its zenith. From the vines the unfruitful branches were cut away so that each cluster of grapes could get the full sun and swell. "The pullets have started to lay," Soeur Thecla was content.

"The new pig is fattening beautifully . . . we have clutch after clutch of pheasant eggs," they sold at a good price, "and I have never seen such plums as we have this year."

"Let's shake the trees and have done," said impatient Lise.

"Shake them! You will bruise them." Some had to be shaken, they were so high, but the ladders came out, the blue-pinafored nuns went up to pick; baskets were carefully lowered to be carried in. "The earth is the Lord's and the fullness thereof," said the psalm, "but sometimes I wish there were not so much fullness," said Lise, and, "do we *need* so much jam?"

"There are forty-five of us and it's not only for us; there's the guest-house," said Soeur Fiacre.

"Soon it will be tomatoes."

"Well, what do you expect? Be thankful. Besides, you have seen nothing yet. Wait for the apples and cider . . ." but the work was, as usual, broken by feasts, especially one nearer to the heart of Béthanie than even Saint Joseph's, the feast of Saint Mary Magdalen. It was a day of rest and pleasure, with the beauty of its liturgy, telling all her stories. For lunch a cold buffet was spread in the cloister and in the evening when the heat of the day lessened, the whole community picnicked in the forest by the spring which gave Belle Source its name. To interrupt the work again came the respite of another day, Saint Dominic's, and, on the fifteenth of August, the Assumption of Our Lady, with its procession and Solemn Mass, acolytes helping the aumônier and the chapel crowded with visitors. "After that, I always think summer abates and we begin the slowing down and quietness of autumn," said Soeur Thecla.

"Quietness? Slowing down? I think you have forgotten the cider," said Lise.

In September the garden was lovely with late summer flowers and there was mist on the lawns in the early morning, and those minute spider webs spun on the grass that, as a child, Lise had called fairies' cradles—but there was little time for fairies; not only had the main crop of potatoes to be got up but, in October, the apples were ripe; this time the fruit could be shaken down and the cider apples were piled in a great heap in the courtyard; a few rotten ones among them were left to ferment until the last week of November which brought the hardest work of the year;

first the apples were brought into the cellars and put into the heavy wooden press; from the press the juice was poured into barrels and left to work for a month. The knocking out of the bungs was skilled exciting work with the sisters standing by with jugs and buckets to catch the gush. Even the smell was potent. "You can be quite drunk without touching a drop," warned Soeur Thecla.

As for cleaning the barrels—"I never imagined!" gasped Lise. A chain was put through the hole, the barrel filled with boiling water and soda and the chain worked round and round as the strongest of the sisters pushed the weight of the barrels to and fro. The sisters were soon exhausted but Soeur Thecla drove them on. "Unless the barrels are *completely* clean, next year's cider won't be good." "Talk of galley slaves!" said Lise.

This too was the season for tidying up the domaine; culling the poultry, seeing to the cold frames, getting up dahlias and storing them, planting bulbs—"There must always be flowers for the chapel." The grapes were picked and sent away to be sold in boxes layered with tissue paper, and, with all this busy-ness, not a minute of prayer or devotion could be left out of the day.

There was one feast though when, in spite of Bella's overriding wisdom, Lise could not help shutting her mind. With the Dominicans, and particularly with Béthanie, there had always been a devotion to the Rosary and, on the seventh of October, its feast, Our Lady of the Rosary, came round with a sung Mass in the morning, a lunch of extra goodness and an afternoon given over to recreation. Lise would have liked to plead a headache and stay in her room; instead she volunteered for the tasks that, feast or not, still had to be done; she washed dishes, relieved the infirmarian, fed the hens and the pig; Soeur Thecla seemed to sense she needed any and every distraction. "I wish I could milk," Lise told her as she watched Soeur Thecla with Bienvenue.

"You haven't the hands," Soeur Thecla said flatly, whose own were broad and strong. "They're too nervous," which Lise supposed was true on this day of all days. Nobody commented, asked any questions; only the Prioress said, "That's enough, Sister. Go into the chapel and rest."

In the chapel there was rest, and Lise was always glad that, each year, when cider-making was over, harvesting done, the eight-day retreat was held, when the convent was shut to all outsiders and a priest came to take charge; not their familiar aumônier, but a priest from outside, "who will open our minds, give us to think—I hope," said the Prioress.

"I always wonder," said Lise, "why, in Britain and America, we make Hallow'een into a frightening thing with, for children, ghosts and skulls, witches, spiders and black cats, when it is the eve of one of the most radiant feasts of the year—All Saints, all those men and women who have shone out light and goodness, courage and faith into the world."

"And All Souls is radiant too," said Soeur Marguerite —it followed the next day. "For us there is loss, but for the dead, for him or her, it is the culmination, the crown. . . ."

"What of the people who die badly—in their sins . . . ?" That was what Lise, from the first, was haunted by.

"How do we know they do?" Soeur Marie Alcide had answered. "No one knows except God, what happens in those last few seconds."

"No," and Lise remembered that smile, Patrice's strangely sweet smile and the whisper, "Chérie." She would hear that forever.

"And don't let me catch you being morbid on All Souls," Soeur Théodore too had always told her aspirants. "Pray, yes, for every soul you know, but leave them to God. That they are with Him should make us joyful."

"The weather doesn't, though." Lise found it difficult to find joy in the darkening year, usually wet, day after day of Normandy rain . . . the frost too mild to be sparkling and invigorating. "The weather doesn't, particularly when you have to get up mangolds in the mud, dirty heavy slippery things," and yet there was a satisfaction in piling up and earthing the heaps. "The cows will be fed all winter and, if they are, so will we be, with milk and butter and cheese . . ." but, "getting up mangolds isn't work for you," Soeur Thecla told Lise.

"It is, Sister. Sometimes I need to do hard, dirty work."

"Exorcising devils," but wise Soeur Thecla did not wait for an answer. She took action though, and Lise was put to transplanting endives into the cellars where, cut, they would spring up in six weeks. "So we shall soon have salads again." Soeur Thecla herself had begun ploughing and, to her satisfaction, great wheelbarrows of pig and cow manure were wheeled by those she called her "stalwarts" down the paths to the furrows. "Phaugh, Jehoshaphat!" Bella, Soeur Marie Isabelle, had said on a visit to Belle Source and added, "It's not what goes into a man that defiles him, it is what comes out. I didn't know that applied to innocent animals!"

And then, as if it had stolen into these dwindling days without notice, as Christ had stolen in almost without notice, came Advent. It's odd—Advent always comes as a shock, thought Lise. *"Rorate Coeli*—Drop down dew" was sung at Benediction. It reminded Lise of the old carol:

He came all so still
Where His Mother was
As dew in April
that falleth on the grass . . .

A new dew, a new refreshment, was coming into the world.

The days of December were like a hush, expectant, though the world was at its darkest; when she, Lise, came out in the morning to help Soeur Thecla, the stars were still out until the sky paled and they faded, leaving one, her evening star; she knew now it was the morning star as well and, as she turned Bienvenue or Bibiche in the stall ready for milking, rubbing the Jersey's head, hard and firm under its soft hair, Lise could see the star through the broken rafters of the cowshed, incandescent in the pearl of dawn in the sky. No wonder the Magi had followed it as wise men had done ever since.

She held her hand under Bibiche's soft muzzle and felt the warm breath, sweet with the smell of grass and hay, the breath of life. You don't have to try and be wise, Bibiche, thought Lise; you simply have to live, you lucky little cow. You don't know when you fail . . . trample on someone else's heart. She was thinking of Lucette's present.

It had happened at Christmas, Béthanie's homely joyful Christmas when, after Réveillon, Lise had gone up to her room and on her bed was the usual packet from the Prioress.

To Lise's intense joy, Soeur Marie Emmanuel, having done twelve years as Mother-General, the utmost limit, had been appointed the new Prioress of Belle Source—Soeur Raymonde was Mother-General now. Lise opened her packet, warmed by its message and affection, then turned with a sigh of happiness to take off her veil, and stopped.

There, between two lit stubs of candles, obviously saved from the chapel and carefully stuck into a pair of shards—from a broken flower-pot, Lise guessed—was a picture, a collage or an ikon. Lucette! It must have been Lucette, but what was Lucette, Lise wondered, doing in her room. Then Lise came closer; to Lucette this—travesty, Lise could not help thinking—was an ikon, holy enough to excuse any trespassing—but Lise only understood that, and with anguish, afterwards; unfortunately, what she saw in that first moment was a garish daub, a picture of the Mother and Child cut from a newspaper and coloured with crayon in kindergarten colours, bright red cheeks, bright blue eyes, bright yellow hair, the Virgin's hair not as yellow as the Child's which was spangled with gold. How did Lucette get the gold, Lise asked herself when she came to examine it. She must have picked up a snipped-off end of the gold cord Soeur Elizabeth tied the cornets of sugared almonds with; Lucette had minutely shredded it and, to make the Child's robe white, she had used icing sugar on glue and varnished it. "So it won't come off, ever." Lise could imagine her saying that and the same of the frame which was of sugared almonds, glued down and varnished too. Lucette would never have taken them without leave, but she was a pet of Soeur Elizabeth who would every now and then give her one or two; they were eked out with a few beads and pebbles. The Virgin's robe was red translucent paper which Lise recognised as being from crackers sent to the community for Saint Joseph's Day; her sleeves and neckline were bordered with the minute flowers of lavender, rubbed from the spikes. "It must have taken hours." The figures were backed by a gold paper lace doyley spread on a cardboard base and varnished too. All this Lise saw afterwards but, as she had turned, the yellow and red, blue and gold hit her eyes and, for a moment, her face betrayed her.

It was only a moment but Lucette, hiding full of joy and pride behind the door and peeping round it, saw, and "You don't like it." It was a cry like a wounded child.

"Ssh! It's silence," whispered Lise, and, "Like it? Of course I like it. It's just . . . it's such a surprise. How *did* you do it?" but, even to Lise, it sounded false and, "You don't like it." It was such a wail that it brought other

199

sisters to their doors but, when they saw it was Lise and Lucette, they went in again.

"Lucette." It had been no use; Lise had tried to hold her close—she made herself do that—and whispered, "Isn't it enough that you did all this wonderful work for me?"

"No, it isn't enough." Lucette tore herself free, darted into the room and took the imitation ikon. She tried to tear it across but being so encrusted and firmly glued it would not tear, so she crushed it, threw it on the floor and ran sobbing down the corridor to her own room.

Lise had stood, sick, dismayed and in something of a panic; holding Lucette had been like holding a human sparrow, her bones were so small and light, so frail. I must go after her—but to go into another nun's room was forbidden and Lucette was now almost a nun. After a moment Lise went to Soeur Marie Emmanuel.

"Ma Mère . . ."

The Prioress, already undressed and in bed—where she must need to be, thought Lise—came at once to the door, a shawl over her nightdress. "Ma Mère, may I go to Soeur Lucette?" and, as Lise told, she found she was suddenly sobbing too.

The Prioress listened, her eyes on Lise, her hand steady, then, "Go to bed," she said. "Leave Soeur Lucette to me."

"Ma Mère. It's past two o'clock. You must be tired."

"Not too tired for this," and she put her hand on Lise's shoulder. "Soeur Marie Lise, don't grieve. It wasn't your fault."

"It was. It was. I should have been more controlled."

"One can't control oneself all the time," and, "Bed," ordered Soeur Marie Emmanuel.

On New Year's Eve, after Vespers, the nuns met in the community room to wish one another a happy new year and eat the bonbons the Prioress provided, and on New Year's Day, at recreation, the aumônier brought in a basket and each nun drew out a motto, an augury for the coming year; for Lucette it had been, "They took sweet counsel together and walked in the house as friends," and it was at Lise that Lucette beamed.

Another year was rounded, and nothing anyone could write or say, thought Lise, could tell the whole meaning of each succeeding year, of its unfolding; what is a day-to-day miracle is unexciting because usually it's so sure—and yet it is a miracle; only if it's taken away, as in a famine or drought, do we see that. I never saw it, thought Lise. Long before I went to prison, I was in a prison, the prison of myself and, thinking of Soeur Thecla, she thought, The paradox is that the nearer you are to earth, the nearer you are to heaven. My motto was fitting, too: "My lines have fallen in pleasant places." I don't deserve it but thank God, thought Lise. Thank God.

Then the Mother-General, Soeur Raymonde, sent for her. Why, thought Lise. Why?

Soeur Raymonde was at Belle Source for the "visitation" the Mother-General had to make to every house of Béthanie at least once in three years, for a minute examination of the affairs of the house. Lise had already had the long and private interview that was given to every sister in the house, just as every corner, every least thing was seen. "How does she find time?" Yet Soeur Raymonde never seemed hurried and this sudden summons must have been premeditated and Lise could not help a feeling of apprehension.

"Soeur Marie Lise, sit down," and, when Lise had arranged herself, her hands under her scapular, Soeur Raymonde said with a smile, "You have been here at Belle Source seven years."

She is going to move me, thought Lise in dismay, but she only murmured, "Yes, ma Mère, except for the years when, as you know, I filled in at the novitiate."

"Yes. Well, as we both know ..." and the words familiar now and dreaded came, "... you have great sympathy and tact in dealing with girls and women."

"Not sympathy."Lise had to be honest "Tact, perhaps. I . . . I learnt that in a difficult school—had to learn it." Lise gave a wry smile.

"Well, it has stood you in good stead. You have been elected, Soeur Marie Lise, as a missionary, one of our prison visitors."

"Prison!" and emotion overcame Lise. Soeur Raymonde waited until she was able to speak. "But ma Mère, I was there. Not at Le Fouest, of course, but at Vesoul."

"Naturally that made us have to consider carefully, not to say gravely—still, after fifteen years, and in a different prison, it isn't probable you would be recognised."

"This is a small world," Lise said desperately, "and there's my scar."

"Sister, that shows to you far more than it does to us. I doubt if anyone in the outside world would notice it unless you deliberately drew back your veil. Besides, the mark has grown so pale."

"Except when I'm angry or excited or moved. Then in spite of myself. . . ."

"It reddens. I know. I have seen it."

"Yes. Suppose . . ." Lise twisted her hands under her scapular.

"Well, suppose, which isn't likely," Soeur Raymonde was calm. "Wouldn't it be a wonderful witness to our Lord that this woman, once La Balafrée, is a Sister of Béthanie now? Naturally you must be extremely careful but, as it happens, there is no one here now at Belle Source as suitable as you and, my daughter, there is terrible need." It was the same Soeur Raymonde, "bringing you up higher than you think you could go," as Bella had said. "Terrible need, perhaps more now than ever before. As, physically, things get better for these poor unfortunates, the spirit seems to get worse, and Soeur Marie Mercédes, in spite of her courage, is beginning to fail." Soeur Raymonde laid her hand on Lise's. "Think what it was like for you when you first saw Soeur Marie Alcide."

"But—Soeur Marie Alcide . . . she is a saint."

"How do you know," said Soeur Raymonde, "that Soeur Marie Alcide may not once have been exactly like you?"

"For your prison visiting," Soeur Raymonde said a little later, "I shall ask you, Soeur Marie Lise, to think about two things: the first comes from a story often told—you may have heard it before: it was when, during the war, the Americans had a detachment near a leper colony. One young soldier watched a nun washing an old man and dressing the leper wounds where the fingers were dropping off. 'Sister,' he said, 'I wouldn't do your work for ten thousand dollars a day.' 'Neither would I,' said the nun."

"Ah!" whispered Lise.

"And if you do take the work, remember the parable our Lord told his disciples after he had sent them out and they came back delighted with what they had done and expecting praise. 'What man,' asked our Lord, 'when his servant was out all day, ploughing the fields and came in at the end of the day, would say to him, "Sit down and I will get you something to eat." No, rather he would say, "Go and wash and make yourself tidy, then wait on me while I dine. You can eat and drink yourself later," because the servant had only done his duty.' "

"Ah," said Lise again.

Chapter
Nine

LISE HAD TO CONFESS, when she saw the gates, the heavy portico of the Maison Centrale of Le Fouest, her heart almost failed her. I can't go behind prison walls again, I can't—and the thought came, But Lucette did—and not as you are doing now, Lise reminded herself, not free but under duress; Lucette endured and came through, yet *you* think of her as a feeble little creature.

All the same it seemed incredible to Lise that her companion, Soeur Marie Mercédes, could go calmly up to those gates and ring the bell, an everyday ring. The grid that opened was not "everyday"—no one could pretend that—nor the uniformed guard who looked through, but, without question, he opened the door, the same sort of little door that had let Lise out of Vesoul. This time the guard not only opened the door but saluted. I wonder what he would say if he knew whom he was saluting, thought Lise.

There was the same sort of courtyard she remembered, but here were trees in flower, magnolias—"We hadn't anything as beautiful as those," she almost said to Soeur Marie Mercédes. Behind the beauty of the trees was a huge, four-storeyed building, bigger than Vesoul and grim in its dark brick and the four stone staircases that penetrated and divided it. Think about the magnolias, Lise urged herself, not about walls; shut out the sound of locks and keys. "But we didn't come here to talk about magnolias," she found she had said that aloud.

"We could," said Soeur Marie Mercédes, "or any other pleasant thing. The difficulty for the women is to talk about the . . . the nub, shall we call it . . . the thing that really matters and that usually doesn't happen for a long long time." All the same, Lise felt the little nun stiffen herself as for an ordeal.

There were questions Lise longed to ask: "Do you still come here in chains?" "Do you still have that shaming search?"—but of course you must. "Do you still have that same prison régime?" There has to be a régime, but how it had altered! Lise soon saw that. The bell still went at half past six, the wardress on duty opening the judas to be sure the women were up; slops still had to be emptied—no more than Vesoul was Le Fouest an up-to-date prison. Cells still had to be tended and cleaned—mine was always bare, thought Lise—a few books, a photograph of Coco—but now she saw that some were almost cosy, an odd word to use for a cell, but women with long years to go had made their cells into bed-sitting rooms with rugs they had made in the workshops on the floor, the walls covered in photographs, pictures, pages torn from magazines, perhaps a statue, a vase of paper flowers. "For many their cell becomes their home—they haven't any other," said Soeur Marie Mercédes.

The food too was good. Nowadays for breakfast there was good bread, often from the prison's own kitchen. "There is a school of cookery now"—Le Fouest had come a long way from the stinking soup trolleys of

Cadillac—Lise was astonished at the menus. Roast beef or beefsteak, fresh fish, omelettes, all appetisingly dressed with herbs. She could not believe it. "They are taught in the cookery school to do things properly and they can buy extras in the canteen; they earn more money now," Soeur Marie Mercédes explained.

If they had had these workshops in my day, what couldn't I have brought to Béthanie, thought Lise. The prisoners no longer toiled at heavy and boring tasks, but at what they chose to learn, tie-making and dressmaking, cooking, to professional standards for city shops. I could have learned to be a secretary, even take a university course, thought Lise. There were sports and yoga—where else would most of these women and girls have ever heard of yoga? When the bell rang for meals, each went back to her own division, not herded by the hundred, but only twelve to twenty women, each division with its own refectory or sitting-room; they could take their trays into their cells if they liked and Lise thought of the old great room filled with the sound of crockery and rough utensils where not a word was allowed to be spoken. "Who is behind all this?" she asked Soeur Marie Mercédes.

"The Adminstration Pénitentiaire are, I suppose, but here I think you will find it's mostly the imagination and force of Mademoiselle Signoret, the Directrice, and her staff, helped by the Sisters of Marie Joseph. As a new visitor, you must come and meet Mademoiselle. She will be in her private office now."

The Directrice! There was not a prisoner in Lise's time whose heart did not beat so that it seemed to choke her, whose knees did not feel weak, when summoned to see the Directrice; even the defiant ones who tried to brazen it out, who called her behind her back "gouine" or "enculée," felt the same. Perhaps it was the punishment, the cachot—not a dungeon any more but a bare room without any comforts, not even a bed—in which case not only the Directrice, but her "second," the Sous-Directrice and Madame Chef, the chief officer, would be there. It might be what was even worse, bad news from the family, in which case Mademoiselle Signoret would see the prisoner alone. Now and again it was good news, a remission, two or three months of grace, but it had been always intimidating, standing facing the desk. "I suppose there has to be distance," said Lise, but nowadays, she was told, Directrice or not, Mademoiselle Signoret would often go and talk alone with a prisoner in her cell.

No one had told Lise the history of this Directrice, her name either, but when the sisters were ushered in by a young secretary and a tall, slim, dark-haired woman stood up to greet them, for a moment Lise stayed still. She knew that intelligent face, the dark eyes under shaped brows, the clear cut nose and mouth, clear but sensitive, and Lise remembered the young wardress of, was it 1948 or 1949, at Vesoul, whom she had heard protesting, "To give them that disgraceful bedding!" and Lise remembered the heavy coarse blankets, dark grey as almost everything was; they pricked as did the straw palliasses. "Straw, and thin—and some of these women are old!" said the indignant voice. Evidently Mademoiselle had got her way; now there were real mattresses, white sheets and pillowcases and the blankets were green.

But if I remember her, will she remember me? thought Lise. But, if Mademoiselle did remember, she was too controlled, too well-bred, thought Lise, to show it. There was only an even "Bonjour, mes Soeurs. Please sit down," and, when Soeur Marie Mercédes said, "This is our new visitor, Soeur Marie Lise," Mademoiselle simply said, "Welcome, Soeur Marie Lise."

"Though they have asked to see us, to begin is always difficult," Soeur Marie Mercédes told Lise. "You must remember they are all, or almost all, unhappy and prison is emotional." Lise almost smiled. So, Soeur Marie Mercédes, in the true Béthanie way, knew nothing of her junior's experiences.

207

And, for all the alleviations, Le Fouest is still prison, thought Lise. There were still the bleak iron-netted courts where newcomers walk round and round in those first days of solitary confinement or, more usually, sit hopelessly on benches; still the punishment wing; still the women in identical blue work-smocks washing down the staircases while a wardress, her white uniform covered by a blue cloak, gold-starred, kept a strict eye on them. There were still locks and keys. It was when all the women came out of their workshops to go to their divisions that the full force of prison was seen; they were like ants, numbers, not people.

"That's what we have to fight," Mademoiselle Signoret told Lise, "to keep them people."

"Yes, they must be somebody, not nobody! Somebody—each one," said Soeur Marie Mercédes.

"Soeur Marie Lise, this is Marie Dupont," said Soeur Marie Mercédes. "She is one of our regulars . . ." but Marie Dupont could not wait for politeness. "Ma Soeur, did you see them? Oh, did you?"

"Indeed I did. As your mother wrote, they are well and happy. Look, I brought these snapshots. One of our sisters borrowed a camera and took them." At the sight of the photographs, two schoolboys, one with a football, the other with a racquet, smiling, eating peanuts in some snapshots, or grimacing in others, the mother broke down and, "For her it's terrible," Soeur Marie Mercédes told Lise. "She got twenty years and has done twelve; in a year to two she might be released, but her parents don't want her home; there is no husband. They took the boys and brought them up on condition she didn't ask to see them again. They don't want their grandsons to be shamed by their mother, the boys think she is dead. She agreed—what else could she do? But now. . . ."

"What can happen to her?"

"She wants to come to Béthanie but she hasn't a vocation and a convent is no refuge for a broken heart."

"Contrary to what most people think," said Lise.

"Contrary to what most people think." Soeur Marie Mercédes smiled. "We shall try and get her work on one of the farms until she finds a way."

Soon Lise began to see how she, particularly, could help—after all, she knew the sore places—but she had to be careful not to betray herself. "Don't you hate the noises . . . the sound of the keys in locks . . . the banging of trays . . . the smell of the slops trolley?" would have been too close, but she was learning; there was so much to learn and she soon came to admire and reverence Soeur Marie Mercédes as she had revered Soeur Marie Alcide—Only there should be a thousand of them, sighed Lise, and even then they wouldn't be enough.

Soeur Marie Mercédes was as adroit and astute as she was sympathetic. "Ma Soeur, it's my birthday on Friday and you'll be coming then, won't you?" It was a prisoner called Yvonne. "I know you stay the week and my mother wants to send me a box of little cakes she has made herself. If they come through the gate I shall have to share them with the whole division and there wouldn't be enough, but if you could bring them, ma Soeur, five or six of us could have a private fête . . . ma Soeur—it's my birthday."

"Yvonne, you know perfectly well I can't."

"But little cakes. What harm could there be in that? She'll leave them at your hostel. . . ."

"Yvonne!"

There was no ill-feeling. "It was just a try," said Soeur Marie Mercédes. "They know we can't even bring in gifts of our own. All parcels are forbidden."

"It seems inhuman."

"Is it? I once brought in a bomb."

"You!"

"Yes, it seemed so innocent. The girl asked me to bring in some knitting wool. She had started the tricot before she came and couldn't match the colour in the prison. I had to go to a particular shop she told me of to get it. Fortunately the parcel seemed rather heavy—

209

bombs were not as small then as they are now—so I took the box to Mademoiselle."

"We can give cards," said Soeur Marie Mercédes. "Often when talking you can find out their birth-date and without their seeing write it down, then, on their birthday, they get a card. It seems nothing but when you are a surname or a number, a birthday card. . . ."

It was strange, Lise often thought, to be on two sides at the same time; she was one with the nuns—thank God, thought Lise—yet still one with the prisoners. There was so much I didn't understand then. "The moment a prisoner realises it is justice that she should be here," a Sister of Marie Joseph, those experienced prison workers, told Lise, "is a wonderful one. When she sees she is making amends in a way, paying for what she did, she gets a new dignity." Many had it and Lise was often astonished, as she had been after her baptism when she had found a fraternity, women who had a deep devotion, "far far deeper than mine," she told Soeur Marie Alcide, "yet it was to me that the vocation was given. How . . . funny," said Lise.

"Perhaps they were meant to stay in the world," said Soeur Marie Alcide, "Even this world," and it was true that from each of those women spread, not a combat—because they were not fighting—but warmth and sanity in that hotbed of resentment, hate and despair. "We could do with more of those," Mademoiselle Signoret sighed.

In Mademoiselle's office Lise seemed suddenly to find herself on the other side of the desk with a woman who had what must be one of the most difficult tasks in civilisation and such responsibility. "To be second," Soeur Marie Emmanuel had once said, "yes, that I could do, but to be the first!" Yet Soeur Marie Emmanuel had been Mother-General of the Order for twelve years, re-elected twice, and Mademoiselle Signoret, Directrice of Le Fouest for fifteen years; and no more than with Soeur Marie Emmanuel was there ambition. Lise was sure of that, nor a desire for power.

How much Mademoiselle knew of Soeur Marie Lise, Lise could not guess, but a friendship grew up between them. "The first friend I have ever had outside convents," said Lise, marvelling, "at least, if one doesn't count Henri, but that was such a short time: or Maître Jouvin or Marcelline—but she was like family." Soon Mademoiselle was coming to Belle Source for a long weekend. "Pagan as I am, you still have me and I love it," and she said, "I wish I could make a domaine like this at Le Fouest. Do away with those dreadful courtyards, let those who wanted to make gardens, but it's always money, money, money. We are accused of spending too much as it is . . ." she broke off, brooding.

"I believe you think about those women day and night," said Lise.

"No, I don't." Mademoiselle was too honest to say that. "If I did, I couldn't go on. I have to have my books, music, friends to keep my mind sane . . . but you, you have none of those."

"Indeed we do. Don't we have our community, our chapel, prayers," yet, though the nuns only went to Le Fouest four times a year, the visits haunted Lise, a constant shadow of evil and despair. Yet I ought to be accustomed to it, thought Lise. For all of us at Béthanie, it's never far away.

Jacky, for instance, had finally and irrevocably "thrown herself in the river," only this time it was from the top window of a house where Soeur Marie Mercédes had again found work for her. Jacky had fallen on to railings below. When the news came, Soeur Marie Mercédes had merely tightened her lips and gone to the chapel to pray. Lise had taken her to the funeral, a pathetically lonely one, they two the only mourners, with only one wreath, homemade from Belle Source. "But why? Why?" asked Lise, as, long ago, the disciples had asked Jesus why they could not cure the possessed boy, and he answered, "That kind can come forth by nothing but fasting and prayer." "We did not fast or pray enough," said Soeur Marie Mercédes, "but there

211

are so many, too many!" and, for the first time Lise saw the intrepid little sister crumble. It was only for a moment. Soeur Marie Mercédes stiffened herself upright. "Still, we must do what we can," and it still went on: the telephone or gate-bell ringing with a message or a need, a traveller; it might even be a gendarme bringing a woman or girl drunk or lost, but for anyone wretched there was a room ready.

"That must often be abused," Mademoiselle had said.

"Not as often as you would think. Perhaps it pays to be defenceless; there is nothing here to fight," said Lise.

"That's a key I can't have." Mademoiselle got up and stood with her back to Lise. "The Governor of a prison can do no right; either we are soft, too lenient—people say our prisoners have more chance than many in the world which unfortunately is true—or else we are tyrants, oppressors, avid for power. I can put up with all that," said Mademoiselle, "because I know neither is true—we strike the best balance we can; what I can't bear are the failures, the irrécupérables, the ones we can't reach or help."

"Are they really irrécupérables—irredeemable?" Lise asked and said slowly, "We're supposed to be made in God's image so, in every one, there must be some spark."

"Of the divine? Unfortunately the devil is divine too," Mademoiselle said. "I don't know if I believe in God, but I know I believe in the devil. I have met him," said Mademoiselle.

It happened when Lise had been a prison visitor for six years, "and had grown in confidence—I thought," said Lise, taking more and more responsibility; Soeur Marie Mercédes had grown even more frail—she had broken her hip again and this time it would not set properly, "because my bones are old," she said, but she still managed to struggle along on her caliper. Lise had said Soeur Marie Alcide was a saint but Soeur Marie

212

Mercédes was like a flame, though it was burning her out; only this little carcase of brittle bone and sallowed skin was left—and those eyes! When they looked at a prisoner they burnt away all pretence and saw to the heart of the unhappiness and sin, and yet Soeur Marie Mercédes was gentle and endlessly patiently charitable, and, "Was I glad to have her with me that day?" Lise told the Mother-General. "Though it was for her I really feared."

They had been coming down the staircase at noon to the officers' dining-room when they met a party of prisoners coming up with a wardress on the way from their work-shops to their division for lunch. There were fifteen or sixteen women and girls, all dressed alike in the prison uniform, well cut grey skirts, grey cardigans, blouses of different colours. Most passed with a smile or a word of greeting to the Sisters but one, in a scarlet blouse, stopped. She and Lise were on the same step and face to face.

There was no mistaking; Lise saw the bronzed hair, no longer silky, the regular perfect features though the flesh was sagging, the grey eyes that Lise guessed had been dimmed but were bright now with surprise—and the old spite. Vivi had grown plump, her figure had gone, some of the pretty teeth were broken and black, but there was still the independent neck, the proud carriage, and I, thought Lise; in spite of what Soeur Raymonde had said, she was sure no habit or veil could disguise her height, the way I walk and I expect my eyes and, to her chagrin, the scar had begun its immediate expected throbbing.

There was not as much as a breathed "Toi!" but Lise saw hatred blaze. "Allez. Faites vite!" called the wardress and Vivi went on up the stairs as Lise went down.

"That new prisoner, Vivi—does she call herself Branzano or Ambard—when did she come?"

"Vivi?" Though Lise knew Mademoiselle could have told her at once, she typically reached for the file, "because one can always make mistakes." "Yes, Vivi Ambard. She came five months ago; we had to keep her in the Division d'Accueil for the full three months. I'm afraid she's going to be one of the difficult ones; though she has only been in her new division a few weeks she has already ganged up with two of the least desirable, Joséphine—they call her Big Jo, a boxer's name—and Zaza. I shall have to separate them. For another thing, when she came she was still only convalescent. She was taken to the Maison d'Arrêt, half-starved and riddled with syphilis."

"Half-starved." Lise was startled. "Vivi!" Mademoiselle asked no questions but presently Lise herself asked, "And her sentence?"

"Five years. She was in the Rue Saint Denis—you know what that means. She robbed one of her clients while he slept; he was a salesman travelling in tools and she used one of those, a small hatchet, to attack him. No one, not he or others or even she, seems to know why."

"But Vivi! That spoiled darling. What happened? What could have happened?

"Get up and get out."

I was in bed when Emile came in, still half asleep, not ready to get up. Gaby had not brought my coffee; the blinds were not up, nor the curtains drawn back, but a slant of sun shone on the carpet and showed how dirty it was. We had not enough staff—I had told Milo that but he only shrugged. I stretched and yawned. "Where's Gaby?" Emile did not answer. He looked pale, his tie was wrinkled and he hadn't shaved—fastidious Milo. "What time is it?" but I had no need to ask; the church clock was striking twelve. "Where's Gaby? She isn't doing her work properly."

"She can't. She's gone," and Emile said—he hadn't lost his sneering calm—"We have escaped so far but now they are closing us down. There are to be no more 'houses.' "

214

"No more . . . what do you mean?"

"What I say. You will have to look out for yourself now." He patted my leg. "You have been a little blind, poupoule. You had better wake up and get up. The vans will be here soon for the furniture. If I were you I should pack a little suitcase quickly—not too big or I might see it—and go."

"Go? Go where?" Emile shrugged.

I still could not believe it; he was teasing me. "But—I haven't had my coffee."

"Without your coffee . . . in any case, it wasn't your coffee, it was mine and there's not going to be any more. Without anything, poupoule."

"But you—what will you do?"

"I have made my arrangements, my arrangements."

I lay on my back and looked at him. "But . . . us?" It was the wrong word. There never was an "us"—for me there was only "me."

Emile said, "I am taking the young ones."

"The young. . . ."

"Yes. Not you."

"Not me." I had to whisper it but it was true. I . . . Vivi . . . was forty-four. Vivi . . . la petite pouponne . . . the favourite.

"And I brought you all that money!" I shouted at him. "You made a fortune out of me."

"You had some too."

"I spent it."

"Silly you. I have mine tucked away," and Emile gave his frog smile.

"Monsieur Patrice would never have done this. He wouldn't have let them turn me out, take my things." I stormed at him but he only smiled. "If Monsieur had lived. . . ."

"But he didn't, did he? So get up—and get out."

In a slave-market you are sold by someone else and for work. That doesn't shame you, but standing in doorways or at corners you have to sell yourself. Funny, I never thought of it as shameful before but you're just an animal, for animals and beasts. Beasts! They look you over and pass along. You smile at them and they laugh in your face and you know they are right—you have nothing worth selling. I know now what Madame Lise meant when she talked to me, but I never thought I would be old and why did she talk and not do something—la salope.

At the Rue Duchesne I still looked young; I had a masseuse and Leo to do my hair; it soon had scabs in it and we, us of the streets, sat on the stairs and caught the nits in each other's hair. Emile used to keep me in trim; he stopped me eating cakes and bonbons. Well, there weren't any more cakes and bonbons; if there was any food we could beg or buy we brought it back and cooked it on a gas-ring in our room—when there was a room.

At first two of us older ones took a flat, a little apartment, and worked from there or tried to work; we were soon turned out—in any case, we couldn't pay the rent. Then it was bars. Clubs wouldn't have me, I was too old and when I told them I was Vivi Ambard, they said, "Who's she?" I was on the streets when Madame Lise found me but then I was a bony little ragamuffin and it was fun. I was used to being hungry and I didn't mind how hard I slept or if I slept at all, but now I was soft. One by one my things went—what I had taken from the Rue Duchesne—my fur coat, my earrings, clothes. They were my stock in trade, but. . . .

Sometimes I thought of Luigi; if he knew he might have helped. Luigi was always kind, except that day; but where is he now? I wrote to Italy but the letter came back. Giovanni-Battista Giuliano, my Morpion, must be grown up now. I was his mother but I don't know where he is either. There was no one and all the time the hate grew in me—until that fat pig of a man.

"You're no good," he said, "but at least there's a bed. Let me sleep and you needn't try to take my wallet. I made the precaution of taking all my money out and putting it in my hotel safe—and my watch and cuff-

links. Here's ten francs for you, pute." Ten francs, for a
whole evening!

"And a waste of money at that. Let me sleep," and the
hate burst like a gush of blood in my head, but the blood
was on him.

He had a case with his samples of tools, beautiful,
shining, all shown against purple satin; they had never
been used but they were sharp. There was a little hand
axe, the kind used for splitting faggots, and I split him,
his head, though I missed, but I got his cheek and his
shoulder and the great fat belly he had, the fat pig. He
screamed like the pig he was too, screamed and screamed,
and they came running in—there was no lock on the
door. They took away the axe but they couldn't put it
back against the purple satin; it was bloody and covered
with bits of him. I wished it had had more and when
they shouted at me, I laughed. I laughed and laughed. I
laughed because I didn't care—even when they took me
away.

"She asked questions about you," said Mademoiselle
Signoret afterwards, "but they were the ones to be
expected. 'Who are those frangines? Do they belong to
the prison?' and, 'When they visit do they come here
every day?'"

"Where were they going when we met them?" asked
Vivi.

"To lunch? The same time every day?"

"Ah! those questions ought to have put me on my
guard," said Mademoiselle.

Lise heard them coming. Perhaps they made more
noise than usual but she felt a tingle of warning,
enough to make her stop and put Soeur Marie Mercédes
behind her. The stairs of Le Fouest had never seemed
so steep; one could fall a hundred feet down their stone
and, "Hold to the handrail," Lise told Soeur Marie
Mercédes. "Keep your caliper close."

The three were foremost. Lise immediately recognised

Big Jo, her big front, huge forearms, close-cropped hair, and the one with the thin spiteful face must be Zaza; between them was Vivi. The wardress was behind, and the others were peaceably going on up the stairs when Vivi, flanked by her henchwomen, stopped on the same step as Lise and this time said, "Toi! Toi!" Vivi's voice shrilled through the shaft of the stairs. She burst into laughter, but then slapped Lise full in the face.

"You a nun! *Toi!*— une frangine! Mes amies, I'll tell you who she is—Madame Lise, Mère Maquerelle . . . La Balafrée." With a quick twitch she switched back Lise's veil. "See that scar? Look at it. She got it in a fight between two drunks. Ask her. Ask if she isn't a murderess and a whore. *Ask* her! Madame Lise—a holy Sister! It was she who kept the bordel where she took me when I was fourteen and, when our patron protected me, she killed him. She, your angel, was in a prison like Le Fouest for fifteen years, just like us, like you, like me, but worse, because she's a fake. Fake! Get at her!" screamed Vivi, and before the stunned listeners could move, Vivi, Big Jo and Zaza set to work. They wrenched Lise away from Soeur Marie Mercédes; Zaza tore off her veil, quite off, Big Jo her tunic; one of Jo's fists pounded her in the eye while Vivi's nails tore her face and neck.

It was only a moment. "Non! Non! Non!" It was the other prisoners who interfered; perhaps they had divined there might be trouble but not like this. Still, they were quick. Two moved in to protect Soeur Marie Mercédes; two went to Lise; one of them pulled up her tunic; the other, sobbing had her prison handkerchief out, trying to stanch the blood. The wardress, who had blown her whistle and run up, was still at the back and a fight was in full battle on the staircase. Big Joe had already thrown one girl down the flight; the steps were a horror of flailing arms and kicks. Vivi and Zaza, already seized by the women, were shaken like rats, but Big Jo held her ground until two more wardresses came running down from the floor above; they stayed to lock the doors of their division behind them. "We might have had all the prisoners out," and Madame Chef was quickly on the scene. All the while, Soeur Marie Mercédes, her caliper held to her side, her hand necessarily clinging to the rail, stood, her lips moving in prayer. "It was all I could do," she told Lise afterwards. "Ah! God forgive me, how I should have liked to join in!" but, when Vivi and Zaza and Big Jo had been taken away, the others came and kissed her, some were trying and, "It was almost worth it," Lise told Mademoiselle afterwards, "worth it to feel that protection and love, and from some we hadn't even seen."

"Ma Soeur, you are terribly marked," said the prison infirmarian Soeur Justine of Marie Joseph, in distress as she finished cleaning Lise's face.

"Worse than before?" Lise tried to joke through the pain and smarting.

"Much worse. Those scratches are deep. She really clawed you." Indeed, the marks showed for weeks.

"Somebody has scratched you—hurt you." Lucette came running as soon as, back at Belle Source, Lise left chapel after Vespers. "I know. It was somebody in that prison."

"Lucette, it's only scratches."

"Only!" Lucette was shaken with emotion and pity. I thought she had learned to be calm, thought Lise. At Belle Source, Lucette, Soeur Lucie, now in her temporary vows, was invaluable; as under-infirmarian, she seemed to glory in the work no one wanted—if they were honest with themselves—that of looking after the very old nuns, one bedridden. No matter how cantankerous they were, difficult or confused, sometimes incontinent, Soeur Lucie bore it all, did all the sordid things with infinite patience and love; by day or by night, strength seemed to be given to her puniness. "They love her and she loves them!" Soeur Marie

Emmanuel said in wonder, but now Lucette was like a tiger. "Someone did it. If I knew who she was, I would kill her, and Soeur Marie Mercédes said you went back next day."

"Of course I went back."

There was surprise at Le Fouest when Lise had appeared next morning and with some a backlash: a few of the women came expressly to look at her. "So—you were one of us." Usually it was said with astonishment, but sometimes with arms akimbo or a toss of the head. "One of us!"

"Yes."

"Quel dommage! Pity!" And the tongue came out.

There was also genuine bewilderment. "Why did you pretend?"

"I didn't pretend."

"If she were pretending she wouldn't be here now, would she?" For once Soeur Marie Mercédes's voice was rough.

"I—suppose not. I never thought of that."

"Well—think." Then the voice became as tender as it had been severe and Soeur Marie Mercédes quoted what Père Lataste had said and she had quoted a thousand times before. "It's not what you were, but what you are now and what you want to be, that God beholds with his merciful eyes."

Only one prisoner asked, "Ma Soeur, could I do the same?"

During the week presents were brought, touching in their smallness but each a sacrifice: a bar of chocolate bought at the canteen: a handkerchief made in the work-room: a miniature bouquet of feather flowers fashioned from snippets dropped on the floor. They were put on the table in front of Lise with a shy, "Pour vous," or left with a note, "For Soeur Marie Lise."

"Mademoiselle, should I see Vivi?"

"Certainly not. She's like a wild cat. She would tear you in pieces if she could."

Vivi was in the punishment block, as were Big Jo and Zaza. Now, Mademoiselle left her desk and came to sit by the fire, near Lise. "Soeur Marie Lise, do you know anything about Vivi's life before you found her? Where she came from? Who she was?"

"She wouldn't tell me anything. She told the others tales."

"Which she is still telling," said Mademoiselle. "The latest is that she was stolen by gipsies."

"Now and then, when she wanted to be pathetic," said Lise, "it used to be an orphanage, which was probably nearest to the truth."

"It was worse than an orphanage." Mademoiselle looked into the fire. "It was the local Maison Dieu, part or old people's home, part lunatic asylum, where she should never have been put, but it was wartime. . . ."

"Was the Maison Dieu run by Sisters?" interrupted Lise.

"No, by the town. Vivi's father . . ." Mademoiselle stopped. "What is it, ma Soeur?"

"I know there are facts," said Lise, "but what concerns me—I expect it seems beside the point but it isn't, it really does concern me—is how did she get that rosary?"

If Madame Grebel had held out her hand to me, Vivi, if she had held out her arms that day in the Grande Salle, would everything have been different? I don't know.

"What can I give you, ma petite?" Madame Lachaume used to ask me in despair. It was after they had given me the baby doll and I went into hysterics so dreadfully they had to call the doctor to me and Pom-Pom was so frightened he hid under the beds. "What can I give you?"

I said, "Beads." She had a string too, I had seen them, but they were wooden and ugly. "Beads, but pink, like Renée's."

Madame smiled at me, "One day, when you know what to do with them. Ask Mamaine to teach you," and she was pleased and put my hair back as she always did when she was pleased. "She has a good disposition, this little one. P'tite bien aimée—poor little love." What she didn't know, poor Madame Lachaume, was that I had had the beads for six months. I stole them from Renée. They were pink, pink pearl on a silver chain, and divided into tens, and at the end of the necklace a few beads hung down and on the end was a tiny cross in silver. When Mamaine was not looking, I used to take them and put them round my neck and loop the end over my ear so that the cross hung down like an earring.

It was a funny thing; when I put the beads on the way I said, Pom-Pom did not like it. He pulled my dress and whimpered. Rico, of course, didn't notice anything; he had his coloured pencils and was doing his kind of drawing, smiling as if he saw the pictures in the air. Renée went to sleep over her knitting because she ate so much at dinner. Mamaine went down for hers so then I brushed my hair with my brush and put on the beads and the silver cross hung down and caught the light. I looked very very pretty but there was no one to show them to, so I thought, One day I'll show them to Stefan.

Though Stefan was wrong in the head which was why he was in the men's wing, he was not as wrong as the others; and, by and by, because there were so few guards, he was let out to get the dinner trolleys; every day he wheeled them from the kitchen and every day he wheeled them back again, before we came down to the courtyard—before, because we were not supposed to see Stefan. Mamaine had the key to the staircase door, but sometimes when she went to her dinner she forgot to lock it; if she did forget, I used to open it and go a little way down just to look at Stefan. Mamaine went for an hour so there was plenty of time. I watched him wheel the trolleys away; I watched him come back and sometimes the guards didn't let him in at once.

Mamaine didn't know I watched him, but I think he knew.

When I came back from the Grande Salle that day I wouldn't eat my dinner. Renée laughed. "Pauvre petite! Pauvre petite fille." It was in imitation of Madame Lachaume and I threw a plate at her. The plate broke and Pom-Pom began to cry. Mamaine scolded and I threw another plate at Mamaine; it had gravy and haricots on it and made a mess all over the table. Pom ran to hide under the beds but I didn't care. After dinner I unravelled Renée's knitting and it was I who pinched Rico.

When Mamaine went down to her dinner she was so upset she forgot to lock the door.

Renée was crying over her spoiled knitting and wouldn't notice me; Rico doesn't notice anyone and Pom-Pom was under my bed.

I put the beads round my neck. I brushed my hair and looped the end of the chain over my ear so that the cross hung down to catch the light. I looked in the mirror and laughed. It was true what Madame Grebel said—I am too beautiful.

Then I went downstairs in my beads to show them to Stefan.

"The father, a labourer, Paul Sordeau, got fifteen years for assault and infanticide," said Mademoiselle. "It wasn't only Vivi—Viviane is her real name—it seems there was an older girl who had a baby which was smothered under grain sacks. The girl disappeared. When Vivi was found she was sleeping on a heap of old turnips on the farm for fear of her father, but the damage was done. She escaped from the Maison Dieu with one of the inmates, a Russian who was simple; they found them of course, that poor wretched creature and Vivi; it seems they were just in time. Vivi was only eleven but already. . . . She ran away from every place she was put in, and you can imagine how difficult it was to find anywhere in those war years; the last was an experimental school run by the famous Ralph Marise; for a while it seemed successful—Ralph is an attractive person but, like everyone else, he hadn't enough staff and Vivi, with an older girl, Suzanne . . . but you know the rest," and Mademoiselle looked from the fire directly at Lise. "Ma Soeur, why does she hate you?"

"I think," Lise said slowly, "what I did, or tried to do, should have been the other way round; the opposite of all they tell you about dealing with delinquents, and I suppose Vivi was delinquent; that you should always show them you believe in them and that, given a chance, they have a better side. I think the rosary she loved misled me. I believed Vivi was good under it all, touchingly good—and she wasn't good, so, of course, she couldn't be. If I had accepted her just as she was . . . but I suppose I was as blind as Luigi. Poor Luigi."

"Not quite as blind. He couldn' forgive her, while you. . . ."

"I always could, and did," Lise admitted. "Over and over again. But I could never get near her."

"Just as well." Mademoiselle rose. "I am having her transferred to Vesoul—for her sake and for ours. Too many emotions have been stirred up and, in any case, she must be—separated from Big Jo and Zaza—and I hope, Soeur Marie Lise, that you need never encounter her again."

"No," said Lise, "and yet . . . I have a feeling it's still not completed."

Chapter Ten

AMONG ALL THE CHANGES, there was a new innovation for Béthanie: Saint Xavier sent their novices to make a tour of the different French houses and a party was coming to Belle Source. "God help us," said old Soeur Anne Colombe. "They'll make a nice mess of my clean floors."

"I'm sure they won't," said the Prioress. "We'll probably find them most helpful."

"In my day, novices were strictly cloistered; we weren't allowed to go gadding all over the place."

They certainly went "all over the place," but not to gad; they not only took courses in Paris; all of them met, mingled with and talked to the groups of men and women, often from overseas, who came to stay at Saint Etienne or the bigger guest-house newly built at Saint Xavier. "Ironically," said Lise, "they probably meet more people than they did before they entered what is called the 'cloistered life,' and certainly more different nationalities. It's wise because now they may be sent anywhere in the world." The light from that tiny ray kindled at Cadillac was spreading like the beam from a lighthouse across the sea, a searchlight; "searching." That was a great word with the nuns, "She is searching." "Has she a vocation?" "Only time can tell, but she is searching," and, "It's not that there are more Sisters of Béthanie; in fact, as we spread, the houses necessarily grow smaller—in all we are still only five hundred, still so few."

"But I have seen what that few can do," said Marc, and he laughed. "Perhaps I have lost my box-office attitude at last, thank God."

How different he is now, thought Lise. Two short years at Belle Source. . . .

"It's our milk and fresh food," said Soeur Thecla.

"Our salads," said Soeur Fiacre.

"It's yourselves," Father Louis was firm.

Twice Father Louis had chosen to spend the short annual holiday he allowed himself with Marc in the aumônier's little house. "I love this Belle Source of yours," he said. It was a gala day for the sisters when Father Louis came.

To have Dominicans again! This for Belle Source was wonderful luck. "So often our convents have to share the parish priests, good holy men, but not like having our own aumônier," Soeur Thecla told Lise. "One should be grateful for anyone, but secular priests are not trained in the Rule of an Order." Marc, for instance, came naturally to Lauds and Vespers, not officiating but as part of the community. He said his Midday Prayer and Compline. On Saint Dominic's Day, sometimes on other feasts, he was invited to recreation when usually the lower domaine was closed to all outsiders. Unless he had guests at the aumônier's house, and often then, especially if the guest were Father Louis, he ate in the guest-house. "It might help in the work," he said diffidently.

"Indeed yes. Just being with people often helps them," said the Prioress.

He relieved Lise of some of the driving, "and if anyone is taken ill, or there is an emergency, we can call on him day or night."

The nuns, in fact, had found a brother. "I haven't had a brother before," said Lise. "It's pleasant."

"I wouldn't have believed it would be pleasant to have some forty sisters," said Marc, "but it is."

Marc, though, was astonished at the novices. "But where are the white veils?" he asked, "I thought all novices wore them."

"So did we—once upon a time," said Lise. "In fact, I had to, but perhaps we have grown wiser and more merciful."

"Merciful?"

"Yes. You see, some who come with . . . difficulties, may have to remain novices for a long time, and that white veil is distinctive. Now, when anyone is Clothed, she goes straight into the full habit, so that no one who isn't intimate knows who are novices, who in temporary vows, who professed."

For five hilarious days the three novices—habited as Lise had said—and two postulants, wearing jeans and tee-shirts, joined in the life at Belle Source and already Soeur Marie Isabelle was pleading for at least one; Soeur Marie Isabelle—Bella of the old days and now Prioress of a new American house—was back in France to attend the Chapitre Général of the Order and, to Lise's joy, had been granted a holiday at Belle Source. "Just one little novice," she pleaded. "That would be riches."

"And I'm pleading too," said Soeur Thecla, "for that little Marie Jeanne. She wants to come here."

"To milk?" Lise teased, smiling.

"It's no smiling matter." For once Soeur Thecla was sharp. "I can't last for ever and what will happen to Belle Source and our cows then? You don't know how I have prayed and prayed that God would send us someone capable and He has."

"I shouldn't have teased," Lise told Marc in contrition. "What Soeur Thecla says is true. We still need our domaines. There are still bruised and uncertain souls who need the peace and health."

"Still?" said Marc. "More—many many more."

The novitiate did not please all the nuns. "They argue," said the older ones, scandalised. "I think they should," said their Responsable, Soeur Magdaleine Martine who, after two others, had succeeded Soeur Raymonde of Lise's time. "Our Lord dearly loved an argument and, after all, He always had the best answer, didn't He?"

In particular, there was Anouk, the second postulant. "She's dirty," Soeur Anne Colombe said what she meant, and others, more gentle, begged the Responsable, "Soeur Magdaleine Martine, can't you get her at least to brush her hair?"

"She does sometimes," Soeur Magdaleine Martine was unperturbed, "but it's difficult for Anouk. She's a born scruff."

"La pauvre!" said Soeur Marie Isabelle—Bella— remembering her own struggles with her shock of frizzy hair.

"But Anouk's language! Sister, she *swears*!"

"So did I," said Bella and, "She tries hard not to." Soeur Magdaleine Martine defended her chicken. "In fact, she tries hard over everything. She's one of the most sincere but she must have been brought up roughly, and she's a little naïve."

"A little!"

Each of the visiting five took her turn for the half-hour watch or Adoration before the Exposition. "But ... they sit on the *floor*!" expostulated Soeur Anne Colombe.

"At Saint Xavier we all sit on the floor if we want to," said Soeur Madaleine Martine. "It is, you know, good for contemplation. Give them a cushion," she said and, each morning after Mass when the monstrance had been put on the altar, a flat cushion was laid on the floor beside the customary prie-dieu.

The novitiate visit coincided with a time of pressure at Belle Source; the infirmarian was away; one of the older nuns had fallen ill, another was in hospital; it was, too, the time for fruit-picking and jam-making, so that the house was grateful for the young ones' help, especially knowing that one of them could always be called on to come to the chapel to reinforce or keep steadfast the worship and prayer that was the core, the heart of Béthanie.

Often they watched alone. One day Lise, over-busy with car-driving, helping the porteress, acting as infirmarian, had had to miss her half-hour and, having a lull, slipped, on the quarter, into the back of the chapel for fifteen minutes' respite. She knelt, hidden by the height of the cantor's music stand.

The half-hour struck and into the chapel came Anouk. She genuflected, going reverently down on both knees and touched the nun on the prie-dieu gently on the shoulder; the two exchanged smiles; before going out the sister gently touched the girl's hair, that disputed hair, as Anouk settled cross-legged on the cushion.

Anouk glanced round; seeing no one, she obviously thought she was alone and put on the floor beside her a small transistor. For a few minutes she sat motionless, praying, thought Lise, then bent, turned a switch and the chapel was filled with rollicking raucous music.

Lise herself almost jumped upright, then waited and watched to see what would happen. Anouk sat rapt, her fact uplifted to the star of the monstrance, happy and dutiful, but the noise was so loud it penetrated the thick glass doors that usually shut out all sound between chapel and ante-chapel; outside there began to be conternation; scandalised faces were pressed against the glass doors; frenzied sisters gathered, someone ran—for the Responsable, guessed Lise—while Anouk sat on, her body swaying slightly to the rhythm, lost in the music and her joy.

"Well! What could you say about that?" the indignant sisters asked Soeur Magdaleine Martine.

"First I had to find out why Anouk did it; whether, for her, it was a programme she wanted to listen to herself or whether it was from the best of motives."

"*What* best of motives?" As several sisters asked that together, it sounded like the burst of a grenade and, "Let Soeur Magdaleine Martine explain," said the Prioress.

"If she can," and there were glowers.

"Anouk played her transistor because she thought our Seigneur would like to hear it," said Soeur Magdaleine Martine.

"*Like* it. That hullabaloo!"

"Granted it isn't exactly Bach's Jésu, Joy of man's desiring," Soeur Magdaleine Martine admitted and Soeur Marie Mercédes laughed, that unexpectedly rippling and infectious laugh, and some of the nuns began to laugh as well.

"Ma Mère," Anouk had said to Soeur Magdaleine Martine. "It was from *Godspell*. That's the English musical about Jesus, all the rage in London. The words are from an old old prayer . . . 'Let me see you more clearly, Love you more dearly, Follow you more nearly, Every day,'" and Anouk said, "Our Lord may have heard it in London, but I'm certain He hasn't heard it in Normandy, so I tried to pick it up for Him on my transistor and I did."

"Pah!" The posse was still outraged.

"Mes Soeurs," said Soeur Marie Emmanuel, "would you condemn Le Jongleur de Notre Dame, the poor lay brother in the story who juggled to amuse Our Lady?"

After that, "Anouk, our petite jongleuse," the sisters called her with pride.

Marc had hired a small bus and drove the novices, "a merciful dispensation when we are so busy," said Lise. "I can guess Father Louis was behind that."—Father Louis was spending yet another holiday at Belle Source. Marc drove them far down in the countryside to Solesmes where they heard the beauty of the Chant, the magnificent ritual carried out by some hundred monks. "But you know," said Marie Jeanne, "I like our simple little Vespers better." He took them to Chartres, "Surely the most beautiful cathedral in the world." They went on picnics to the sea and in the nearby woods and every day he gave them a short conference. "Not a conference, it's more like questions and answers." He smiled. "It's they who usually supply the answers," but the smile was tender.

"For someone who was going to stagnate you seem remarkably busy," said Father Louis.

It was not the convent; the villagers had begun to come to Marc; with the Prioress's permission he had started a catechism class in the guest-house, "And he's an excellent confessor," said the nuns. Even Soeur Marie Mercédes, with her exacting standards, granted that. "He preaches without pretence," she said with satisfaction. Not only preached; shyly at first, he had revived the Sunday conference the sisters used to have. "It takes me hours to work one out," he told Father Louis.

"It would," and more difficult still Marc sometimes gave one in the week, light and often amusing, on current affairs.

"Can't the novitiate hear one of those too?" begged Soeur Magdaleine Martine.

"I think one day," said Lise, "they will ask for you at Saint Etienne or Saint Xavier."

"Do you think they will?" His face lit up. He had come to post his letters and found Lise acting as porteress.

"Where you wouldn't be wasted?" Lise teased him. "In a rut?"

"You have been talking to Father Louis."

"No," said Lise. "I guessed that you fought against coming here, but, as you see, there isn't a rut and these girls are new life—and perhaps more real. When Bella and I were made novices, given the habit, the priest, as was the ritual, offered us two crowns, one of white

231

roses, the other of thorns—we wondered what would happen if one of us chose the roses."

"It had to be the thorns."

"Yes. To be a nun of Béthanie isn't easy and many of us were such innocents, but now there's not the same need to warn. These children have grown up among thorns."

"Yet I suppose," said Marc, "it's perhaps a hundred, even a thousand times more difficult to be a monk or nun now than it was fifty years ago."

"I don't know," and Lise said, "There are still a few—they have always been few—that have such faith that once it has been kindled they see nothing else. Most of us, even after the 'call,' waver; we have to struggle, but a few mysteriously go straight to the crux."

"Am I too old?" asked Big Jo.

It had been two days after the battle on the stairs at Le Fouest that Big Jo had asked to see Soeur Marie Lise and Soeur Marie Mercédes, but particularly Soeur Marie Mercédes, "Madame Foret, the wardress in charge of the punishment block, thinks you should," said Mademoiselle. "But are you nervous? I can send a wardress with you."

"That would be against everything we are trying to do." Soeur Marie Mercédes was decided. And, "I'm not nervous," said Lise. "I never have been of Big Jo. Of course, I have only seen and passed her; she hasn't visited us. It's Zaza who gives me the shivers."

"Yes, she's one of those." Mademoiselle Signoret said it sadly. "Mal dans sa peau—evil personified."

"Pauvre femme," said Soeur Marie Mercédes.

"Everything we try to do she twists and distorts," said Mademoiselle. "Big Jo was never like that, only mulish and violent. If we let her in to the workrooms, she wrecked them; she terrorised the other women. I should have said she was one of the 'irrécupérables,' but I was wrong. You'll see."

Big Jo came into Madame Foret's small office, but was this Big Jo? With her heavy stride she strode into the little room seeming to fill it. She's as big as a lorry driver, thought Lise, but she was washed and clean, her hair, though still rough, was brushed back with an attempt to hold it by a comb and the face that had always been sullen was radiant. She went straight to Soeur Marie Mercédes and knelt down and took her hand. Lise made a quick movement—those bones were so brittle—but the huge red hands were gentle, and reverent. "Ma Soeur," said Big Jo—the voice was husky—"ma Soeur, you didn't know but I nearly punched you."

"I thought you might," said Soeur Marie Mercédes, unmoved.

"If I had, I would have broken your arm or your shoulder and I should never have forgiven myself, never ... these little bones." For a moment Big Jo looked almost disbelievingly at the hand in her own, at the fine skin and bones. "If I had!" Lise had seen that the small eyes were sore, red-rimmed as if Big Jo had been crying—For a long time, thought Lise—and now a tear fell on Soeur Marie Mercédes's hands, then more. "Excuse me," said Big Jo, but the sister held her fast.

"These are good tears," said Soeur Marie Mercédes and, "Ma Soeur! Ma Soeur!" Big Jo's head went down on Soeur Marie Mercédes's lap; the hand that was free stroked the rough hair. "Ma fille," said Soeur Marie Mercédes. "Ma pauvre fille."

Big Jo dried her eyes on her sleeve, knelt up and faced them. "Am I too old? Does one have to be a girl?"

"For Béthanie?" Soeur Marie Mercédes had understood at once. "Well, we once had an aspirant—someone who comes to try—of eighty."

"Did she turn into a frangine—I mean a nun?"

"A very good nun."

"Bon!" A huge sigh. "I have three more years to serve. Then I shall come."

"Dear Jo," said Lise. "This doesn't happen in a moment."

"It has." Big Jo was triumphant.

"But do you believe in instant conversion?" Lise asked Soeur Marie Mercédes afterwards.

"Of course. Wasn't there Saint Paul?" asked Soeur Marie Mercédes, and then, "Remember what Big Jo said."

"It was as if I was given new eyes, ma Soeur," she had said, turning to Soeur Marie Mercédes. "I saw you shining with sunlight."

"Nonsense," said Soeur Marie Mercédes. "There is no sun on those stairs."

"Exactly." Big Jo was even more triumphant. "Yet you were shining and I knew, because he told me so."

"He?"

"Le Seigneur. Who else?" asked Big Jo impatiently. "One day I shall be wearing that white habit."

"Well, I'll be damned!" said Lise when Big Jo had been taken away.

"We have had her before," said Soeur Marie Mercédes. "Yes, other Big Jos. At Belle Source, with our visit from the novices, we have been looking forwards; that is good but perhaps we should look back too. Big Jo is like the 'petites soeurs' of Père Lataste's time, or those poor women of Cadillac our first sisters visited. They had to talk to them through the shutter of their cells; it was years and years before they were allowed to see prisoners in privacy. There was one called Hélène, condemned to twenty years. She used to cling to the shutter, watching them out of sight, poor soul. She said their white clothes shone in that gloom," said Soeur Marie Mercédes. "You see Big Jo was right about the light." Mère Henri Dominique wrote of another called Alice, in for twenty years too. "Don't go near Alice," the sisters were told. "Don't put your hand through the shutter. She is a brute." A brute! When they spoke to Alice, she burst into tears. When one took her hand, she drew that sister's hand in and covered it with kisses. "It's a continuing miracle," said Soeur Marie Mercédes, but it was a difficult miracle.

"We'll bring you some books," Lise told Big Jo.

"Books! Mes lapins, I can't read—read or write," said Big Jo.

"Then in the years you still have to spend here, they'll teach you. I'll talk to the éducatrice."

Big Jo gave a pitying smile. "Ma fille—pardon—ma Soeur—I'm made of wood, wood!" Odd, thought Lise, I once said that of myself. "Thick as two planks," said Jo cheerfully, "I'll do the work of two men when I come; I was a fishwife at Le Havre, used to lift crates and barrels, blocks of ice, but don't ask me to read or write."

After the novices and the postulants had gone Belle Source seemed extraordinarily quiet. "We needed that visit," said Soeur Marie Emmanuel and, except Soeur Thecla who mourned for Marie Jeanne, of all the girls, the sisters missed Anouk most. "Who would have thought it!" To Lise, though, the peace was balm—"The days get richer and richer." There was her friendship with Mademoiselle and Marc and Soeur Marie Mercédes who had had to admit she had become too frail for prison visiting. Lise was the senior visitor now but often came to sit by the older nun and ask her advice.

When Big Jo was released it presented a problem. "We can't send her to a foyer," Soeur Raymonde, still the Mother-General, said to Lise when she went to Saint Xavier to talk it over. "Yet she isn't ready for Saint Etienne." In the end, Big Jo went to work in a market garden near enough to Belle Source for her to visit Soeur Marie Mercédes and Lise every month. "A little patience and you will come to Béthanie completely, enter Saint Etienne as an aspirant. This is only for now." To Big Jo it seemed nonsense; the old Jo would have fought it, but this new one said, "If they want it that way. . . ."

"But she must learn," said Lise. "She knows nothing."

"Except the one thing that matters," said Soeur Marie Mercédes. "But certainly she must know a little of scripture, customs, prayers."

"How?" asked Lise. "It would mean *hours* of patience. We only see her once a month and the local priest has several parishes to serve and he is getting old. It needs someone who would understand, read a little to her at a time, explain, get her to repeat, slowly bring her. . . ." Soeur Marie Mercédes and Lise looked at one another and both said, "Père Marc."

"Would he?"

"I know he would."

"It's quite a long way to drive—just for one person."

"One can be more important than the ninety-nine."

"Yes," said Marc when he heard, and with fervour, "Yes!"

For him too something unexpected had happened—not as surprising as Big Jo but unexpected, "and maybe glorious," he said, trying to keep excitement out of his voice. "I may be wrong but it makes me feel that nothing, nothing at all is wasted." A Chinese girl from his parish at Kowloon was coming to Saint Etienne. "First as a visitor of course—just to see—then, we hope, as an aspirant." She was not an indigent girl, one of Marc's "rags and tags" as Father Louis called them, but the daughter of a well-to-do family whose father was a Christian. "Lee Wan Tsui is educated—for instance, she speaks French—this would be impossible for her without that. Perhaps it is a sign," said Marc and, "I think—believe—she has a vocation."

"Are you sure it's a vocation and not Father Marc?" teased Louis.

"For a time perhaps it was Father Marc," Marc was serious. "But I haven't seen her for two years. There have, of course, been letters."

"Constant letters."

"Necessarily so, but Wan Tsui knows when she comes to France it's unlikely I shall see her, at any rate for some time. She will be at Saint Etienne, I here, though

236

I might be at Saint Xavier if she comes there later on. Besides, long before she met me she had wanted to be a nun: she tried one of the Orders in Hong Kong but teaching or nursing didn't seem right for her. She was searching, then suddenly Béthanie. . . . I don't know why."

"Except somehow it always seems to happen like that," said Lise.

"For Wan Tsui it will all be so strange, no one can tell how it will turn out, but. . . ."

"All the same you have brought us Béthanie's first aspirant from the Far East. . . ."

"Perhaps it *is* a sign," said Marc.

"More like a sign-post," said Lise.

In farewell, Mademoiselle Signoret had given Big Jo what seemed an extraordinary present, "and an extremely expensive one," said Lise, "but priceless to Big Jo." It was a museum reproduction in a limited edition of a Book of Hours with page after page of miniature paintings showing scenes from the Bible in borders of flowers, leaves, jewels, minute portraits and grotesques. "For Big Jo!" Lise had been dumbfounded but, "Don't you see," said Mademoiselle, "It's like stained glass windows which were the Bible of the poor. Big Jo can't read but she can conjure up the meaning of each picture."

When Big Jo first took the book into her hands, they trembled. "For me?" but, as she turned the pages, the trembling was forgotten in wonder. She kept the book wrapped in a cloth and washed her hands before she touched it. "The little pictures," she said, looking at the background landscapes of castles and farms, hills, rocks, meadows; her coarse forefinger endlessly traced the intricacies of the borders; her eyes loving the flowers and fruit, laughing at the monkeys, the ass laden with faggots, the bee-hives, symbol of purity. "I believe she looks at it every day," Lise told Mademoiselle. "And to think," said Big Jo, "I called that one 'cette enculée!' "

* * *

Summer, autumn, winter, spring, summer came and went, "like a flash," said Lise; now it was autumn again and an uncommonly hot one. As she carried up baskets of apples to the cider heap in the courtyard, Lise was sweating. She had spent the whole morning picking up windfalls, shaking the trees and climbing them. "No one would think you were over fifty," Soeur Fiacre had called up.

"Fifty-five," Lise called back. "But it's funny—I feel younger now than I did at twenty." All the same, with the weight of the baskets and the sun she was panting; Lucette appeared, small, reproachful. "Soeur Marie Lise, you shouldn't be carrying that basket by yourself. It's far too heavy."

"I don't need a nounou, thank you." The inevitable irritation broke; Lucette shrank back as she always did when Lise was sharp—Lise could not forget that. At the same time as Lucette, the porteress, Soeur Elizabeth, ran out from the lodge. "Soeur Marie Lise, telephone."

It was Mademoiselle. "Marie Lise?"

"Yes."

"Vivi Ambard was released last week."

"Vivi!" It was like an arrow—no, a bullet—shattering the peace. "Vivi! I had almost forgotten about her."

"That's what I guessed," said Mademoiselle, "which is why I'm ringing. Vivi hasn't forgotten. She came here yesterday, ostensibly asking to see Zaza, but I think it was really to find out where you were. We wouldn't allow her near Zaza, of course, but I saw Vivi. I saw her myself simply because I was worried for you, and I think I'm right. Prison has done a great deal for Vivi, physically—regular food and sleep and exercise. For all her age she is blooming, still beautiful—attractive—and she knows how to wheedle. I'm afraid of a leak."

"But what leak could reach me?"

"I don't know," said Mademoiselle, "but for some reason I'm apprehensive. Lise, I beg you . . . take care."

"Take care. Why?" But Mademoiselle had rung off.

They think they can stop me from finding out where that salope, that pute, Madame Lise, is—but they can't. It's all her fault, always has been her fault, and when she broke my beads, she broke my luck I'll find her somehow. This time she won't escape.

"What do you want?" Madame la Directrice said it without the least flicker of pity, like the monument she is. I had hoped it would be the éducatrice, or even Madame Chef, anyone but her, that old cow. "What do you want?"

"Just to be allowed to see Zaza, my friend, for five minutes."

"You know very well you can't."

"If I knew that I shouldn't be here, should I?"

I couldn't stop myself being impertinent—she's like a lighted match on petrol. She tried to quell me with a look but I am still myself, Vivi, and "If you won't let me see Zaza, at least give me Big Jo's address."

"I can't do that either."

"Why not? You can't stop me seeing Big Jo. She's free."

She did not answer, only pressed her bell and sent for a wardress. "Take Vivi out, right out."

As a parting present I spat full on her papers. I wish it could have reached her face, but outside the gate I didn't know what to do. It's like a chain; I knew before I left Le Fouest for Vesoul that Jo—big silly—had gone over to the frangines . . . she was blubbing and bellowing about her sins. She could never keep her mouth shut and she would have told Zaza where she would go when they let her out and I could have made Big Jo speak, easily—but now. I sat down on the curb to think.

The devil looks after his own. Monsieur Patrice used to tease Madame Lise by saying that, and it is true—I sat there and I was so furious I began to cry. I cried and cried and then the girl came along.

She was a wardress. I could see the white uniform

239

*under her coat but she was young and her gold hair was
fine and pale, like Rico's; I think, like Rico, she was not
altogether here—she was smiling at everything, the sky,
the trees, the street, humming a little tune, and walking
as if the pavement was made of air—perhaps she was in
love. I cried harder than ever and she, the ninny, stopped
as I guessed she would.*

"Madame, something's wrong? Why are you sitting
on the pavement? And you're crying. Are you hurt?"

"No." *I made big tears fall and rocked myself.* "They
have hurt. Hurt me."

"How? Who?"

"Madame—Madame la Directrice. Oh, she's cruel."

"Madame cruel? Never."

"You know only one side. You don't know the other.
You can't—you're one of them."

"There must be a misunderstanding," *but I shook my
head.* "At least get up. There! Here's a handkerchief,"
and, as I wiped my eyes and blew my nose like a child,
"When did you see Madame?"

"Just now. She threw me out."

"But why?"

"I don't know—except she always had it in for me. She
sent me away before to Vesoul . . . I only came out
yesterday. I didn't want to come here but I had to . . . I
had to. I had to ask. . . ."

"For what?"

"Only if I could see Zaza—just for a minute."

"Zaza!" *That shook her and for a moment she was
wary, careful. I had to cry again.* "I know nobody likes
her, poor Zaza, but Mademoiselle, if they told you you
were an irrécupérable, went on telling you, wouldn't you
be one?"

"I never thought of that."

"Nor do they. Zaza's a good friend," *more crying.*
"She would have told me at once."

"Told you what?"

"I need—I have to know where my dear Big Jo is."

"Big Jo. I have heard of her, not seen her, but I haven't been here very long."

I could have told her that! "Big Jo was here with us and should have come out two years ago. She promised when my turn came she would help me, find me work, so I could go straight . . . give me a chance. Now," I sobbed. "How can she when I don't know where she is?"

"If you explained this to Madame. . . ."

"I did. I did. She wouldn' listen," and I mocked just like Madame, "It's against regulations for a prisoner to see an ex-prisoner. . . . No matter what, or how hurtful."

"It seems—inhuman," said my little rabbit.

"It is. We're not poison, Mademoiselle. What harm could there be in an address?"

"I'll ask Madame Chef if I. . . ."

"Not Madame Chef—she's against me too—but Mademoiselle—if you could yourself. . . . You haven't had time to grow hard, callous, you have only to ask Zaza. I know Big Jo would have told her. Zaza wouldn't have to write anything—you could scribble it down yourself. . . . I would wait here till you come off duty."

"That won't be till evening and—I have to meet somebody. . . ." She blushed.

"I'll wait. I would wait all night—and I won't be in the way. I'll disappear at once. Oh, Mademoiselle, please, please."

Chapter Eleven

IT WAS TWELVE O'CLOCK, time for dinner, but Lise was in the chapel, "watching." This was the half-hour she always chose because of the silence. The refectory was at the back of the old château and thick-walled, as were the kitchens beyond, so that while they were busy the whole domaine was as quiet as it was empty; the glass doors shut off all sound from the ante-chapel. It was also the watching time that no one else wanted; women who began their day at six, had only a cup of coffee and bread for breakfast and worked all morning needed no excuse for being famished at midday. "But you, ma Soeur, what about you?" Soeur Marie Emmanuel was far too careful of her flock to let any of them go hungry. "I can have mine afterwards," said Lise. "For years I was used to eat at any time. Please, ma Mère."

This was what Lise still loved best, to be alone in the chapel, alone with Him; to be, for a few minutes, really like Mary Magdalen who, ignoring everything else, chose that "better part," to sit at His feet and hear Him. For Lise it could usually only be half an hour—one of the others would come and relieve her; most days it was not a relief but an interruption because sometimes Lise would lose herself utterly, only for a moment, or what seemed to be a moment—she often found, to her surprise, it had been the whole half-hour; then the tap on her shoulder came as a painful shock. She had soared—there was no other way to put it—into a nothingness, a mist, the Cloud of Unknowing in the book of all books she loved best to read; a cloud but perhaps, one day, some day, she would pierce it and be truly lost into infinity, and she was finding more and more the way to that was not through prayers and thought; it seemed simply to be the repeating of one word. Just as the book said, someone burning to death does not use sentences but cries "Help!" or "Fire!" so one word seems to deliver me, thought Lise; sometimes "Lord" or "Seigneur," sometimes simply "Love"; often even that one word gave way to silence and oblivion.

Then no sound or whisper reached her, not the ticking of the clock, the door opening quietly or, through the window, birds in the garden: a car in the road: nothing. It was only afterwards when she tried to stand up and found herself stiff that she knew how still, even rigid, she had been; it took time to bring herself back.

This autumn day, when she took her place, a bowl of chrysanthemums had been put on the floor before the altar, blooms grown with pride of Soeur Fiacre in the glasshouse; the colours, bronze and pinkish brown, were beautiful in the candlelight but the scent was pungent and bitter, and Lise remembered that for the French, chrysanthemums are the flowers of death—but, if I should die in one of these "cloud" times, thought Lise, I'm sure they wouldn't have to bury me. I should be gone. But that was presumptuous—"Who do you think you are? The Virgin Mary?" and it was stupid, because such moments are "vouchsafed"; when

one thinks consciously about them, they don't happen.
You can't command nor even ask them, thought Lise.
You can only watch and wait. . . .

Now, for the first few minutes, she was filled with
distractions, needs and worries; the cider press had
broken down again—it's getting old, how are we to
replace it? Soeur Thecla's bronchitis: why did the Prioress, Soeur Marie Emmanuel, look so tired? Then it
was of a birthday card she, Lise, had forgotten to send
to a prisoner. How could I forget! "One keeps on discov-
ering these holes, failures, in oneself." "Lord, help
me," prayed Lise. "Lord. Lord . . ." and then it was
"vouchsafed"; as if a cloak had fallen round her, Lise
was taken up and forgot.

Suddenly, and as frighteningly, as if she had been
thrown down from space, Lise found herself back on
the prie-dieu. She was used, at such times, to feeling
cold—it was part of being rigid—but not as cold as
this. She glanced up at the clock; it had only been a few
minutes and then Lise knew it was the cold of fear—why
fear?—and then there came a sense of evil, such evil
that she could only hold to the wood of the prie-dieu
and keep her eyes on the round of white in the monstrance; she could not even pray, only hold on, and it
seemed to her there was a stench, not of the chrysanthemums, bitter as that was, but a smell of . . . blood,
thought Lise?

She knew she must not move, not even dare look
round, only hold; she had heard no sound, seen no one,
but someone or something was there, standing behind
her, standing over her. She thought she was going to
faint and shut her eyes, but only for a second; the only
way was to keep them fixed on the Host. Lord. Lord.
Beads of sweat broke out on her, not only on her
forehead and neck but over her whole body. "You had
that too, in the garden of Gethsemane when you too
were afraid. Let this cup pass from me," prayed Lise.
Then, "But your will, not mine, be done," and she

raised her head waiting, for what she did not know—a blow? a stab? a horde breaking into the chapel? a stroke?

And then the chapel was as it had been when she came in, empty, filled with autumn sun; there was only the scent of the chrysanthemums, the steady flame of the candles and, "Really," said Lise to herself, "you must go and see Father Marc. You are having hallucinations."

Then she heard footsteps and a touch came on her shoulder but it was not the sister to relieve her; it was not time yet for that. It was Marc himself. "Soeur Marie Lise. You must come. Come quickly. We must get help."

It was then that Lise looked down; beside her priedieu, on the floor, was a cluster of pale pink mother-of-pearl, a rosary, its chain broken into pieces, making a little heap of beads.

"So, it was there." Marc noticed she did not say "she," but, "Indeed she was," he said and shuddered. "Mon Dieu! It might have been you."

"But she didn't. . . ."

"She did. Come quickly," but a voice rang out from the ante-chapel, an old voice, shrill with anger. "What have you done to my nice clean floor—and I washed it this very morning." It was Soeur Anne Colombe. "*Look* at the mess. It's wine, that's what it is. Get up you lazy girl and go and fetch me a bucket. Don't just lie. . . . A-ah!" Soeur Anne Colombe's scream rent the convent, but Marc and Lise were there first.

It must have been a desperate silent struggle; Lise guessed that Vivi's strong hand had been clapped at once over Lucette's mouth.

"Lucette must have been watching, as she always did." Lise could hardly get the words out. "She knew, as she always knew; she may even have overheard that telephone call from Mademoiselle. She went without her food to watch over me."

245

Lucette was still breathing but as Lise lifted her head and shoulder, more blood flowed out onto Soeur Anne Colombe's clean floor and the white tunic grew redder and redder.

The Prioress and infirmarian were there. Soeur Elizabeth had run to the telephone; the other nuns kept back, out of the way, silent, only their lips moving. Soeur Marie Mercédes held Soeur Anne Colombe who was weeping with remorse. At a sign from the Prioress they knelt, as Marc knelt too. With infinite tenderness, he took the holy oil he had hurriedly fetched from the sacristy and made the sign of the Cross on Lucette's forehead; then the words came strongly. "Through this holy anointing may the Lord, in His love and mercy, help you with the grace of the Holy Spirit," and quietly the voices echoed "Amen."

"I saw her," Marc told them. "I was saying my Office in the garden when a woman ran past me. I thought she was one of the visitors, or a penitent perhaps, because she was sobbing. Then she threw something away— this," and he showed the knife, an ordinary kitchen knife, but sharpened to a blade like a razor. "She used it five or six times on little Soeur Lucie. She could have stabbed you in the back, Soeur Marie Lise. It would have been so easy."

"Then why didn't she?"

"Because you were where you were," said Soeur Marie Emmanuel.

"But it was meant for me. Why couldn't I have been the one?" That was Lise's agony in the next days, that and the memory of those last unkind words she had said to Lucette: "I don't need a nounou, thank you." She had thought of them at the beginning of her "watching," and had vowed that, when it was over, she would go and find Lucette and tell her she was sorry. Now. . . . "Too late," Lise said in bitter reproach of herself.

"It wasn't too late." Soeur Raymonde spoke firmly.

246

She, the Mother-General, had come straight from Saint Xavier on the afternoon train to help Soeur Marie Emmanuel. "Soeur Lucie died where she had never dreamed she would be—in your arms. Soeur Marie Emmanuel tells me that at the last moment she looked up and, as your tears fell on her face, she put up her hand and touched them and said, 'For me?'"

"Don't. Don't," said Lise.

"She—didn't hurt you?" Lucette's words had come painfully.

"No, because you. . . ." Lise had been unable to go on.

"Good. Good!" and there had come a smile as, at the last moment, Patrice had smiled, but Lucette's smiles were rarer. "Good."

Then a terrible convulsion had shaken the little body and Lucette was gone.

They had to let the police take Lucette's body away. "I'm sorry it's necessary," said the Inspector in charge of the case but, "An inquest on one of us!" the nuns were shocked.

"And she won't be laid out properly." Soeur Anne Colombe's tears had never ceased to flow. "Where are the candles, the flowers, the prayers?"

"We can say the prayers," said Soeur Marie Emmanuel.

"You shall have her back as soon as possible," the Inspector promised.

He and the other gendarmes tried to be as gentle and unobtrusive as they could, dealing courteously with Lise and Marc, treading quietly in the chapel. "But with their cameras and big boots," moaned Soeur Anne Colombe.

"Shoes. Policemen don't wear boots these days."

"Boots," said Soeur Anne Colombe firmly.

"And you saw and heard nothing?" the Inspector asked Lise incredulously, over and over again. "True, the doors were shut."

"I heard nothing—only felt. . . ."

"Felt?"

"I knew there was someone—some . . . thing, rather, because Vivi couldn't have been in her senses. . . ."

"I think she was, and so does Mademoiselle Signoret. Ma Soeur, you have had a miraculous escape."

"That is the bitter part." Lise could not say it to the Inspector but she could to Mademoiselle.

Mademoiselle had come because, "I blame myself," she said. "I was right; there was a leak. I should have been more vigilant. One of our young officers had too soft a heart, was too inexperienced. She carried a message from Zaza to Vivi; it told Vivi where she could find Big Jo—and poor Big Jo did the rest."

"I told you I was thick, thick as two planks," Big Jo had said in anguish, "and to think I begged my Responsable to let me see cette connasse—that cheater —because she had just come out of prison, she, like the weasel she is, after her prey. Oh, she knows how to do things, that scum. She began by abusing Soeur Marie Lise, our angel."

"It's the first time anyone has called me an angel," said Lise. "Dear Jo." ". . . trying to dirty our angel with filth and lies, as I told her roundly." How roundly they all could imagine. "I told her what Soeur Marie Lise is, what she does, how she works. I told her," and Big Jo gulped a great sob, "I told her to go to Belle Source and see for herself. Idiot! Idiot! But when I lose my temper, I blab."

A hiding-place had been found up in the loft above the cowshed. "She must have watched me milking," said Soeur Marie Jeanne who was now in the community. "Watched us! Ough!"

"And stolen some of the milk; I had been puzzled," said Soeur Thecla, "and eggs from under the hens." The guest-house had been broken into and bread and butter taken—*"Butter!"* said Soeur Joséphine Magdaleine to whom the butter seemed worst of all. "I should have been more suspicious," but suspicion was not encouraged at Béthanie.

"She must have been watching and spying for days, perhaps a week, to find out where I went, what I did. To think she hates me enough to do that." Lise trembled and Soeur Raymonde's hand came over hers. "You must pray for her, ma Soeur."

"Pray for her!" Mademoiselle was indignant. "Pray that they may catch her."

"If they can." Soeur Raymonde was calm. "So far there is no trace. Justice must be done, of course, but. . . ."

"If we depended on justice," Soeur Marie Emmanuel smiled, "we shouldn't go far—and, dear Mademoiselle, remember we don't know how the poor soul has been driven."

"Soul! That creature!"

"Creatures have souls."

"But think of Soeur Marie Lise!" and Mademoiselle asked Lise, "How can you ever feel safe?"

"I was safe then—at that extreme moment. I think I'm safe now."

"I don't understand," said Mademoiselle.

Lucette came back to be buried in Belle Source's small cemetery where she could still be in the companionship of the house and her sisters.

For two days she lay in the pavilion; as soon as dawn came its doors were opened and all the daily life of the domaine was round her: washing blew in the wind, apple-picking went on, the cider press, mended, perhaps for the last time, creaked and groaned. The muscovy duck came by with her last brood of the season, eight ducklings, yellow and brown: birds flew down to pick at the berries of the cotoneaster and the hips of the roses that grew round the pavilion.

Lucette lay in a clean habit with no sign of the wounds; her hands held her wooden rosary and a nosegay of late flowers Soeur Fiacre had found for her; her eyes with strangely long lashes were shut. Candles burned beside the bier and, always, at least one of the sisters kept vigil. Lise was there a great deal of the time but, "No histronics," Soeur Marie Emmanuel, with her good sense, had warned Lise. "Remember, no matter if sometimes you were brusque with her and that wasn't so often, if sometimes she knew you found her tiresome, you still brought her what we can guess was perhaps the only happiness she had known—and what happiness! And isn't this what she would have chosen?" asked Soeur Marie Emmanuel.

On the night before the burial the nuns gathered in the pavilion; there was no electricity there, only the warm light of candles. Lise, coming from the porteress's lodge where she had been on duty, could see white figures flitting between the chapel and the pavilion as everything was made ready. Marc read the prayers; then Lucette was lifted into her coffin which was closed and sealed; it was no bigger than a child's. It was carried into the chapel and put on a stand before the altar. There was no pall, only a bunch of flowers, only candles and the steady light of the tabernacle.

The next day was brilliant with crisp sparkling frost and sunshine. "Lucie, light," said Soeur Marie Mercédes who could not walk to the cemetery but had to follow in the convent car, with others even older who had to be helped even the few yards from the path to the grave. When the long Mass of the Dead was over, the procession went back through the domaine.

Usually, at a nun's funeral, there were many neighbours, but no one outside the house had known Soeur Lucie, and no one inside had ever guessed her strength and her love, thought Lise, except perhaps the old and feeble. They were inconsolable for themselves, not for Lucette. "If anyone is sure of going straight to heaven, it's Soeur Lucie," said Soeur Anne Colombe. "She's there already, I know she is and forgiving me for what I said about the floor." More tears ran down the withered old face.

If Lucette could have looked down, Lise thought, she

would have said what she had said in wonder at Lise's tears. "For me?" The beauty of the ceremony, the nuns coming one after the other to sprinkle holy water into the deep grave. "For me?"

"Not to be afraid." Lise came often to visit Lucette's grave and sat by her as if they were still talking. "Do not be afraid." How often had Jesus had to say those words to his disciples as, in this little cemetery, Lise said them to Lucette. It was the old habit of reassuring, though Lucette, Lise was sure, was now far wiser than she. "Though earth closes over you or, even, as nowadays, you are burned to ashes and scattered, it is wonderful," whispered Lise. "Listen. Listen, there are a million tiny voices and movements, rustling, crumbling, disintegrating, disappearing, as you become one with creation. Your body will be earth, water, wind, stars." Lise knew that would happen to her too and it did not frighten her—she liked to think of it. Lucette herself was in God's keeping; Lise was sure of that too. How? When? That did not matter. We are not meant to know. We can only try and live as if we knew. But those who won't? And the old cry woke again. Patrice? He had smiled at her as Lucette had smiled, so surely Patrice . . . but Vivi? Vivi?

Where was Vivi? It was amazing that the police had not found her. Had she escaped to some shoddy bar in Algeria? Morocco? Or was she driving her pitiful bargain in one of the polyglot town streets, Marseilles or Toulon, where people like flotsam and jetsam came and went. Had she joined that throng of misery who came shambling out at night, the meths drinkers? Or was she lying dead in a ditch somewhere? Lise did not know, but the cry, Vivi, Vivi, was in her still. Lise could not stay in the cemetery any longer.

Marc came to say goodbye before going to Saint Xavier. "We are hoping," he said, "that perhaps in the New Year we shall have Big Jo."

"What a day that will be," said Lise.

"It will indeed! and Wan Tsui is an aspirant now, but . . ." his face grew grave. "I feel anxious for you, ma Soeur."

"Not anxious," said Lise. "That's the wrong word," and she said, as she had said to Mademoiselle, "I have a feeling that it's not completed. I'm probably wrong. Vivi may be back on the beat in some other city, God help her. She may be in the Seine, but. . . ."

"But?"

"Every time I go to make my adoration," said Lise, "there, where it happened in the chapel, I take her rosary—I have mended it where I broke it—I can't forgive myself—I put it down on the floor where she left it as a sign to me. Perhaps one day she will come back to fetch her pretty beads."

ABOUT THE AUTHOR

RUMER GODDEN is a novelist, and a translator and writer for children. Her many books—some of which have been turned into equally memorable films—include THE RIVER, BLACK NARCISSUS, AN EPISODE OF SPARROWS, THE GREEN-GAGE SUMMER, IN THIS HOUSE OF BREDE, and THE PEACOCK SPRING. She now lives in southern Scotland.

CLASSIC BESTSELLERS
from FAWCETT BOOKS

ALL QUIET ON THE WESTERN FRONT by Erich Maria Remarque	23808	$2.25
TO KILL A MOCKINGBIRD by Harper Lee	08376	$1.95
SHOW BOAT by Edna Ferber	23191	$1.95
THEM by Joyce Carol Oates	23944	$2.50
THE SLAVE by Isaac Bashevis Singer	24188	$2.50
THE FLOUNDER by Gunter Grass	24180	$2.95
THE CHOSEN by Chaim Potok	24200	$2.50
NORTHWEST PASSAGE by Kenneth Roberts	02719	$2.50
THE RABBIT RUN by John Updike	24031	$2.25
JALNA by Mazo de la Roche	24418	$1.95
SPORTS IN AMERICA by James Michener	24063	$2.95

Buy them at your local bookstore or use this handy coupon for ordering.

COLUMBIA BOOK SERVICE (a CBS Publications Co.)
32275 Mally Road, P.O. Box FB, Madison Heights, MI 48071

Please send me the books I have checked above. Orders for less than 5 books must include 75¢ for the first book and 25¢ for each additional book to cover postage and handling. Orders for 5 books or more postage is FREE. Send check or money order only.

Cost $_____ Name _____

Sales tax*_____ Address _____

Postage_____ City _____

Total $_____ State _____ Zip _____

*The government requires us to collect sales tax in all states except AK, DE, MT, NH and OR.

This offer expires 1 June 81

8061

NEW FROM FAWCETT CREST

Let COVENTRY Give You
A Little Old-Fashioned Romance